GUADALAJARA BURN

A Skip Reid Adventure Thriller
by Garr Kuhl

TINA —
nice meeting you,
Enjoy the Ride!

G. Kuhl

This is a work of fiction. All of the characters, events, and organizations portrayed here are either products of the author's imagination or used fictitiously.

GUADALAJARA BURN
A Skip Reid Adventure Thriller

Copyright © 2015 Garr Kuhl

First edition printed 2015

10 9 8 7 6 5 4 3 2 1

ISBN-13: 978-1505652611
ISBN-10: 1505652618

Adult - Mystery - Adventure - Thriller - Mexico

Don't miss any of the novels and plays of Garr Kuhl

Middle Grade

SNAGGED: The Door to ZEE
A Coming of Age Fantasy
"Compelling. Loved the story and the adventure, and so will young readers. This book should be in classrooms and school libraries everywhere.

—**Judge**, Writer's Digest 21st Annual Self-published Book awards.

Young Adult

CAPTURED A Retro Ransford Adventure Novel

Plays

WESTCHESTER GRAFFITI
BRIMS—THE SEQUEL (with Wynn Allen)
PEACE ACCORD (with Wynn Allen)

Look for Garr Kuhl's newest novel
BETRAYED The second book in the Retro Ransford adventure trilogy

This book is dedicated to Mitch, who didn't pull the trigger that day on Lake Chapala.

GUADALAJARA
BURN

CHAPTER
ONE

The unforgiving early afternoon heat ripped the breath out of Guadalajara. I had blown fifteen pesos for a cheap seat facing the sun in The Plaza de Nuevo Progreso, tolerating a bull fight and drowning in buckets of sweat. A half-empty bottle of Dos XX warmed in my hand as I watched the matador offer one of the dead bull's ears to a corpulent Mexican man in a black cowboy hat and a red, open-necked guayabera shirt.

One *corrida* did me in. I needed out of there, needed some fresh air that didn't smell of blood. Even though the bull had fought well, the odds had not been in his favor. I peeled myself off the wooden bench seat and headed for the exit, reminding myself that I needed to file a story soon, somewhere. I was short on cash and long on time, searching for a story that would pay my way down to Panama. With the exception of a few dollars, I was running on empty. My life seemed to be in a downward spiral that could easily auger into the fertile earth of the Jalisco countryside. 1971 had beaten me up worse than the scandal-ridden years of my ice hockey days.

Having spent the last two months of my year in

1

Mexico surfing and racking up one-night stands with desperate divorcees drying out in Puerto Vallarta, I had come to Guadalajara for respite – to research an ancient Tabachine ruins outside a town called Teuchitlán a few miles northwest of the city. With its adjacent shaft tombs, I was hoping it would lead to a story and a few bucks.

As I was leaving the arena, I noticed a narrow corridor at right angle to the main exit. Curious of the loose security chain strung across its width, I stepped over the looped links and followed the dim light down a musty tunnel toward a tiled, three-sided, tin-covered outdoor stall that opened onto a side street. Several local butchers were deftly dressing and quartering the bull I had just seen killed in the arena. The sour, metallic odor of blood still floated in the air like cheap perfume. Watching the men butcher the bull, their sweat-soaked shirts hugging their backs and chests in the oppressive heat, I thought about the once enraged and confused bull, never really having a chance against the picking, stabbing, and torture it had endured in the ring.

But this was Mexico, and somehow it all seemed so natural.

"He was a strong fighting bull," a gruff voice filled with authority resounded behind me, addressing the butchers. It was the man who was offered the bull's ear earlier. "And Miguel, this time make sure *all* of the meat gets to the orphanage."

The admonished butchers responded by waving their cleavers at the man and quickened the pace of the butchering. Turning to me, the man laughed and said in perfectly polite English, "We should all die that way, eh, *gringo*?"

I stared at the man for a moment, taking in the long-sleeved guayabera shirt that neatly fit the contours of his thick, rounded shoulders, yet clung like wet tissue over the beefiness of his stomach. A pair of well-buffed snakeskin, silver-tipped cowboy boots peaked out from beneath the cuffs of his twill khaki pants. He smelled of arrogance.

"I don't relish dying by the sword," I countered.

"But you have to agree, it is swift."

"Tell that to the bull, even if you did get an ear."

"Carlos Huerta," he laughed as he introduced himself. "I happened to sit in the right seat. It also pays to own the bulls." His hand was meaty, hard, and strong. He could have crushed mine if he chose to. He was the type who always seemed to be in shape, no matter what shape he might be in. The type you might want at your back if things turned nasty. He may have been a street fighter in another time.

"Skip Reid," I offered, looking past his thick, black mustache and wide pock-marked face into his narrow-set dark eyes, not sure I liked what I was seeing.

"I can tell you don't approve," he said, smirking beneath his grin, looking at the bull being slaughtered in front of us. "The *corrida* is not for everyone. Why did you bother to come?"

"My curiosity got the best of me," I replied. "I was looking for a quick story. The quick kill was disturbing."

"It's all a matter of perspective," Huerta said with the firm coolness of a man in charge. His speech suddenly slowed as he glared past me to the street where an open Jeep was crawling by. From inside the Jeep, a cropped-haired, wiry American and a Mexican boy the size of a boulder shot Huerta a menacing stare. "I hope you are enjoying your stay in our beautiful city," Huerta added, the words measured and tentative as his eyes tracked the Jeep down the street. "Yes, by all means, take advantage of everything our beautiful city has to offer."

* * *

To clear my head of the effects of the beer and my quick, rather odd encounter with the man called Carlos Huerta, I walked the six blocks down Avenida de Independencia to the Mercado Libertad, thinking about a late lunch. I chose a *fonda* on the second floor next to the railing where I could look out over the main market below and ordered a fish lunch. Amidst the heavy odor of fried fish and overcooked meat floating up from the stove grills, a troupe of mariachis were serenading an older American couple through the tightly packed labyrinth of shops on the first floor. It was a snail trail of out-of-tune guitars and ambitiously decorated *charros.* Amplified by the tin roofs of the shops, the discordant notes wafted into the vast expanse of the forty-foot ceiling and drifted away.

When I turned back toward the *fonda,* I noticed the wiry American and the big Mexican I had seen driving by the bull ring earlier walk off the wide, concrete stairway. The American, in jeans and an oversized T-shirt, limped his way through the crowd, trying to mask some hidden pain with a troubled, stiff smile. He was short and taut as a rope; his eyes dark as gun metal. He eased his right leg over the bench at a carved up wooden table that was anchored in a slab of concrete at a *fonda* next to me, grimacing as he gently set his foot down on the floor. The scratches on his forehead and cheek were red and raw. I noticed part of his right earlobe was missing. The Mexican was as big as the bull I had just seen killed. He lowered himself next to the American. His knuckles were an angry red; his thick, black, mustache and tightly-pulled ponytail intimidating.

Looking at the two men made me think of a friend of mine who had lost his surfboard and crashed head first onto a coral reef off a beach in Hawaii. Besides the infection that took over his body for a time, he, too, lost part of his ear. To this day, he still wears the scar like a bogus badge of courage. I thought whatever these two were mixed up in, they came prepared to show off the spoils.

"Was anybody left standing?" I said smugly from my table. "You didn't kill the referee, did you?"

The short man's dark eyes bit into me. "And if we had?" The words rasped above the sounds of the crowded Mercado. He then gave me a twisted smile and laughed. "Just clearing brush up at the ranch," he said and nodded toward the man who was sliding my fish plate across the counter.

I knew better. The wounds on the American and the cuts and scabs on the big Mexican's knuckles looked more like street fight residue than scrapes from brush clearing. I didn't know much about cutting brush, but I had had my share of bruised knuckles and bloody noses in my few years of professional hockey. I let the lie go.

"And don't eat Edgardo's fish," the American added, giving the cook a crooked smile.

Edgardo responded with a smirk and a flip of his index finger. He said in slow English, "Señor Garret, you are not helping my business."

The man called Garret ran a hand over his inch of mud-brown hair. "You'll be heaving your guts out," he said to me. "Eat with us." Even though the invitation seemed playful, the words had teeth in them. He waved me over.

"A bit late with the warning," I said. The two sized me up as I gathered my fish lunch into its day-old, front page newspaper wrapper and started for their table. Turning to grab a napkin, the wrapper split open, spilling the fish. I caught it before it hit the floor. It was one of those times when my reflexes were in my favor. The two men sitting at the table had not missed it.

"I'll be on it next time," the man called Garret said after taking a quick look at my hands. "Maybe you'll be lucky. Garret," he introduced himself, and then nodded toward his friend. "Manolo."

"Reid. Skip Reid," I said, taking Garret's lead. "Saw you drive by the bull ring."

Garret snickered. "Just cruising."

With the palm of my hand I brushed old food chunks that hadn't yet glued themselves to the table and laid out my fish. Seeming to mirror me, the big Mexican laughed and picked at the table with his fingernails, flicking crusty food particles into the open spaces around us. He reminded me of an ex-teammate who blew out his knee and became a bouncer in Manhattan Beach. He was a big, muscled, no-neck with a clear complexion. His innocent, boyish looks didn't fool anyone. He would, without hesitation, or on a dare, tear a fender off a late model car or an arm off some-one's body. I once saw him break a beer glass on a bar and eat the smaller shards, using a beer to chase them down. The Mexican at the table had the same look, only he was bigger.

Then Garret asked, his smile fading, "Who was the dude you were with at the bull ring?"

"I wasn't with anybody," I stated. "He said his name was Carlos Huerta. I just met him. Seems to be an arrogant ass as far as I'm concerned." I shrugged and smiled. "Says he owns bulls. He looks more like a roadhouse bouncer."

"You think he might be something else?"

"Who knows? Everyone seems to be something else in this part of the world."

"You're right about that," Garret laughed, casually glancing at the macramé belt keeping my short cargo pants cinched, my fading Hawaiian shirt, and my tired old leather sandals. "California?" he asked.

"L.A.," I said. "That obvious, eh?"

"Americans can't hide," he said, still sorting me out, eyes tracking mine. "They don't know how."

"We've never had to think about it," I said, looking at Manolo, whose big hands were tearing the head from his half-eaten fish. "What would we have to hide from?"

Garret shrugged. He pulled a six-inch hunting knife from the sheath on his belt and cut into his fish. "You'd be surprised. Hell, I'm not a teacher," he said sharply with an unnerving coolness that slowed the moment. "Stay out of the States for awhile. Maybe you'll learn something."

"I've been out, and the lessons are tough," I said, wiping the grease from my fingers onto the headline of the newspaper, the inky letters bleeding a tattoo onto my right palm. "Leaving stateside problems behind is a challenge."

"Stay in Mexico long enough and you won't even remember your name," Garret said.

"Seems you've been here awhile," I said. "How many brain cells have you lost? And what have you learned?"

He went quiet, still looking me over as though missing a piece of who I was, trying to finish a puzzle. "That things are seldom what they appear to be," he finally said. "I came over after I left 'Nam, five years ago. Rangers and Recon. 'Nam and this place have taught me a few things. One is that it's okay to be an ex-pat. You learn to live with it." He looked at me suspiciously and asked, "What brings you down here? Nobody comes to Mexico unless they're running from something, Skipper." He hesitated as Mano-lo tapped his watch then added, "What demons are chasing you?"

"I quit my job as a writer in L.A. and kissed off my fiancée," I said, wondering about his sudden interest in me. I didn't mention that there was a warrant out for my arrest.

"Fucking everyone?" Garret asked.

"Got that right," I said. "She finally took off with a Kiwi. There was nothing left to hold me in place. But I got lucky, had a high number in the draft. So here I am in Mexico, surfing my way to Panama."

There was a flicker of sensibility in Garret's disturbing, dark eyes when he said, "I don't hold court on anyone. We do what our conscience tells us is right."

"Or sometimes wrong," I said somewhat relieved, picking up a better feel for Garret. "I'm sticking around for a while," I added. "Writing a story about the Day of the Dead from the perspective of the ruins at Teuchitlán. There's also rumor of an artifact that was stolen from a museum last night. It apparently came from the same ruins. It's worth checking out."

"The Tabachine Warrior," Garret stated. "Nice piece of ancient sculpture. Heard about it going missing."

"What do you know about it?" I asked, noticing an almost undetectable flash of alarm shooting across his face.

He stared off into the open space of the Mercado for an instant, then said, "Only that there has been a lot of controversy about it in the past. And now it's gone." He paused again, long enough to jab the tip of his knife into the tabletop, his muscled forearm displaying a silver dollar-sized tattoo with a wild-eyed tiger face over a five-pointed star. He caught me staring at it and reflexively pulled his shoulders back. "That bother you?" he asked. He was looking at my sun-bleached, premature gray hair and couldn't quite manage a smile. It was quick, more like a nervous tic that pulled on the corner of his mouth.

"No," I said. "Unusual, that's all."

He looked quickly at his forearm. "It was an unusual situation."

"Garret," Manolo broke in. His English was broken, guttural, gravel deep. "*Vamonos.*"

Garret wiped his knife on his jeans and slid it into the sheath on his belt. "Sorry, business doesn't wait," he said flatly. "Demons or not, we do what we have to do." The two pushed themselves up from the table, Manolo rising a good eight inches above Garret's head. "You've been published, Skipper?" Garret asked without looking at me, favoring the pain in his right leg.

"Mostly human interest, personal experience for the magazine I worked for," I said, snaking my way up from the low table. Standing next to Manolo, I suddenly felt a lot shorter than my six feet, two inches and two hundred pounds. "Now I'm just working on a few bylines for magazine articles," I added, feeling Manolo hovering behind me, his fishy breath fouling the air. "Why?"

"Don't have time to explain now," Garret said. "Meet me here tomorrow at eleven. I'll buy you lunch. We may have something of interest to talk about."

Garret's limp was more obvious as the two headed toward the stairs leading down to the main market area. He stopped long enough to slide a few dollars across the counter to Edgardo, who flashed a wide smile and gave him a thumbs up. "Always take care of your friends," Garret said over his shoulder. It was meant for me.

At the top of the stairs he shifted something in the waistband of his jeans and pulled the tail of his shirt down over his belt. My imagination took it from there. *Was he an ex-combat soldier that didn't know what to do without a gun? And if it was a gun, why did he have it with him in the Mercado?*

I trashed the rest of my lunch and headed downstairs, the heat and the crush of people in the Mercado wrapping around me like a pair of tight wool socks. The air was filled with musk and sour body odor along with fresh aromas of fruit, vegetables and flowers, and pungent scents of herbs and spices. I pushed aside the webs of party-colored piñatas and clothing that hung like stiff laundry drying on a line and found myself in a maze of jewelry stands, the silver flashing in slivers of sun that found their way through the cracks in the high wooden ceiling of the Mercado. Carved soapstone figurines of Aztec and Mayan gods peered at me from behind rows of pottery and leather bags as I made my way to the sidewalk and into the glare of the early afternoon sun.

Through the crowd of outside vendors and shoppers congesting the sidewalk, I spotted Garret's Jeep parked at the curb a short distance away. He and Manolo were loading boxes and bags into the back of the Jeep.

I started toward them, slowing to sidestep one of several puppies wriggling between my feet. A small boy jumped up, corralled the pups and put all but one back into a cardboard box next to the wall. He looked at me with pleading doe eyes and pushed the puppy toward my chest. A dog was the last thing I needed at this point in my life. I held it and ran my hand over its soft coat then handed it back to the boy, all the while keeping an eye on Garret and Manolo.

Garret seemed suddenly on edge. He was pacing the length of the Jeep. It didn't take long to understand why. A square-jawed man whose nose looked like it had seen too many punches was stalking Garret through the parting crowd, straight-backed as though consciously counting the rhythm of his steps. Beneath his elephant-hide face and deep-set eyes, his upper torso bulged as big and solid as an engine block.

When the man was within an arm's reach of Garret, he stopped, small mountains of muscle pushing the limits of his khaki-colored polo shirt. He considered Manolo for a moment who had pushed himself off the fender and was towering over the man. The man laughed, ignoring Manolo, as the words between him and Garret picked up heat. The two men moved within inches of each other. Then with lightning reflexes the man grabbed the neck of

Garret's shirt, yanking him closer, whispering angrily into his face. Manolo, just as swiftly, jumped behind the man and grabbed his biceps, pulling him off Garret and holding him a foot off the ground. As the man twisted, turned, and kicked trying to shake him off, Manolo tightened his grip, the beginnings of blood deprivation forming in pink blotches below Manolo's hands. Then with a signal from Garret, Manolo slammed the man onto the sidewalk.

The man bounced once, sprang to his feet and started after Manolo. He missed with a leg kick to Manolo's knee. Manolo, with one punch to the face, sent the man reeling across the pavement. There was contempt in the man's eyes as he dragged his forearm across the steady stream of blood flowing from his mangled nose. A peculiar chill swept through me when I saw the same five-pointed star and tiger-face tattoo on his forearm that mirrored the one on Garret's.

Who were these guys?

"This isn't over, Garret," I heard the man say as I moved in closer. "There will be a time when you won't have your goon watching your back."

"You may never live to see that time, Kopek," Garret countered.

"Don't bet against me, Garret. The odds are not in your favor."

Garret laughed. "Life's a crap game. You taught me that."

"And all bets are off," Kopek said. He took a few steps toward the sidewalk away from Garret and Manolo, turned and shoved his right index finger into the air. "Fuck you, Garret. What's yours is mine. You owe me."

"Even though we've been through hell together, Kopek," Garret said. "I'd be stupid to think we could settle this peacefully."

"There is no peace in our world, Garret." He turned away then spun back around. He aimed his forefinger at Garret and using his thumb as a hammer, fired a phantom round. "Watch your back, Garret," he said. "So we wasted a few dinks in 'Nam. That doesn't make us soul mates."

He marched onto the sidewalk, rage burning in his eyes. I reflexively took a step back when he flicked his head and took a longer than comfortable look at me. Without breaking his stride, he viciously kicked the puppy into the wall of the Mercado. The puppy bounced off the concrete with a heart wrenching squeal and wobbled to the boy as the man stuck his middle finger into the air again. I didn't know the man, but I already hated him. When I saw the fury in Manolo's eyes as he pushed himself off the fender, I knew I wasn't alone in my abhorrence of the Neanderthal.

It has always been the curious side of me that feels it needs an answer. That curiosity has put me in harm's way a few times, but never with anything I couldn't handle with tact, diplomacy, or when either failed, a fist to the jaw.

"It's none of my business," I asked when I reached the Jeep, "but what was that all about?" Garret had calmed Manolo again. After looking at the big Mexican, standing large and ominous beside me, I said, "On second thought, would I want to know?"

"I told you I was in 'Nam," Garret said dryly. "Kopek was with me. He's a delusional asshole. Thinks everybody owes him something."

Taking a step away from Manolo, I asked, "Do you?"

"Don't be a smart ass." Garret slid into the Jeep and fired up the big-bored engine as Manolo swung himself into the passenger seat. "I doubt you're doing anything important for the next couple of hours, Skipper," he said playfully. "Manolo and I are going fishing at Lake Chapala. You're welcome to come along."

"Thanks, but I'll stick around here. Catch up on some letter writing. I'll see you here at eleven tomorrow."

"We'll keep that meeting, and the letter writing can wait," Garret said forcefully. "Get in. I have a story for you that could make us both rich."

CHAPTER
THREE

Garret kept the Jeep at high speed for the forty-minute drive south on Highway 23 to Chapala. Manolo's massive presence hovered over me from the back seat, an enormous, storm surf wave that could crash over me at any time. He was, fortunately, at the moment preoccupied with a hand-held radio squawking at him in Spanish.

"What's with the radio?" I asked Garret above the roar of the road and the wind whipping by us. "Manolo seems to have a lot to say to someone."

Garret's face was empty of disclosure. He was intently focused on the road. "It will be a lot clearer soon."

After more rapid-fire Spanish into the hand-held, Manolo leaned over Garret's shoulder. "*Está bien,*" he said, "*esta noche.*"

"Just some business tonight at the ranch," Garret said, anticipating any questions I may have had.

At Chapala, Garret parked the Jeep in a dirt and gravel lot off Paseo Ramon Corona across from the lake about one hundred yards from the cement pier that jutted out toward Scorpion Island. The water side of the street was lined with vendors selling their wares in the open air under shabby tent-like shops. Garret, favoring his left leg, pulled a small shoulder bag out of the rear of the Jeep and tossed it to Manolo as we headed past the sellers toward the concrete pier. Garret then drew a needle-thin joint out of his T-shirt pocket, flipped the hood of his Zippo lighter, and held the flame to the end of the joint. He took a long drag, held it for a few seconds then passed the joint to me. I handed it to Manolo who sucked in a hit, and we started out onto the long, low pier, avoiding the creeping, thick green vegetable carpet of water hyacinth working its way onto the dock. Halfway out, two men were tossing a metal cooler and fishing gear into a long *ponga,* each had a beer bottle in his hand. They finished loading and cast off in a direction south of Scorpion Island. I took another hit while Manolo quietly dropped into the rear seat of a small boat tied to a cleat at the end of the pier and fired up the outboard motor. Garret took the shoulder bag from Manolo and eased himself into the front seat, facing me.

"We'll pick up bait and poles on the island," Garret said in sync with my suspicious looks around the boat.

With the sweet smell of cannabis in the air, I sat looking out over the bow of the boat into the glare of the sun on the lake as the clatter of a loose piston in the old motor rang out over the silence. Other than the two fishermen we had seen earlier, we were alone on the lake as Manolo guided the boat out toward Scorpion Island over the midday smoothness of the water.

"Do you know how deep this lake is?" Garret asked, pulling his palm across the sweat bubbles on his forehead, exposing the tiger tattoo on his forearm.

"About nine feet in the shallows and maybe ninety in the deep," I said, recalling the numbers from a pamphlet I had read my first day in Guadalajara.

He stared at me with those coal black eyes. "You do keep up on things, don't you?"

"Call it research. Nothing that's going to change the world."

"Deepest part is on the backside of the island," he said. "About three miles out. You can get a better perspective from out there."

We had gone past the tip of Scorpion Island and were in the heart of the lake when the outboard sputtered and died, leaving us adrift and bobbing for a few silent seconds on the back side of the Island. When I turned to look at Manolo sitting in the back of the boat, staring out at the ominous, gray-blue water, his arms folded across his big chest, waiting, I knew we had not run out of gas. I turned back toward Garret and was staring at a .45, the barrel pointed at my forehead.

Manolo grabbed me, his big hands cutting the circulation in my arms.

"Jesus, Garret! What the hell?" My life never had a chance to flash before me. No isolated childhood events; no great moments left over from years ago. My mind was as cold and sterile as the ten-inch piece of steel in Garret's hand. I had confronted bullies on beaches, on the ice, and in bars; but this was far beyond throwing a few punches. Fiction had mutated into a five-foot-eight inch miscreant with a bigger caliber gun than his presumed I.Q.

"Fun's over," Garret said. "Your reflexes are too quick for a writer. Those calluses on your hands didn't come from a typewriter. Be straight with me, or this thing might take on a mind of its own."

"Straight? About what?" I managed to choke out, thinking he had me mixed up with someone else. "I played a few years of professional ice hockey out of college. I wouldn't have gotten that far if I didn't have quick hands. Then I discovered surfing and journalism. Is that straight enough? I'm not looking for any trouble."

"Trouble doesn't mean anything when you're dead," Garret said. "You just could be in very deep shit. Interpol and that asshole from my past you saw earlier have been after me since I got here. You're not that asshole, so I'm going to ask you once… are you with Interpol?"

"I'm just…Interpol? What the hell are you talking about?"

Manolo tightened his grip on my arms as Garret repeated his threat. "If you *are*, you're fish bait!"

"Hey, I'm heading to Panama!" I exclaimed. "To stay with friends. Just traveling. I've never belonged to anything, sure as hell not Interpol." I wrestled against Manolo's grip. I might as well have been in a straight jacket. "I don't have anything you'd want."

"I want to know what you have going with Huerta."

"Huerta? Carlos Huerta? I just met the guy this morning."

"So you said. Prove it!"

"How? How can I prove that? We're in the middle of a god damn lake!"

"Find a way, quick," he said calmly. "You have ten seconds."

"But…"

"Nine."

"I don't know any more than what I've already told you."

He pushed the barrel hard into my forehead. "Five. Come on, Skipper, you can do this."

"I'll tell you anything you want, but I can't tell you what I don't know. If you're going to kill me, there's nothing I can do about it. But I'll die wondering why you hadn't taken the time to find out that I'm nothing more than what I say I am. What a shitty way to die."

Garret pulled the trigger, the deafening sound of a round shot past my ear and out over the lake. My ears were ringing in high C when he said, playfully, again, "I'm just messing with you, Skipper." He patted my cheek as he gave me a blistering stare then lowered his gun, resting it on his thigh. "I have to be sure. I have to know I can trust you."

"And scaring the shit out of me is your way of developing trust? Asshole." I felt Manolo's hands tighten even more. "If we're talking trust, tell your Mexican friend to let go."

"Sorry, Skipper. Can't do that. Trust factor hasn't been established yet."

"Trust me for what? What the hell's going on?"

"I believe you have a certain… integrity. But if I find out you're anything other than what you say you are, I'll put a bullet in your head. *¿Comprende?*"

"Completely," I said, relieved that he believed me, yet haunted by the fact that if he changed his mind a bullet could be chasing me around Mexico. "What do you want from me?" I asked again.

"I have a proposition for you," he said. "I don't write. You do. I want you to write a book about my life down here."

"You put a gun at my head to tell me that?" I tried jerking away, but Manolo's grip was too strong. "You son of a bitch!"

"I put a gun at your head to show you what you'd be getting into if you choose to do it."

"You'd trust me that way?"

"No. You're in this boat, and the water's damn deep.

It's not a matter of trust as you know it. It's business, and my business can be extremely unforgiving."

"It might help if you told me what you do," I said angrily. "Let me decide without a gun at my head and my arms free."

"You're not stupid, Skipper. I think you've already guessed," he said. "Cannabis and coke are big business. I want you to write the story. I'll pay you to live here until it's done, then more when it's published." He reached into his shoulder bag and pulled out a stack of cash. "There's twenty thousand dollars here. It's yours if you stay. But you'll have to know everything about me and what I do. This is not fiction. Our meeting was by chance, but the rules are still the same. Turn on me, and no one will ever find your body." He peeled off five one hundred dollar bills and stuffed them in my shirt pocket. "Call it incentive."

"My timing may be off a little," I said, eyeing the gun on his lap, "but guns have never held much sway with me. Just a nasty means of persuasion."

"In my business, decisions are made with guns. They're an occupational necessity." He snapped on the safety, put the gun back in his shoulder bag, and nodded to Manolo. I felt the blood rush back into my arms as Manolo released me.

I flexed my shoulders and rubbed the circulation back into my arms and looked straight into Garret's eyes. "You son of a bitch!" I yelled.

He never saw it coming. With Manolo sitting behind me, I knew it had to be fast. I slammed my fist into Garret's cheek. He fell straight back, his head hitting solidly on the small anchor in the open space at the bow of the boat.

Manolo had me by the throat before I could go after Garret. Air was leaving me fast, and I was getting light-headed and dizzy. I saw Garret give the Mexican a nod, then as quickly as Manolo had grabbed me, he let go. Garret was back on his seat instantly, leaning forward inches from my face. With air rushing back into my lungs, I heard him say smugly, "That was your one shot, Skipper. I'll let this one go, but don't ever try it again."

I leaned closer into Garret's face, matching the intensity of his stare, knowing that at any second Manolo could toss me into the lake for fish bait. "I like to keep my options open Garret," I declared. "Now, get me the hell back to shore!"

Garret gave me a light tap on the chin then signaled to Manolo to fire up the outboard and head us back toward Scorpion Island. He looked to the island coming up fast on our right and said with a wry smile, "So I guess you're in, eh, Skipper?"

"In?" I said, still feeling the remnants of Manolo's hands on my biceps and the sting in my hand. "I haven't agreed to anything. You seem to think we have a deal."

"We do," Garret said, running a finger over his swelling cheek. "I like your style, Skipper. You may claim to be a writer, but you've got fight in you. This was a test of your meddle."

"That test won't help raise my GPA," I said with disgust.

"Don't worry, you'll be protected and obviously well paid."

Fighting against my anger, I thought about my dwindling finances and the chances of finding work in Mexico. Twenty-thousand dollars was more than I'd seen in years. With that much money and with Manolo protecting my back, it was worth considering. *How bad could it be?*

"Why?" I asked. "Why would you want anyone to know about this? Writing about it puts a pretty bright light on you. Everybody'd be looking at you and for you."

"They already are. Maybe I have a death wish," he said, "but I've always wanted to be a legend, or a folk hero, or whatever you want to call it. Be nice to have people sitting around in their living rooms talking about me. I want to have some record of my life before a bullet finds me. Mariachi songs or *corridos* would be even better." As Manolo eased the boat next to the wooden dock at Scorpion Island, Garret grabbed the bow line, tied the boat to a cleat, and said casually, "Ready for an early dinner? We'll seal the deal. Great restaurant here."

We sat at a table under a thatched umbrella and ordered beers from a callow, pigeon-chested boy who seemed obsessed with my pre-mature gray hair. "You don't mind if I don't eat," I said to Garret. "I haven't got the stomach for it right now." The waiter continued his stare. "Natural," I said, picking at the short curls.

"Diego," Garret addressed the waiter. "Two specials, *por favor.*"

"*Sí, sí,*" the waiter said. "I will buy."

"You won't buy anything, Diego," Garret declared and pulled a wad of bills from his pocket.

"*Señor* Garret," Diego responded, "I owe you for giving my cousin work. *Muchas gracias.*"

"*Por nada,*" Garret said, shooing the waiter back to the open food stand behind us.

Both Garret and Manolo were now staring at my full head of gray hair. "It *is* natural," I said, "unlike some of the other things that have happened today."

"Cut the smugness," Garret said. Then with a quick, twisted smile, he said, "I've been wanting to ask you. Are you the same Skip Reid? The All-American from Michigan?

"Past life," I said, "but, yes."

A spark came into his eyes. "Cover of *Sports Ilustrated* a few years back. Hockey's Enforcer they called you. "Rumor is you busted up a few guys pretty bad outside a bar. Supposedly killed one of them."

"Supposition doesn't kill," I said. "They were getting a little chippy. It wasn't the best of times for me."

He looked me over, seemingly reviewing his thoughts about me. "I saw you play once. You took no prisoners. I was a fan."

"Let's keep it that way," I said. "All I'm looking for now is a good story and great surf. No more bullshit."

"I'll see what I can do about that," he said as the waiter returned with two plates of Chapala white fish. Garret cut into his fish. "Meanwhile, we've got business to take care of. You in?"

Who are these guys? I thought as I looked out to where Manolo had killed the motor. *And what is this curiosity that has found a foothold, attached itself, and is blowing holes like hand grenades through what few rational thoughts I had left?*

"Sure," I said. "Why not?"

I t was six o'clock at night when Garret dropped me at my hotel near the Mercado, reminding me that it would be inadvisable to consider leaving town. I was free of him for the moment and had five hundred dollars of his money. It would be easy to pack and skip out, and it didn't usually bother me in the least taking money I hadn't earned. But with Garret and his goon throwing their weight around, it made me think differently. The thought of being buried in a hole in the sand somewhere in Mexico was not a good idea at any time. Manolo's bulk alone should have told me to get on the next bus out of town, to head to Panama, and to catch a few waves with friends. Yet, I had agreed to meet Garret the next day in the Mercado. There I'd give him his money back and then catch the next bus south.

My room was a three-dollar-a-night escape in a seedy hotel. I'd been there two nights. The title above the slot in the cage separating the main lobby from the hotel desk read "Concierge." Armando, a five-foot ball of a man with a scraggly mustache was, as usual, reclined in his arm chair reading the newspaper, one leg crossed over the other as I approached the cage. Without lowering his paper, he gave a frustrated sigh and mumbled, *"Completo. Vas de al lado."* Full up. Go next door.

In the few days I had been there, I had not seen more than a handful of people going or coming at The Hotel Libertad, and those were normally renting by the hour. For him to say the hotel was full would be like saying the Hilton was empty. Both would be suspect. Armando was using his self-declared busyness to avoid dealing with most of the hourly-rate transients. When he lowered his paper and saw that it was me, he groaned and pushed himself out of his chair, flushing scraps of food out of his thin mustache with his thumb-like fingers. He started to shove my key through the slot when I caught him staring at me. He shook his hand in front of his chest then gave me a look that I thought might be pity.

"Quit looking at me like that," I said in my best Spanish. Then I noticed my reflection in the mirror behind his desk. My afternoon with Garret hadn't helped my hygiene at all. My shirt was torn at one sleeve. My throat was red and raw from Manolo's strong grip. I looked a mess. "I need the directions to the Archeological Museum of the West," I said. I had the rest of the evening and had read that the museum was open until nine. I thought I'd do some research on the Tabachine culture.

"Sí, sí." He thought for a few seconds and said, *"16 de Septiembre Avenida."* His lazy mind seemed to be working. He waved his stubby fingers toward the door. *"Sigue derecho, luego gira a la derecha."* I followed his hand as he pointed straight then gestured a quick turn to the right.

What I had discovered about Mexican directions is that they always require a backup. I don't know if the people intentionally mislead you, or if they are too proud to say they don't know. What I do know is I would have ended up back at the bull ring had I followed his fingers. I checked my map and discovered the museum was only a block away between Independencia and Campesino streets.

16 de Septiembre was busy with late-afternoon commuter traffic. Dusk was closing in to temper the exhaust smoke that rolled in acrid, gray waves from the buses, taxis and trucks pulling loads down the wide avenue at the speed of growing grass. The cloak of twilight, however, did nothing for the choking stench of burning oil and gasoline that floated through the shops and small restaurants lining the avenue. The smoke filled my lungs making it difficult to breathe. I hadn't felt this kind of chest pain and nausea since the mid-fifties before L.A. banned back-yard incinerators.

The Archeological Museum of the West was a truncated pyramid set back off the street, its roots buried deep in pre-Columbian architecture. Fortunately, the structure was built 500 years later, and I was relieved to feel the cool breeze of an air conditioner as I swung the glass door open and walked into the narrow lobby.

A nicely dressed woman in a crème skirt and red blouse with bands of crème color running through it was fidgeting at a desk in the middle of the foyer. Except for a telephone near her right hand, a few brochures neatly fanned on the corner, and a name plate with Graciela Gonzales engraved in gold letters, the desk was clear. I had just started toward her when three official-looking men in suits rushed out of an office in the corner of the lobby. They had an urgency in their step. Their speech was clipped and sharp as they prattled intensely to one another. Seeing me, they slowed for a moment, staring hard. Apparently not seeing what they were looking for, they accelerated through the door like children at the gate of an amusement park.

I shrugged at the woman behind the desk. She was

sitting straight and tall in her hard-backed chair, her wide butt rolling over the edges, giving her the appearance of a full-figured paper weight. She had the worn look of a laborer in a Diego Rivera mural. She flicked her eyes toward the door, shook her head twice, shrugged at me in return, and asked with a tight-lipped smile, "*¿Qué puede servirle?*"

"I'm a writer," I said, "and I'm looking for information about the shaft tombs in the Guachimontones region."

Her oblique stare told me she thought that *I* had just been excavated and pulled from the dirt. After a quick inventory of myself mirrored in the glass of an encased ceramic model of a seated male figure with an upraised weapon in his hand, I couldn't blame her. My Hawaiian shirt, besides the tear in the sleeve, was soaked through with sweat and needed a lot more than just pressing. My shorts hadn't been washed in a month, and my hair was a tangle of gray knots from the Jeep ride. A moment of silence passed until she pulled a strand of her own gray hair off her face and said with a replica of politeness, "*Un momento, por favor.*" She picked up the receiver and pressed a button on the telephone, saying a few rapid words in Spanish that didn't sound like they were in my favor.

A long minute later, a tall, lithe woman in her midtwenties seemed to float out from the corner office where the three men had appeared earlier. Her stride was soft, seductive as she approached me with her hand outstretched. For a moment, time seemed to stop. She was wearing the same crème and red skirt and blouse as the receptionist, but she wore it with style. Her narrow waist was tucked tightly above the roundness of her hips, her breasts round and firm with just enough bounce to make them interesting. Her black hair was pulled tightly to the back of her head, with small curls dropping just in front of her ears. She looked fresh and alert, her eyes bright and forth-right, but they held a fire that could wound you. The danger, however, had bypassed my brain and gone straight to my groin. My cave man instincts kicked in for a second. Thoughts of pulling her into a dark corner of the museum and backing her up against a wall, raising that crème and red skirt up to her shoulders and...it had been a while.

"Itzla Abarco," she introduced herself, looking me over, interrupting my fantasy. In her high-heeled shoes, we were nearly eye-to-eye. "I'm the director here at the museum."

I took her outstretched hand, and for a few seconds we stared at each other. She appeared to be no older than some of the teenage girls I taught surfing lessons to on the beaches of Southern California, the ones who had to work on getting as brown as Itzla Abarco was naturally.

"Skipper Reid," I finally said. Her hand was cool and soft, the kind you never want to let go of.

"May I be of some help to you?" she asked, sliding her hand out of mine.

She was one of those women who could set you on fire, destroy your confidence, make you want to max out your credit cards. My fire was a year into its ashes, though, my comfort around women well-guarded, and I gave up my credit cards when I left for Mexico. What I had left was a sense of primal urge that could only get me into trouble. She'd be good for a few days, I thought, reminding myself that commitment and accountability had long ago been erased from my emotional thesaurus.

"I could only hope," I finally said smiling, dropping my eyes to her mouth, to her soft, full lips. "I could buy you a cup of coffee, and you could tell me all you know about the Teuchitlán burial sites."

"I'd be happy to talk to you about the burial sites, Mr. Reid. But as you may have noticed, we are in bit of a crisis right now, and coffee is not on my list of things to do this evening. Now what is it you'd like to know?"

How is it that some of the most beautiful women can exude so much sex appeal and still be as cold as a side of beef in a storage locker? She had everything to make any man's juices flow, but I doubted anyone could get near her without an ice pick.

"Just thought maybe it would warm you up," I said without thinking.

"I have no time for games, Mr. Reid." She turned and began to walk away, her well-toned calves flexing in a rhythm that could make a poet sigh with envy.

"*Lo Siento,*" I said. "I'm sorry. I could use your help. I promise I'll be good."

She turned, saying, "Mr. Reid, I will gladly give you the information you're looking for, but I will not put up with your arrogance. Do we understand each other?"

After negotiating with Garret for my life earlier in the day, Itzla Abarco's question was piss in the wind. I said, "Yes," and added, "I could take a shower, clean up a bit. You know, shine a little?"

The glacier seemed to be heading back in my direction, and I doubted seriously if I even wanted to try to thaw it out. My ex fiancée's betrayal had closed down my emotions, and my trust factor was in the negative. The only attachment I wanted was an occasional erection given to a no-name stranger. My smile was my only bit of bravado, and it didn't look like Itzla Abarco was buying even that.

After a nod from me, we headed into the main gallery and into one of the five small rooms that housed the Tabachine heritage.

"Why Itzla?" I asked. "It's an unusual name."

"My parents wanted to keep the Aztec culture alive, even if it is in name only," she said. "It's an Aztec word that's difficult to translate."

"If I translate it correctly," I said with a grin, "it means 'girl who needs dinner.'"

She glared at me but didn't move away. "Mr. Reid. I haven't time for this. What is your interest in the burial sites?" she added with the detached coolness of a clinical entomologist.

Breaking through to her soft side was comparable to being blindfolded while trying to hit a moving piñata with a toothpick. Not impossible, but highly improbable. I knew what I looked like at that moment; and as she looked me over, I knew she wasn't going to let me forget it.

"You don't exactly have the demeanor of an archeologist," she said.

"Well good, because I'm not," I replied. "I'm content with being a writer and a damn good surfer. I'm interested in the ruins at Teuchitlán. And now even more interested because of a stolen limestone warrior. It was a Tabachine piece from what I understand, discovered in those ruins back in the '40s by three men from Teuchitlán."

Her eyebrows lifted just enough to show surprise. "How…,"she stammered. "How do you know this?"

"I research things that interest me. You don't mind if I pick your brain a little?"

She checked her watch. "I have little time." Her voice filled with the stress of necessity.

"We'll start with an easy one," I persisted. "How did you get this job?"

"I did my doctoral dissertation on the architectural and ceramic chronology of the Atemajac Valley."

I straightened up after that. Beautiful *and* smart.

She must have noticed my surprise because her face softened for an instant. "UCLA," she said.

I smiled. It still wasn't working. "Well, then, I guess that makes you the expert."

"Yes," she said slowly. "Thank you for acknowledging that."

It's difficult playing with the competition when the competition is a league above you. In just a few short minutes I was on the ropes, struggling to come up with some sort of defense to salvage what little testosterone I had left. I'd have to play her game.

"Your uniform has the same colors as most of these pieces," I said. "Not a coincidence, I'm sure."

"Red and crème bichromes," she said, hastily leading me to a display of obsidian tools and ceramic artifacts. "Most of the ceramics during the Late Tabachines period, about 600 A.D., used these colors. The motifs were predominately geometric, some had more organic motifs. Bands, crosshatching, drips, propeller shapes, horseshoes, clusters of dots, and hardly ever seen, rectilinear spirals referred to here in Mexico as *xicalcoliuhquis*. The Tequila valleys seem to be the sites where a much more complex iconography took place, possibly because there was more emphasis on symbolic signaling. But Graciela told me you're more interested in the shaft tombs and burial sites, no?"

"I know you're in a hurry," I said. "Tell me what you know."

Following her to a color-coded map of the Atemejac Valley was like stumbling behind a prima ballerina gliding across a stage. My body was telling me it had been too long a dry spell, and the sensuous outline of her legs moving beneath her skirt was only making it worse.

"The Guachimontone site is here." She pointed a long finger at a small blue ring circling the site. "As you can see, it covers a fairly large area."

I studied the map for a moment. Teuchitlán and Guachimontones were highlighted in yellow rings. "How many tombs have been uncovered?"

"We aren't so interested in the burial shafts themselves although they are extremely important in our work. Our focus here is to locate and preserve pre-Hispanic artifacts and to establish architectural chronology phases. Since the shaft tomb complex is scattered across a wide area of western Mexico, you can see that it is quite a challenge. To answer your question, we have just begun excavation on five shaft tombs."

"Have any been excavated before this?"

She tapped the map. "On a small scale in the central valley and some north of here in El Arenal and Huitzilapa. We usually find that someone has been there before us."

"I would imagine they're prime sites for looters, given the potential for profit."

"That is a problem we are dealing with, yes."

I thought I saw a pout on her full lips as she sighed and flicked her head away from the map. "Sounds like a pretty big task given the area to be covered," I said.

"Too big for our small museum. But Carlos Huerta..."

"Carlos Huerta?" I said with surprise. "The barrel-body under the cowboy hat? The bull breeder?"

"He is a little overweight, and yes, he does raise bulls, among other things. How do you know Carlos?"

"I met him at the bull ring earlier," I admitted. I didn't feel comfortable telling her that his was a name of interest to Garret when we were out on the lake.

"That would be Carlos," she said with a quick laugh.

"He is our self-proclaimed goodwill ambassador for Gua-dalajara. He is also an investigator for the central region of the National Institute for Anthropology and History here in the state of Jalisco. He and I have enlisted the government's assistance and, with its limited resources, it is doing what it can to help us."

"Any luck?"

"The people of Teuchitlán keep a vigil and have caught a few teenagers having fun on Saturday nights. The kids climb into a shallow tomb and tell ghost stories, maybe walk off with a few shards, but we haven't gotten close to the thieves who break into unexcavated tomb sites and steal priceless artifacts."

She was silhouetted in front of a warm spot light and a backdrop of richly-colored tapestries, her skin glowing with the sumptuousness of someone who has found her passion. I felt raw and undeveloped standing next to her, out of the light, not knowing where I would be tomorrow, or the next day. *How could I offer her champagne when I could barely afford beer?* And the thought of holding Itzla Abarco, if only for a moment, shook me to my core. I hadn't had a meaningful embrace since before the Kiwi came on the scene and stole my fiancée. Talk about looting. Itzla, too, seemed to have lost something dear to her, beyond the looted treasures she was so committed to retrieving. Her coolness, I thought, might be evidence of something deeper.

"Carlos and I," she went on, "are currently investigating the disappearance of one of the pair of hollow warrior sculptures you mentioned earlier. The pair is from the Early Tabachines period, around 300 A.D. My uncle and my father and Carlos discovered them many years ago. It was stolen from the museum last night. It's priceless, and clues to its whereabouts are as rare as it is. You probably saw the security people leaving when you came in."

I nodded as she led me to an eighteen-inch high earthenware figure. It sat in a dimly lit, glassed-in alcove toward the rear of the room on a round, five-foot tall sandstone column. A matching column sat next to it, its platform empty. She pressed the palm of her hand against the glass casement, saying, "Its large size in relation to others, the baton, the special headdress, and his heroic stance all indicate that he was something special, probably a warrior chief. Its twin is the one that was stolen."

"Twins usually stick together," I said. When she didn't respond, I said, "Whoever stole it had the opportunity to take both. Why just the one?"

"I don't have the answer to that, Mr. Reid."

"But doesn't that make you curious?"

"I'm only interested in getting its twin back."

"Then you must have some confidence that it will be found."

"With Carlos' and the government's help, everything that can be done will be done," she said. "We can only hope it hasn't left the country."

"Too many needles in too many haystacks, I assume."

Itzla backed away from the glass. "In a manner of speaking, yes. It would make our job much more difficult."

I smiled. I couldn't help it. I was looking at her smooth, unblemished skin that could easily have been fired by the Aztec gods of beauty. "If there's anything I can do to help. Maybe investigate, or, as I mentioned, have dinner and talk about it."

"Mr. Reid, I have to go," she said and hurried back toward the entryway. "Feel free to wander around."

Your body would be choice wandering, Ms. Abarco, I thought.

I spent another ten minutes in a cursory tour then picked up a brochure and map of the Guachimonton from a stand near the door. Itzla and a man resembling a poorly-sculpted obsidian figurine under a black cowboy hat were in a quiet conversation just outside the door. Her colorful skirt and blouse made her even more strikingly beautiful when compared to the short, thin-legged block of a man standing next to her. Itzla was a good two inches taller than he and at least fifteen years younger. The man was Carlos Huerta.

When I approached them and made it known I wasn't going away, she turned to Huerta and said coolly, "Mr. Reid, I think you know Carlos Huerta."

"*Con mucho gusto*. We meet again," Huerta said. "And what brings you here?"

"Research," I said. "As someone once told me, there are a lot of stories here."

Itzla took over. "He's interested in the history of the Tabachine shaft tombs. I told him about the stolen warrior."

"Ah, the great mystery," Huerta said with a wry smile. "I doubt that you'll discover anything other than what we already know. But if you happen to get lucky, I'd like to hear about it."

Huerta's self-righteousness touched a nerve in me. I returned his mocking smile. "Whatever I discover, you can read about it," I countered, turning toward Itzla.

Huerta snickered. "By all means. I'm an avid reader."

CHAPTER
FIVE

Armando, the little concierge at my hotel, looked at me with a suspicious grin as he pushed aside the coarsely-woven, cotton fabric that separated the kitchen from the reception area. He smelled of dust, sweat, and molé. Without a word, he slid my room key under the wire barrier and started back to the kitchen.

"Armando," I called before he could disappear behind the curtain again. "*Un momento, por favor.*" I had been thinking about Itzla's passion for the Guachimontone and the mystery of the stolen warrior. The ruins warranted a visit. "How would I get to Teuchitlán?" I asked.

"*Ahora?*" Armando's eyebrows rose in surprise.

"Is there a problem with going now?" I said.

"No. No problem. The bus goes once a day from Teuchitlán to Guadalajara," he explained. He went on to describe how it toted the women of the village into Guadalajara and dropped them off near the bus depot where they spent the day at the Mercado Libertad selling their fruit and live poultry. At seven o'clock at night the bus took them back home.

It was six-forty-five by the clock behind Armando's desk. "*De Prisa.* You will have to hurry," he smiled, the thin hairs of his mustache crawling down over his upper lip.

I raced up the rickety, wooden staircase, splashed some water on my face and changed my shirt and shorts. I slid the five bills Garret had given me earlier into my shirt pocket. On my way out, Armando gave me the name of a family who would rent me a room for the night and, he guaranteed, wake me in time to catch the five a.m. bus back to Guadalajara if I chose to return. Fortunately, I didn't have to rely on Armando's directional finger. The bus station was right around the corner from the hotel on Niños Héroes off Calzada Independencia Sur.

Because Guachimontone was not yet an active tourist attraction, the bigger bus lines bypassed the village of Teuchitlán on their way to Santiago de Tequila. My bus was obvious. It sat alone at the far end of the terminal, huffing black smoke and sitting on well-worn tires in need of air, the rattle of loose valves echoing across the yard. With all of the sleek, air-conditioned busses humming in the yard, why was it that the mud-covered Teuchitlán bus was the one I drew? The one with windows-down air conditioning, the salty-sweet stench of sweat-soaked seat leather and the ever present fragrance of live chickens, dust, and hot bodies?

To the well-dressed tourists climbing aboard the newer busses, heading for Mexico City, Oaxaca, or Merida on the Yucatan peninsula, the Teuchitlán bus must have seemed like a romantic dream from which they woke up much too early. The old bus, along with the cracking, paint-peeled colonial structures around the city and the colorful local markets, seemed to hold those people in an arc of their own covenant. They knew they don't have to live here. They could always go home. A luxury I couldn't afford.

I dropped the ten peso fee into the driver's hand and

followed the crowd aboard. After a series of linked recoveries while trying to avoid the large woven baskets and cardboard boxes that filled the aisle, I managed a seat over the wheel well near the rear of the bus. With the bus filled, the driver, without even a glance to his passengers, pulled the door closed and yanked a sweat-stained cowboy hat onto his wide head. He revved the already overtaxed engine, which spewed black smoke out the back like an antiquated coal-burning locomotive.

At the gate of the depot we were met by a dozen people flagging down the bus. Locals heading home. The driver simply made room. He recruited a male passenger, and between the two of them, they hoisted cages, baskets, boxes, duffel bags and other non-breakable items up on to the roof rack where they were securely fastened with ropes and a large canvas tarp. Next came five wooden planks that were stretched across the aisle from seat to seat starting at the rear of the bus. Being by the wheel well, my seat got one of the planks. The dozen newcomers then picked their way through the mess of cargo in the aisle and began stepping over the planks to get to the rear seats. When everyone had settled, I found myself being crushed against the window, feet on the wheel well, my legs shoved up into my chest. We were sitting seven across on an eight foot plank, and the twenty mile, forty minute trip looked like it was going to be a long one. As the saying goes, you get what you pay for.

Not long after we left the terminal, the driver bounced the bus onto a roughed up washboard road and slowed to let off a woman passenger. It was only then I realized that the Teuchitlán bus also served as a commuter bus for families who lived in the area. People began to flag down the bus, appearing from under the shade of the trees and bushes that ran along the roadside. The driver, a patient, avuncular man, seemed to know all the people coming and going. I never saw any exchange of money. I surmised that a balance befitting the scales of justice had been established a long time ago and bartering a bag of oranges for a ride kept the equilibrium.

The old bus clattered along, stopping once to allow for a small herd of cattle to be driven across the road by two men on horseback. This gave me time to take in the vast stretches of agave fields that ran for miles along the highway, trailing back into the shadow of the foothills in a carpet of steel blue. Each plant, armored with its six-foot spiky leaves protecting its heavy pineapple type heart, seemed to have an ally in the ominous Tequila Volcano rising behind it.

When the road was clear, a red, four-door Toyota passed us in a hurry. The car's driver honked, and a slender, brown arm waved from the passenger window. The bus driver returned the honk with a tinny, drawn-out version of "La Cucaracha."

Is there anyone this guy doesn't know?

Ten minutes later, the bus chugged its way up a dirt and crushed-rock road toward Teuchitlán, finally wheezing to a stop in front of a small grocery store in the middle of a row of concrete and adobe buildings lining the narrow, rough street. The store, by the signs on the outside walls, specialized in selling Fanta soft drinks and Bimbo bread.

I stepped off the bus and my peripheral vision caught a flash of red in the alley between the store and the building next to it. It was the red Toyota that had passed the bus earlier. I shook it off as coincidence and hopped onto the crumbling, shredded ribbon of sidewalk that heaved and swelled on its way through the town. I had one foot in the store when I saw Itzla coming out of the shadows. My stomach suddenly felt like the sidewalk I was standing on.

"We can't always meet like this, you know," I said, smiling with an awkwardness that made me feel like I was back in the seventh grade trying to get the courage to ask a girl to the Spring Fling. "Hi, remember me?"

Itzla looked me over with those electrifying brown eyes of hers. At least this time I was wearing my best shorts and a clean Ocean Pacific T-shirt that matched my aqua-blue eyes. My hair was a little messed, and I was sweating through my shirt, but all in all I felt presentable.

"Of course. It's Mr. Reid, right?"

"Most of the time it's Skipper," I said, the wave of nervousness fading. "The mister part makes me feel like I've had a family and a steady job. Makes me feel old."

From out of the shadows of the store I heard Carlos Huerta's commanding voice. "We can't seem to shake you, can we?" It was the third time in one day he had put a chill on con-versation.

"We seem to have some of the same interests," I said, watching Itzla greet a woman half her size, kissing each cheek.

The bus driver, having made his way up the street after unloading the baggage and parking the bus, dipped his body toward Itzla, ready to fall on one knee. He gave Carlos Huerta a quick angry stare, then with arms outstretched, he said playfully, "Pino, Pino," as Itzla rushed to him.

"*Tio* Lino," she smiled and the man pulled her into a hug.

Huerta forced a smile. "Family, Mr. Reid. She was born here."

Caught off guard, I said awkwardly, "Those are her parents?"

"Is that so strange to you?"

"Only in the sense that she seemed to be more of a big city girl."

"She lives in the city, but she will always be from here," Huerta said with irritating sarcasm. He tugged at the crown of his spotless cowboy hat pulling it off and wiping sweat from his brow with a square-folded handkerchief. "No one will ever take that away from her. Lino and Nailea? They're her uncle and aunt. They raised her after her parents died. That was twenty-five years ago."

I couldn't take my eyes off Iztla. Her coolness had turned as warm as the Tequila Valley sun. Her presence seemed to make everything glow.

"I'm sorry," I finally said. "Pain like that never goes away. How did it happen? I know you knew her father. And you know her uncle. The three of you discovered the Teuchitlan Warriors."

Huerta's eyes flicked to me for an instant. In that instant I saw the roadhouse bouncer in him begin to stir. I had obviously switched on something that went pretty deep.

"We all feel her pain," he said smugly, returning his attention to Itzla.

"How?" I pressed. "What do you know about it?"

"*Gabacho*," he sneered. "That is something that happened twenty-five years ago. Do not try to dig up old wounds."

"Old wounds can heal." I was thinking about Itzla and the trauma she must have felt losing both parents at such a young age.

"A little advice, Mr. Reid. Do not pursue this," Huerta

insisted. "The family has been hurt enough through the years. Stay out of it."

"I'll try to contain myself," I said, matching Huerta's arrogance.

Huerta broke the tension with an abrupt laugh. "She is quite beautiful, no? However, I suggest you stick to surfing, or whatever you do when you're not freewheeling around Mexico with your clutch disengaged." He said this with a haughtiness that immediately, in my mind, dropped him to the level of snail castings. "She would not be interested." After a moment, he brightened again and asked pleasantly, "How is your research going?"

"Shaft tombs and a stolen warrior are big topics," I said. "I'm feeling my way around them right now. There is something bothering me about the theft, though. Why do you think only one of the warriors was taken? The opportunity was there to take them both."

"That is a question we have been asking ourselves, also," Huerta admitted. "Perhaps the thief miscalculated with his timing and heard the security guard coming."

"Possibly," I said, then offered, "How the thief got in would be my next question. And maybe there was more than one."

Huerta shrugged his meaty shoulders then worked his thumbs into his wide leather belt and said sharply, "There is no story, Mr. Reid. Forget it. It's all being taken care of internally. We don't need American journalists prying into Mexican affairs."

"I'm just speculating," I persisted. "Sorry if I'm stepping on toes, but what if this affair goes beyond Mexico? What if the figurine is out of the country already?"

Huerta snorted a laugh. "What do you know?" he asked with a calmness that didn't quite hide the uneasiness in his eyes.

"Nothing," I retorted. "Just conjecture from a prying journalist."

Before Huerta could respond, Itzla returned, the warmth of the last few minutes trailing behind her like the dust from her uncle's bus. "So, Mr. Reid, are you getting enough local color?" she asked, her coolness returning.

"Other than a bit of chill in the air," I said, taking a hard look at both Itzla and Huerta, "I think there's plenty to write about here." I smiled and nodded toward Lino who was keeping himself a good distance away. "The bus ride alone was worth it."

"Maybe that is all that is here for you," Huerta said flippantly.

"Are you two boys finished?" Itzla said irritably. "We're losing the sun, Carlos. Mr. Reid, we're going to walk the ruins. If you'd like to come along, you may learn something."

"The learning curve on something like this shouldn't be too difficult," I said with a twist of sarcasm. "Thanks, I'll tag along."

We marched up a dusty, narrow path on the outskirts of the town, passing a few shaded pools of a large spring and on to the top of a knoll where several shaft tombs were exposed. The backside of the knoll was littered with shards and ground up pottery debris. From the top of the knoll I could see the Tequila Volcano looming over the valley, pretentious and foreboding in the fading light.

Itzla had been focusing on the ruins below us when she suddenly squatted at the top of one of the tomb entrances. Leaning over the edge, she said in a husky, playful voice, *"El espíritu de La Diosa Mictecacihuatl llegará pronto."*

Huerta started chuckling at the sounds of small voices

and giggling coming from inside the tomb. Itzla put a finger to her lips and gestured for me to move back.

It was quiet for a moment inside the tomb. Then as though a lid had been blown off a popcorn pan, children started pouring out, one by one climbing the step to the surface.

"Itzla! Itzla!" they shouted, running to her, showing off small, plastic skeletons and skulls, and colorful tissue paper with intricate, festive designs cut out. One of the girls wore a dress and a red, wide-brimmed, plumed hat. Itzla hugged each one as they danced and hopped around her. Then she sent them on their way, headed them down the path to the village, yipping and laughing, and shaking their toys.

"*El Día de los Muertos,*" Itzla announced for my benefit. "The children are preparing for it. The second of November. It's a holiday to celebrate children and dead loved ones."

"That second part sounds a bit morbid," I said.

"How can it be morbid, Mr. Reid, when the children are blessed and the dead are remembered with smiles instead of tears?"

"So all those children had big gaping smiles, remembering the skeleton of someone in the grave down there?" I asked, pointing a finger at what lie under her feet.

"Mr. Reid, you are pushing on tradition," she said. "We are born into it. It is a part of us. The Aztecs had a day just like it called *Mictecacihuatl* or The Lady of the Dead. She was a goddess who presided over the celebration of remembering death and the dead. In three days, Mr. Reid, families will be out celebrating in the town's cemetery. It's like your Halloween, only not so grim.

"What do you see down there?" Itzla continued.

I moved to where she was standing and scanned the valley. With the exception of the shaft tombs, I saw only an occasional mound of dirt and cobbled foundations rising out of the otherwise flat, dry ground and the Tequila Volcano looming over us to the north. "A few small streams, mesquite, acacia, agave fields," I said.

"Look again," Huerta insisted. He had come up next to me and was pointing to a low rock foundation.

"Okay, there's a pattern," I said. "What is it?"

Huerta and Itzla swapped looks with each other that told me I was being a pain in the ass. But they were stuck with me because I had no where else to go until her uncle's bus left for the city in the morning.

"That is an unexcavated site," Itzla explained. "The mound that you *now* see is a central pyramid. And if you look closely, you can see that it is surrounded by a circular plaza and an outer ring of platforms which were once residences."

"And probably of more interest to you," Huerta interjected haughtily, "what would a city be like without a sports arena. To the left of all this is the ball court, that low lying stone foundation."

I was getting tired of Huerta's belittling comments. He was definitely scratched off my list of dinner guests. "It's certainly not surfing," I said, "but I guess they could have had some fun down there. Except for a brief time, I never saw much point in chasing a ball or a puck around." I turned to Itzla. "These are not like Teotihuacan or any of the Maya ruins."

"The Tabachine never considered building huge pyramids or stone stelae to ingratiate powerful rulers," she said. "They portrayed their world in the form of earthenware vessels and figurines that were made to accompany the dead. They weren't concerned with grandeur."

"You mentioned at the museum that there were powerful chieftains," I said. "Weren't they honored?"

"Only in a way to commemorate their family lineages. Powerful chieftains built shaft tombs and burial chambers for this purpose. We're standing on one now."

"That's a chief down there?" I asked.

"Yes," Itzla said. "Do you find all this strange, Mr. Reid?"

"Quite frankly, yes."

"By the way, that's a one-step you're standing over," Huerta said peering out over the edge of a circular foundation about six feet in diameter, maybe six feet deep. "One limestone step and you're in the vault. Take a look. Don't fall in," he said with a patronizing grin. "There's a side chamber at the bottom, dug in about ten feet. Sometimes they dug two or three chambers on each side of the shaft."

Staring cautiously over the lip of the shaft, I said, "Looted, I suppose."

Huerta grunted. "Over the last couple of centuries. Look at this shit lying around. Two thousand year old ceramic art turned into a gravel footpath."

This was another side of Huerta I hadn't seen. "Pardon me for saying, but you don't seem the type to let the past keep you awake at night."

"I don't know what type you think I am, Mr. Reid, but I do have a certain interest in history."

Huerta moved to the edge of the knoll and squinted under the shadow of his hat brim into the darkening sky. Backlit, he gave the impression of a bandy-legged gargoyle as he combed out his mustache with his fingers. "The deceased were laid out in full regalia and surrounded by food and earthenware figurines of warriors and ladies," he said.

"I'm sure you like that last part, Mr. Reid. They were offered elegant vessels, figures of musicians and contortionists, shamans and dwarfs. They didn't care so much about sculptures and artifacts depicting gods and pageantry."

"So ending up in a shaft tomb was considered an honor," I said. "Not unlike the Egyptians, only with fewer pretenses."

"Correct," Itzla agreed. "Unlike most of the other Mesoamerican cultures, figures and vessels were made to function as a vital link from the living community to its ancestors. And through them to the greater, all powerful forces residing in the earth, rivers and lakes, and in the sun and moon."

I looked out over the ruins, letting this sink in for a minute. "So the value of the stolen warrior is not only its value as a relic but our human need to understand the beginning of things?"

"Exactly," Itzla said. "It gives us a sense of order and place."

"Mercenaries would never believe that," I said.

"True," she agreed, "but they know people who do."

Huerta was checking his watch. "I must be leaving. My meeting in Tequila won't wait for me. Itzla, I'll walk you back down."

"Thank you, Carlos, but I think I'll check a few more sites up here. Take my car and pick me up in the morning on your way back if you don't mind."

"*Por nada.*" He pulled Itzla aside, and after a rapid conversation in Spanish, they gave each other a quick kiss on both cheeks. He then gave me a look that could have frozen a pot of boiling water. "And I'm sure we'll be seeing more of you, Mr. Reid."

I gave him a small salute. "It would be my pleasure,

Mr. Huerta."

Huerta had started down the path when Itzla called him back. A Jeep was climbing the road that closely skirted the village, on its way into the pine-forested hills. She had noticed the trail of dust in the distance.

"That's Garret and Manolo," I said. "I'd know Manolo's bulk anywhere." The sound of the bullet Garret had fired past my ear on the lake resounded in my memory. My stomach turned over.

"How do you know them, Mr. Reid?" Huerta's sudden interest in my relationship with Garret and Manolo put me on edge.

"I met them in the Mercado Libertad earlier today," I said cautiously. "We had lunch. Not much else." I dared not tell Huerta about the proposition Garret had offered me because of Huerta's status in the government. He was nasty enough to cause me trouble. And I hadn't liked the tension I had seen between him and Garret outside the bull ring earlier in the morning. Getting caught in the cross hairs of intervention was not my idea of a good night out on the town.

"Do you know them, Carlos?" Itzla asked.

Huerta straightened up. His eyes grew hard at the question. He took a long look at the Jeep. "I've seen them around town," he finally said.

"I've never met them," Itzla admitted. "Uncle Lino tells me one's a *gabacho*. *Gringo* to you, Mr. Reid. He came here when I was away at university." She smiled softly at Huerta, lightly touching his shoulder with her fingers. "Lino and Nailea don't talk much about him, and he doesn't seem to be a problem," she continued. "He apparently employs some of the locals, which is good because there isn't much work here."

Huerta looked again at the Jeep vanishing over a hill and then started down the path, his short legs moving him along at a brisk pace. "I'll see you in the morning, Itzla," he barked over his shoulder.

"I guess we're stuck with each other," I said, keeping pace behind her, enjoying the movement of her hips as she began her long strides uphill to another site.

"I'm not stuck with anything, Mr. Reid. I know what I'm doing here. Do you know what you're doing here?"

I looked around at the empty landscape and then at Itzla. It seemed that at this point in my life, no matter where I was, I never seemed to know why I was there. My life had turned into a crap shoot, and I was the dice. I never knew how I was going to be tossed. Discretion, however, told me to keep this thought to myself. "Research, my dear, research," I replied.

"Well then, you're certainly in the right place for providence, Mr. Reid."

T he night shadows had all but taken over the last rays of light as Itzla and I quietly headed down the hill to the town, the endless patch-work of agave plants in the Tequila valley below us still bragged with the lingering sheen of gun-metal blue in the fiery last moments of daylight. At one point, I turned and looked back up the hill, noticing several higher plateaus that reached up to the tree line.

"Are there more sites on those upper levels?" I asked.

Itzla took a long look up the hill. "There is one shaft tomb," she said, "but no one goes up there now. It, too, has been looted. It is the tomb where my father, Uncle Lino, and Carlos Huerta discovered the twin warriors back in the '40s."

"How well did Huerta know your father? And Lino?" I asked. I was hoping for that bit of insight Huerta had refused to offer.

"They were friends. The three of them grew up here together." She noticed my curious expression and added, "There are many strange things that happen in Mexico, Mr. Reid. Not everything is coincidence."

"You said 'were' friends. Not anymore?"

"My father is gone, and Lino and Carlos have gone their own ways. They rarely speak to each other, and when they do there is anger in their eyes."

"Do you know what happened?" I asked.

"Only that it was some kind of feud no one talks about. You have a lot of questions, Mr. Reid."

"Only as many as you're willing to answer, Ms. Abarco," I said, over- exaggerating the playfulness. "After all, I am a journalist. That's my job. I'm pre-wired for *preguntas.*"

* * *

We came off the hill and into the town, she leading me along the thin ribbon of cracked, undulating cement that served as a sidewalk. She stopped at the door of her aunt's and uncle's store. "End of the line," she said flatly and started to lift the latch on the wooden door.

"Wait," I said, suddenly remembering. "Armando at the Hotel Libertad gave me the name of a family who had a room to rent."

"Vincencio and Luz," she said and pointed me in the direction of a wood and adobe building at the end of the street. "They'll take good care of you. Say hello to Pepino."

"How did you know?"

"It's getting dark, Mr. Reid. The only bus leaves at 5 a.m. And that's the only room for rent in this town. Not much to know."

"Let me buy you a coffee or a *cerveza*," I said. "Payment for the tour. Is there a place you can recommend?"

"This isn't L.A., Mr. Reid. My family is here, and we have business to discuss. If you want a *cerveza*, I suggest the cantina across the street."

My attempts at convincing her that the night still had a

lot of mystery and promise left in it were about as plausible as me paddling out to meet a twenty-foot wave head on. Both were inconceivably idiotic.

As I turned to go, I noticed the ruins of a burned out adobe next to the cantina that I hadn't seen earlier. The charred remains of what used to be the roof covered the dirt floor, fire-scorched walls left patterns of gray and black, scars to someone's psyche. "Why not meet me there later?" I said, indicating the cantina. "You can give me a little history of this town. You know, story background, local color."

"Good night, Mr. Reid." Itzla then disappeared into her family's store.

CHAPTER
SEVEN

Vincencio and Luz lived in a dirt floored, two-room house at the edge of town. The room they gave me was a ten-by-ten stable that had apparently been an add-on to the main house years ago. There was no electricity in the room and the only light came from a kerosene lantern that Luz had brought in and set on the sill of a low, open window on the back wall. The smell of freshly-cut hay wafted into the room from the corral outside the window. I tossed my leather shoulder bag onto the bed and listened as it thumped on the hard wooden surface beneath the horsehair mattress. *What was I expecting? Hotel Libertad amenities?*

A short while later, after checking the room for anything that could possibly move in my direction during the night, I asked Luz, who had silently come to stand in the doorway as though anticipating my question, where I would find the bathroom. The look she gave me said everything. Of course, it was outside, behind the house, next to the corral. She told me that the water pump on the side of the house was broken and that her husband, Vincencio, was fixing it at that moment.

Luz led me to the window. On the other side of a small

corral her husband was clamping a large pipe wrench on a vertical pipe in an attempt to fix the faulty pump. His frustration was evident as the wrench would not bite and hold. It was a two-man job. I handed Luz the lantern and stepped over the foot-high sill of the window and out into the corral where I was greeted with wet nudges from a small burro that had somehow sneaked up on me.

"*Pepino!*" Vincencio barked with disgust as he shooed the animal into the middle of the corral. "*Es loco.*"

Maybe it was the full moon that was making everything so crazy, but with it and Vincencio's flashlight the work was easier and we finished before the Mexican intuition network, that system of everyone knowing what everyone else is doing, could be turned on. We had just tightened the last bolt when Lino came around the corner.

"My friend has helped me," Vincencio said to Lino, smiling up at me. "*Vamos a la cantina. Cervezas para mi amigo.*"

The ingratiating words sung in my ears. After my encounter with Garret, the long, dusty bus ride, and a rejection by a Mexican beauty, not to mention a knuckle-scraping pump replacement, and a good sniffing by a thin-legged pack animal, I felt a few beers would put a nice cap on the day. And hopefully take the edge off Garret's proposition.

The cantina wasn't much larger than Lino's bus. The musty smell of old dirt, sweat, beer, and a mixture of undefined aromas from fried food hit me hard as we entered the cantina. I had spent more than a little time in Southern California beach town bars that had similar properties; but unlike those bars, the redolent blends here seemed to fill the cracks in the walls, sealing in a prurient scent of antiquity.

Vincencio and Lino gave an engaging nod to a leathery-faced old man standing behind a short, wooden counter where a few hard-boiled eggs and something that looked like beef jerky sat on sheets of waxed paper. The man had fewer teeth than my hands had fingers. He was wearing a sweat-stained, straw palm cowboy hat and an ill-fitting brown suit. But the man had a presence that took over the room.

"*Tres Dos Equis, Benito*," Vincencio requested of the man, leading me to one of the two heavy tables that seemed likely hand-hewn from scrub oak. They were butted against the side walls, with posters of past bullfighting events and an assortment of black and white photographs plastering the walls at awkward angles above them. Above the counter several strings of small wattage bulbs were tacked in loops to a wooden beam sunk into the ceiling.

I grabbed one of the folding metal chairs that were scattered around the dirt floor, flipped it around to the table and sat down. While Benito was popping the caps off the beer bottles, I noticed a few bottles of whiskey and a half-empty liter of tequila on a narrow cabinet behind the counter, standing next to a lone, old, dust-covered relic of Tres Equis beer. *Serious business had passed through here,* I thought.

Benito stood tall and straight as he set our beers on the table, his eyes bright, his face tight as rawhide, his toothless smile perhaps a cover up for a thorny past. Lino must have seen my curiosity rising. He snorted a quick laugh and took a swallow of beer. Then, in his broken tourist English, he said, "Benito used to ride and fight with Pancho Villa in the revolution. He has been the mayor of our town for many years."

Before that could sink in, Lino pulled a tattered paperback from a shelf behind him and flipped to a page of black and white photographs. There was Benito as a young man shoulder to shoulder with Villa on the last car of a stolen train, rifles raised, and fists held high in victory. I looked at Benito, quietly standing behind the counter, his head buried under his wide-brimmed hat, his eyes flicking back and forth, alert to every movement in the room. In the fifty odd years since the revolution his pride appeared to have been preserved. His dignity was definitely unassailable. And he looked like he could still throw a mean punch.

Benito brought more beer and sat down with us. I could see mischief in his eyes as he jabbed a hard-worn index finger at his face in the photograph. "We fight for the people," he said, his voice strong, his English slow and fractured. "We protect what is ours."

I believed him. He was just perverse enough to scrape the skin off anyone who posed a threat to his way of life.

I wanted to know more; but at that moment my eye caught a colorful poster of Curro Rivera, the matador, on the wall next to Vincencio.

I stared hard at the poster, remembering Coleen and I watching Curro a year ago, in Tijuana, just before I threw her out, before she flew off to New Zealand to be with her Kiwi. Now, listening to Lino and glowering at the poster, I thought about the bull I had seen killed and slaughtered at the Guadalajara arena earlier in the day. With the memory of Curro and Coleen flashing through my head, I couldn't see much glory or bravery in shoving a sword between the severed shoulder muscles of an already dying bull.

We had soaked up a couple more beers when Lino asked, "What is here for you, Skip? Very few people come to Teuchitlán."

"Originally research," I said. "For a story I thought I'd write about the ruins. Now it's even more intriguing with one of the twin warriors being stolen. I understand that you were one of the ones who discovered it."

Benito puffed up his chest and glared at me over the lip of his beer bottle. Lino spat onto the dirt floor. No one spoke. All sound had been sucked out of the cantina.

Lino finally sighed, a sigh with a lot of weight to it. "That is something that happened a long time ago. There are enough skeletons in the cemetery. I won't waste this celebration with more." He took a long pull from his beer. His somber mood then turned once again to high-spiritedness. The three of them tapped their bottles together and laughed.

"There is something else now, Mr. Reid? Besides research?" Lino asked playfully. He emphasized my name, the same way Itzla did, only he did it with a snicker. "People know everything in this town, Mr. Reid. But don't let that stop you. We will probably know what you are doing before you do it."

That may be part of the tradition Itzla was alluding to earlier—an insidious unconscious passed on through history, sometimes going beyond all logic. Only the gods know the truth, and they're usually not around when you need them.

So I didn't have to mention that Itzla was becoming a priority with me, they seemed to already know. I had hovered around her like some silly, star-struck kid all afternoon. No wonder they were laughing. I felt my face flush. Even with my tan I couldn't hide it. Maybe I didn't want to hide my feelings for this woman who probably wouldn't throw me a life preserver if I were drowning. Maybe I'd take my chances with her. She seemed like a good bet.

To relieve some embarrassment, I asked, "What do people do for work? This isn't a tourist town, and I don't see much else to keep people busy."

They were quiet for a moment, until Lino finally said, "*Agricultura.* Some of the people work in the agave fields, but most of them have work on *fincas,* ranches."

"Then you must know Garret," I said.

"Maybe. There are many *fincas* in these mountains."

He took a sip of beer and it became obvious I wasn't going to get any more information. I changed tack, trying to lighten the mood again. "Actually I do a lot of surfing." Quizzical looks was all I got from the three men. "Surfing," I repeated. "On a board, in the ocean." Their blank stares and shrugs told me they had no idea what I was talking about. I jumped onto my chair, then onto the table. I stood over them, knees bent, one foot in front of the other, arms moving to fake my balance. "Surfing," I said again.

Lino seemed to understand. With a beer in his hand, he worked his way up onto the table next to me, laughing and mimicking my posture. He tried explaining it to Vincencio and Benito and got nothing but comical looks from both of them.

"Why would you waste your time playing in the water, Skip?" Benito asked. I didn't have time to answer, because at that moment Itzla walked through the door, saw her uncle on the table, and me with my sandals, Hawaiian shirt, and shorts, pretending to ride the giant waves of Hawaii's Bonzai Pipeline. The look she gave me was indiscernible, but I thought I saw a hint of a smile.

"*Tío,*" she said in a way that brought us all to attention.

Lino leaned toward my ear. "I'm afraid my niece has found us out, Mr. Skip. She has come to take me home. It is late. We'll surf again, *amigo.*"

"Thank you for entertaining my uncle and friends, Mr. Reid," Itzla remarked as I slowly climbed off the table. "But I doubt they'll be renting surfboards in Puerto Vallarta any time soon."

"You never know. They may buy a franchise. They're a pretty lively bunch." Not expecting an answer from the Azteca, but feeling as though I had dropped another number on her scale of credibility, I asked, "Do I look as red as I feel?"

To my surprise, she said, "You needn't be embarrassed, Mr. Reid. You are being who you are. Not many people can say that."

"Is that a compliment?" I asked.

"Good night, again, Mr. Reid."

* * *

Benito swung the cantina's door closed behind Vincencio and me, and I heard the snap of a latch from inside. We started the short walk up the street. He to his house; I to my straw mattress in the stable. Itzla and her uncle were walking across the street through the darkness toward their store. She had one arm draped over Lino's shoulder, the other holding his arm to steady his walk. Her compassion for family was obviously very strong. *Why did it stop there?* Then it came to me. She had to have been hurt badly, a broken, painful relationship. It was the only explanation. My breakup with Coleen had frozen all the juices of intimacy that I once had. And I would bet that Itzla was feeling the same betrayal. It was the loss of love that hurt so much, the pain of feeling you weren't good enough.

After hopping the corral fence near the water pump Vincencio and I had fixed earlier, I was about to step over the sill into my room when Pepino bumped me from behind. I caught my balance in time to keep from smacking my head on the bed frame and then rolled onto the bed. Luz had left a low flame burning in the lantern in the corner of the room. I could see Pepino's neck and head stretched over the sill, reaching for the mattress. He had already shredded one corner of the mattress and strewn hay around the base of the window. When I reached out to scratch him between his ears, he tilted his head and leaned into my hand.

"Hello, Pepino," I said. "Hope you don't mind my snoring."

It seemed only a few minutes had passed, not long enough to get into R.E.M. sleep when Luz quietly knocked on my door. I rolled over, bumping heads with Pepino grazing on the corner of the mattress, his muzzle now inches away from my head, his warm, sweet breath wafting across my face.

Luz handed me a cup of coffee in a ceramic mug; and with a sly smile and an apology for waking me up, headed me out the door to the bus. Several people had already boarded with baskets of ceramic figurines, small landscape paintings, colorful tapestries, and several hundred chicken eggs, hoping to make a day's wages by selling from blankets spread out on the sidewalks in and around the bus depot and outside the Mercado Libertad.

In the darkness of the early morning, it was difficult to tell whether the red Toyota had returned, so I assumed that Carlos Huerta had spent the night in Santiago de Tequila and that Itzla was safely tucked away in one of her aunt's beds. As Lino ground the gears to get us going down the hill, I was relieved to see Itzla wave to him from the store window. Thinking I could recoup a bit of my loss from the night before, I waved to her, a big sweeping wave across the window of the bus. She turned away, expressionless, pulling the thin cotton curtain back across the window.

CHAPTER
EIGHT

Groggy from the night of drinking and little sleep, I was still able to pull up enough reserve to thank the gods of mystery for the comfort of the uncrowded bus.

When Lino swung the door's round metal handle inward, the squeal pulled me out of my reverie of Itzla and Huerta and their quest for the stolen warrior. I was on my seat over the wheel well as the bus unloaded at the Guadalajara depot wondering if all their effort and time was worth the misery and grief they seemed to be experiencing. Itzla was serious enough already. This hunt could nudge her into the no-fun-zone forever. But that wasn't my problem. I had to figure out what I was going to do with my life. And I couldn't do it by getting involved with something that didn't concern me or with a woman who had little room in her life for anyone outside of her family. The best thing I could do would be to grab my backpack and hop on one of the tourist buses going to Panama. I'd surf the Pacific shore with my friends.

Lino's bucket of shaken bolts huffed to a rest at its usual spot across the yard from the mainline buses. "So, did you learn much, Mr. Reid?" he asked, sitting down across the aisle from me after everyone had left the bus.

"Last night it was Skip," I grumbled. "What happened to Skip?"

"It's a formality, nothing more Mr. Skip. It has nothing to do with our liking you or not liking you. Myself, I like you, only there are *impedimentos*."

We both laughed at my new title. I could handle 'Mr. Skip.'

"Obstacles to liking me?" I asked. "You don't seem to be the kind to let things get in the way of friendships, Lino."

Lino's grin spread over his wide, sun-reddened face. He tugged on the brim of his hat, pulling it down onto his forehead. "Me, no," he said.

"And Itzla? What about Itzla?"

"My niece is very good to me and Nailea and to our town."

"Does she have a special man?"

"Why do you ask this?"

"She seems to be interested in nothing but her work. That sometimes means that a woman has a special man, or she doesn't want to have one."

Lino settled into his seat, thinking. "I like you, Mr. Skip, so I will tell you. She is very suspicious of men, especially *gabachos*."

"All gringos aren't so bad. Besides, she went to UCLA. She must have made some American friends."

"Of course," he said. "But one took her heart and then left her. Now her heart is here in this valley. She is not as cold as she appears, Mr. Skip. She worked hard and studied hard and is afraid that she will lose all that she has worked for if she gets involved with a man again. She does not want to give up her career."

I winced, and then reminded myself that I was not in the States where the sexual revolution was in full steam and the women's movement was shattering old traditions like B.B.s shot into plate glass. "She doesn't have to," I said cautiously.

"If she marries a Mexican man, she may have to," Lino went on. "It is our culture. However, Itzla is strong-willed and has a powerful sense of justice."

"I won't argue that."

"If you're honest with her, she can be a friend, *pero cuidado si no.*"

A quick rush of promise swept through me as the two of us climbed off the bus. "Lino," I said, "careful is my middle name."

CHAPTER
NINE

I t was seven a.m. when I brushed through the swinging saloon doors at my hotel. I needed sleep. I needed to collect my thoughts. I needed some room between the events of the last twenty-four hours and my decision to work with Garret. Even with the money that Garret had offered, the price wasn't nearly high enough for being the possible target of a fanatical drug dealer's bullet. Who was I kidding? I had made up my mind on the bus ride from Teuchitlán that I would pack my duffel, leave the $500 in an envelope with Armando, and hope that Garret would pick it up should he come to the hotel. There was a three o'clock bus that afternoon leaving for Panama. That would give me time to catch up on sleep and make a quick visit to the museum to check on Itzla's progress of finding the lost warrior. It was still a story, and Itzla was still on my mind.

The little concierge, Armando, was sitting upright in his chair— a stone icon of the Aztec God Quetzalcoatl, although not nearly as impressive. He was all but invisible behind the newspaper he had spread open in front of him, but I could see in the mirror behind him that he had now slicked back his hair, and from my view he looked like a counterfeit pterodactyl from an Eastern European B-rated movie.

I tapped the little bell three times before he sighed, snapped his newspaper closed, and toddled over to the counter. When he saw it was me, he grinned and pulled the key to my room off a hook behind him. Sliding the useless key over the countertop, he asked, "Teuchitlán is nice place, no? And the room?"

I reluctantly thanked him for reserving the room at Vincencio's and Luz's and told him that I was disappointed that they didn't have a swimming pool.

"Armando?" I then asked as he shrugged and started back to his chair. "Why do you give me a key when the lock doesn't work?"

"Sometimes it works," he declared. "Try it now."

With a little urging the lock did work. I had just opened my journal when my thoughts were broken by the sound of the only toilet on the floor flushing outside my room, the pipes rattling a strange benediction to the god of sewage. The toilet was a selling point for the management. Not so much that room rates were discounted for the noisome, sporadic discord of the plumbing, but rather for the availability of American toilet seats. Armando had shown me my options when I was considering the hotel. "A nice bathroom with American toilet seat," he had said as he repeatedly lifted and dropped the seat. "*Muy comfortáble.* You can use it for twenty-five cents more each night."

"Or?" I asked suspiciously.

"Or you can use the one in the hallway upstairs without a toilet seat. Everyone uses that one."

"Sold," I had said. It was first-floor luxury I could afford.

That was two days ago. It could have been a year.

I grabbed my towel and what was left of my bar of soap and went downstairs to the upgraded bathroom for a quick French bath. While scrubbing the day's grime from my face and arms, I had the most improbable vision of Itzla Abarco riding a long board on a left break in the surf off Malibu. I was smiling at the image when Garret and Manolo faded into the picture. I realized that the only people I had met so far seemed to have a vested interest in the ruins at Teuchitlán. Even though Itzla's and Garret's interest seemed at different ends of the cultural spectrum, they were fervent in their attention to them. I could understand Itzla's interest in the Tabachine culture and her concern for the preservation of its history, but what was Garret's interest?

It seemed my head had just hit the pillow when I rolled over in a half-dream state and saw Manolo looming large and frightening over me.

"*Vámonos*," he ordered and jerked me to my feet. "Garret wants to see you."

Manolo's large mass shadowed over me like a huge storm cloud as we descended the unstable stairs and marched through the lobby. He was hovering too close and I didn't like it; but I remembered his lightning reflexes with Kopek and still felt the bruise on my neck. I dropped the thought. There wouldn't be much I could do even if he decided to get a little more intimate.

Garret was waiting in the Jeep outside the front door. He didn't look happy and his quietness made me uneasy. Manolo jumped into the back of the open Jeep behind me, talking into a crackling, squelching radio. We drove north out of Guadalajara up the narrow two-lane Highway 15 through the latticework of blue agave fields on the hilly terrain of the Tequila Valley. Garret steered the Jeep onto a dirt road fifteen miles from Santiago de Tequila, and we headed west on a kidney-jolting ride over washboard ruts and pot holes toward the foothills and Teuchitlán. It was familiar territory. At a junction just short of the town, Garret turned onto a smaller road that skirted the town in a wide arc and then reconnected with the main road a half mile above the town. It was the road that Itzla, Huerta, and I had seen Garret and Manolo driving up the day before.

As we snaked up into the hills, past the upper ruins of Guachimonton, I said, "Garret, if you're pissed about something, we'd better clear it up now."

"Why would I be pissed?" he snorted guiding the Jeep around a few holes in the road. He rubbed a light purple bruise on his cheek where I had landed the punch that sent him reeling into the bow of the boat. Snickering, he said, "I just need to know if I can still trust you, Hockey Man."

"Nothing has changed," I lied.

"You weren't at the Mercado this morning. We had a meeting. I thought maybe you were running out on our deal. That's why I sent Manolo to find you."

I had written off the meeting, thinking I would be free of the two miscreants by the afternoon. "I had a long night and overslept," I continued with my half-truth.

His stare burned into the side of my face. I was somewhat comforted, however, when I saw no evidence of an imprint of a gun under his shirt. Yesterday's paranoia had deferred itself to the gorilla riding behind me. "I thought I made it very clear that you had to know everything," Garret said.

He was driving more carefully now, maneuvering the Jeep to the left at the fork off the main road. Below us were the sandstone and sage plateaus. Farther down the hill was Teuchitlán, its structures sitting in short, tight rows like a line of a child's wooden blocks. In the lower ruins, a few children were playing in the fields, darting in and out of the broken structures, and bobbing their heads from inside some of the pit mouths scattered over the area.

"Playing with the dead doesn't seem to bother them," I said, watching the children with their homemade skeletons and colorful masks in preparation for *El Día de los Muertos*.

"Why should it?" he said. "Dead is dead. The real cemetery is behind the town, off the road we came up."

He made another turn uphill and headed off into the variant greens of the mountain foliage, leaving the children behind to play their hide and seek games, to disappear into the darkness of the shaft tombs. It was a hard ride over a road creased like leather. I kept a tight grip on the panic bar for what Garret called his "Last miles." We were headed to his "Ranch."

On one thickly overgrown, uphill stretch of rutted road about three miles up the hill, Garret slowed the Jeep. "Watch," he said. His smile, his first real one, had pride scrawled all over it.

I saw nothing until a few bushes alongside the road began to shake.

"That was for your benefit," Garret said. "Didn't want you to panic. Manolo radioed we were coming. You would have never known they were there."

"They?" I said. "Who?"

Garret nodded once, downshifted into first gear as two men dressed in camouflage and carrying small automatic weapons with banana clips came out of the bushes. They stood on either side of the road, their guns an outward expression of their willingness to use them. Even in the open, detecting them was a challenge with their clothing blending into the background of like colors and a dark canopy of green arcing over their heads, making the road a lengthy tunnel of twisted branches and huge leaves. One smiled beneath his soft green cap, leaned back into a bush, and playfully shook the branches.

Manolo, cat-like even with his tremendous size, swung himself out over the rear fender with one arm, using the roll bar as a pivot point. He and one of the guards squatted at the sides of the Jeep and locked the wheels into four-wheel drive.

"Don't try it on your own," Garret said as his soldiers waved us through with a quick two-fingered salute then disappeared into the underbrush as quiet and motionless as a mirage. "Only I know where they'll be. You'd never get inside the perimeter without a bullet up your ass. No one stumbles into this place. If they do, they're either stupid or playing stupid. My men don't tolerate either."

He must have seen the quick flicker of concern on my face. "Don't worry," he said. "As long as you're with me, you'll be safe. Manolo will see to that. We've got a mile to go. Hold on. Things can get a little rough from here."

Garret maneuvered the Jeep through the thick, forest-like growth as we headed even higher into the mountains and bounced it across the rocks in the slow-moving water of several shallow streams. We had encountered a few more guards and eventually came out of the overgrowth into a small valley and into a clearing half the size of a soccer field. The forest growth was taking back the land, creeping into the clear cut, spreading out over the rooftops of several outbuildings as if covering its tracks.

"Welcome to my home," Garret said.

I waited for the punch line. It didn't come. The house itself sat on a knoll about 100 yards up a road on the far side of the clearing, a faded red and yellow colonial hacienda overlooking the open field and outbuildings. It was a nine-teenth century icon of Mexican architecture: columned arches supporting a portico that ran along the inside perimeter of the structure, heavy wooden doors, a small plaza with a central fountain. It was pushed up against the wall of a vertical palisade, planted in the ground, a stubborn reminder of a once remarkable time.

"Home sweet home," I mumbled, prying my numb fingers from around the Jeep's panic bar, looking around, seeing no one, hearing nothing. I knew we were being watched. People were always being watched in Mexico. It wasn't paranoia; it was fact. They would come out of the jungle or the desert, simply appearing. When nothing was around and you could see for miles, suddenly someone would be standing next to you on the road smiling, carrying a chicken or a pot of *mole*.

Garret pulled the brake in front of one of the outbuildings and hopped out. He looked even smaller against the sweeping mountain peaks surrounding us in the small valley, against the backdrop of intense jungle vegetation aggressively challenging the open space around the compound. I reconsidered his height. Five-foot-seven, maybe, I thought, if he was having a good day. Old jeans, a pair of huarache sandals, and now swimming in a black-hooded sweatshirt, he could have been a former surfer, one that hung out with deadheads on the beaches of Southern California.

Manolo gestured toward the building with a twist of his head, his boyish grin returning. He followed me until we caught up with Garret who was hobbling up to the door. I still felt the pain of Manolo's big hands on my arms from the day before, no longer fooled by the illusion of his innocence. Manolo, at the rear, always watching.

"Every story needs balls," Garret said. He rapped his knuckles on the wall of the outbuilding. A crisp, metallic sound echoed like a tack hammer on a steel drum. "Real adobe," he said, laughing in short, low-pitched chirps. "The balls are in here."

In actuality, the adobe was nothing more than a painted veneer, a facade for the half-inch steel plating covering the front and sides of the building. The steel door was painted to look like weathered oak. I suddenly felt as though whatever was coming was going to be rougher than the ride over the mountains into the compound, a lot more gut wrenching than ballsy cockroaches and fearless mice in my seedy hotel room. But that stubborn kernel of curiosity, as always, was bursting in the back of my brain.

Garret shouldered the door open, and the sun threw a bright rectangle of light ten feet onto the dirt floor. Shadows feathered their way out toward the walls and dust danced in the air. "These walls will stop .50 caliber bullets if that's what you're wondering," he said.

The only thing I was wondering was how I ever found myself in a situation where I had to choose between bullets and a bus to Panama.

A generator kicked on. The generator was one of those mysterious things that happened, like people appearing from nowhere and acting as though things were normal. Garret laughed and told me that he had twenty-five men in the compound and doubted that I'd see any of them. And by the way, don't wander off.

As always, Manolo stood silently behind me, a gorilla wired for 220 volts, ready for his switch to be thrown. I searched Garret's eyes for any sign of betrayal, anything that would give him away. I wanted to know if I was going to die here, but the mystery of the whole damn situation was too deep and my suspicions seemed to be growing as simply and honestly as the land that had been taken back by the encroaching jungle. There was one road in, one road out. Manolo, I knew, wouldn't stop me. *Why should he? Wouldn't the jungle do his job for him if I tried to run?*

I faked a grin while I stared at dozens of military, police, and Federale uniforms. Some hung from hooks on the walls, some were strewn over the backs of chairs, some lay in piles on counters that wrapped around the small-windowed room. All ranks, mostly officers. On the counters at the far wall was enough firepower to withstand a raid by a small army. Colt .38's and .45's, small caliber carbines, semi-automatic rifles, compact Uzi's, dozens of nocuous weapons, idling, like Manolo, ready to show their strength. In the corner, rocket launchers lay in neat rows, again waiting to take out anything smaller than a tank. I ran my hand over the stock of a Mossberg 500 assault shotgun and remembered my father searching through catalogs looking for one to add to his gun case at home.

I could smell Manolo's sweating body behind me as I looked over the arsenal. I said to Garret, "You didn't get this shit out of a Sears catalog."

Garret picked up one of the small carbines and pulled the bolt. "I told you I spent some time in 'Nam. What I didn't tell you is that I was an Army captain who volunteered for a unit called Tiger Force." He looked at the tattoo raging on his forearm. "It was a unit of compulsive killers, or as the Pentagon called them, 'Psychological Misfits.' Our job was to clear cut enemy troops and relocate civilians. I went AWOL when the orders came down to shoot anything that moved. I couldn't kill innocent people. That and a blown business deal I had with my C.O.

brought me here. I learned everything there is to know about ordnance and how to get it from him. Now the son of a bitch is set on revenge."

"Kopek?" I said nervously. "Maybe I should have stayed put in the Mercado, drinking coffee in a quaint little *fonda,* catching up on my writing."

"You need the details," Garret said as we walked outside and stood in the open field. "Details make good stories."

Sometimes I don't recognize the depth of my involvement until it's too late. Comes from a dull childhood, from a kid who wanted answers and never got them. "Not if there's no one around to write them," I said.

"Push through the fear, Skipper. Bump it to the next level. If you don't have fear, you might as well be in that quaint little *fonda* drinking coffee. It's safe, and you'll never get the details."

"The fear is more about discovering my own secrets," I said.

"You'd better get over that philosophical crap, and fast," Garret suggested. "Or, you could end up fish bait by someone else's hand." He stood with his hands on his hips, surveying the area. "So, like what you see?"

"I'm not here on a shopping spree," I said, realizing that steel plating for a drug dealer would not be used for street renovation. "What's that one?" I pointed toward one of the outbuildings sitting away from the others at the far end of the compound under an awning of broad-leafed heliconia.

Garret stood motionless and stared out at the building. "Until you have a need to know, it's nothing. Let's walk up to the house. We'll toast our new relationship."

CHAPTER
TEN

We have business tonight," Garret said later that afternoon after a brief tour of the hacienda. We were sitting on one of two oversized fawn skin sofas in the corner of his massive dining room, surrounded by what appeared to be pre-Hispanic ceramic artifacts neatly laid out on entry tables, book cases, benches, and the mantel of the huge stone fireplace. A large colorful tapestry from Mayan weavers that had probably made its way across the border from Guatemala hung above the mantel. Rich, multi-hued rugs were scattered over the sandstone-blushed floor tiles. Garret was becoming an enigma. His grittiness didn't seem to pair with the garniture of the room.

We'd had a few shots of tequila and half a joint brought to us by Esperanza, a rough-looking middle-aged Mexican woman wearing a pair of jeans and cowboy boots. Her blue cotton, long-sleeved work shirt was open at the top; her dark hair stacked and pulled into a braided bun. She fit the house.

I was looking at her when a ceramic piece in the form of a conch shell trumpet sitting on the mantel caught my attention.

Garret noticed my curiosity immediately. "They're real, Skipper. I know what you're thinking, but you're wrong. I paid for every one of those. Well, almost all of them. That's a ceramic pectoral from the valley of Atema. Early Tabachine ceramics fascinate me. It was such a pure, simple period."

"The missing warrior is from that period," I pointed out.

"That's what I understand," he said then quickly called to Esperanza, who immediately reappeared from an adjacent room. "Fix up a room for Mr. Reid. He'll be staying the night."

"I'd rather you take me back to my hotel," I said as Esperanza nodded and left the room.

"Catch up on some writing; some sleep."

"What you'd rather do doesn't mean shit," Garret declared. He threw back another shot of tequila and then settled back into the sofa. Garret's voice told me he had been bitten, probably more than once, by the sting of past lies. It was the same kind of apathetic, don't-give-a-damn posturing I saw in some of my friends who had returned from Vietnam. They had seen the lie too late, and their spirits had been warped by mistrust and horrific death.

"Manolo and I have business to take care of tonight," he continued. "I'll get you back to your hotel in the morning, but tonight you're staying here. You're part of the deal." Grinning with the intention of prompting my memory, he looked at my shirt pocket where the five one hundred dollar bills were still neatly folded inside. He snickered and said, "Come with me."

We walked out into the shade of the portico where he then led me down the road from the house and out across the cleared area of the compound, past the mysterious outbuilding sitting by itself behind the cover of its protective overgrowth, to a series of small buildings half-hidden along the periphery. Manolo wasn't with us, but I sensed his presence. It seemed to be everywhere. When Garret opened the door to one of the larger outbuildings, Manolo was standing next to a palette of packaged kilos of marijuana, counting.

"*Doscientos cincuenta kilos,* Garret," Manolo said when he had finished his tally. "*Listo.*"

Garret turned to me and said sharply, "We're shipping two hundred kilos of weed tonight. Closing off a two-mile stretch of highway five miles from here at three a.m. I've got a plane coming in. Three minutes on the ground. Throw the shit on board and it's gone. We've done it a hundred times." He gave me a quick smile and punched me lightly on the shoulder. "You're free to wander around. Esperanza will give you what you need. I'll send Manolo to get you when we're ready."

Wander around? The statement seemed more of an order than a courteous suggestion. *And where was I going to wander without the fear of poking my head in the wrong door?* I opted for sitting at the fifteen-foot, hardwood dining room table on one of the stiff, wooden, leather-backed chairs in the main house. Esperanza brought me a pitcher of guava juice along with several pens and a notepad. I had written several pages when my curiosity about the artifacts in the room got me to wander. Partially hidden behind several ceramic pieces in the bookcase was a small, unframed black and white photograph, its edges creased and torn. Garret and five other men in jungle camouflage were lined up with their arms around each other's shoulders, all wearing tiger-striped bush hats. One man's face was hidden under the shadow of his hat brim; another had an incongruous wide-mouthed smile that never reached his eyes. Two of them seemed to stare out into space, lost in their own little worlds. I recognized Kopek immediately, his cold eyes glaring out at me like small tombstones. Even being so far removed from the reality of that situation, I could sense the evil heat in the photograph. The word ZIPPO had been printed in bold letters across the bottom.

I replaced the photo just as Manolo rushed into the dining room with a large duffel bag over his shoulder and ten of the men I had seen working around the compound earlier that day. The men were dressed in military uniforms. None seemed a day older than Manolo—late teens, early twenties. They all carried the same look of determination and commitment that I had seen in Garret's lieutenant. Each had been trained from the ground up to be nothing more than a soldier, numb to social consciousness, living only for his loyalty to Garret.

Manolo tossed the duffel bag onto the dining room table, unzipped it, and began passing out weapons to the men.

I watched as Manolo readied the Jeep under the light of a half moon; as two of the men backed a dark panel truck up to the door of the building housing the wrapped kilos. Within minutes the truck was loaded and ready.

Garret punched a clip into his .45 and settled behind the wheel of the Jeep. "We're going out the back way, Skipper," he said. "Less chance of any foul ups."

I pulled myself into the seat in front of Manolo and instantly felt as though the mice in my hotel room had somehow worked their way into my stomach and were scurrying about pouncing on cockroaches.

"This is tense shit," I said. "Guns, drug running, illicit clandestine operations, and God only knows what else."

"We're all nervous enough to piss our pants. It is tense shit," Garret replied. He leaned back in his seat, staring at me. "You're not going to do anything stupid are you, Skipper? We're just making a late night delivery. UPS night service. Think of it as opening night in the barn."

"My fans threw bottles, not bullets," I said. "Besides, I don't think I could do anything any more stupid than I've already done."

Garret laughed. "Sure you could. We all could. Stupidity sits out there waiting for us. It's incentive to risk something sacred. Too bad we don't realize how stupid it is until after we've done it. If we survive it, we move on. If we don't, it doesn't matter, does it?"

"If my life is at stake, it matters," I said.

"It just may be."

Before I could gain my wits, Garret had started the drive up over the mountains behind his ranch. Manolo was busily chattering into his handheld with the driver of the van following us. As Garret cautiously steered his way over the rocky ground, using the narrow swath of light from the headlights to guide him, I gripped the panic bar more tightly.

We drove for twenty minutes until Garret finally hit the brakes and skidded to a stop on a rocky promontory a couple of hundred yards from the road. "We're not stopping any traffic until we get a signal that the plane's in the area," he said. He scrambled out of the Jeep and stood on the rock overhang, surveying the area, curiously watching the few cars that passed below him. The van driver maneuvered the van to the side, ready to make the downhill run on what looked to be an unused fire road.

Then Manolo got the call. The plane was on its way.

Six men jumped out of the van and ran down the fire

road. Each carried a hand gun and a flashlight. Dressed in dark colors, they immediately disappeared into the foliage along one side of the road below us. Manolo barked orders into the handheld, and instantly one side of the road lit up with a series of flashlight beams, lighting the way for the incoming plane. I heard the plane's engine humming as the pilot brought the plane up through the valley toward the makeshift landing strip. The pilot was bringing it in without lights, relying only on Garret's men and their flashlight beams for guidance. At the last minute, before touchdown, the road lit up for two hundred yards when the pilot switched on the plane's landing light. I recognized it as a DeHavilland Beaver, the work horse for bush pilots. It could carry up to 2,000 pounds of cargo and get off the ground in less than a thousand feet. The light cut into the darkness, spreading into the random bushes and sandy knolls lining the road.

Garret took the few yards from the edge of the overhang in two quick strides. He swung himself into the Jeep, chambered a round into his .45, and slammed the Jeep into first gear. "Three minutes from the time we hit the road, Skipper. Let's rock and roll!"

The several hundred yards down the fire road seemed an eternity. Pitch black, no headlights, nothing to guide us. There were switchbacks; and even in the dim light of the crescent moon, I could see that the Jeep would be no match for the 45 degree slope falling off both sides of the fire break. Each time Garret hit the brakes to avoid an obtrusive rock, I could almost feel the five hundred pounds of marijuana following us in a nearly invisible van slamming into the rear of the Jeep and pushing us over the edge.

When we reached the bottom, Garret followed a hard-packed culvert just below the shoulder of the road. He bounced the Jeep onto the shoulder and waved the van up next to us parallel to the road, its side door wide open. The plane, hidden behind the harsh glare of its landing light, taxied down the center of the road, stopped at an idle next to the van, and cut its light.

Manolo ran to the plane with the two men from the van and opened the passenger door behind the struts of the high wing. The pilot opened his door. Manolo threw an envelope into his hands. Packages flew out of the van and into the plane at lightning speed. Garret was right. It would take only a few minutes. The plane would be gone. We'd be gone.

While Manolo dispatched the dope, counting each kilo, Garret was scanning an area across the road from where we sat in the Jeep, looking intently at a rock-covered knoll. "Fuck!" he growled and turned quickly to look at the ditch we had brought the Jeep through. "Get into the gully, now!" He leaped out over the back of the Jeep, grabbing a duffel bag that had been stowed under Manolo's seat. We both hit the gully at the same time, rolling the few feet down the hill, making our way toward a small outcropping of rock where Garret unzipped the duffel bag and pulled out several compact automatic weapons.

The pilot must have also seen what Garret was so nervous about. I could see the panic in his eyes from the glow of the lights on the instrument panel as he accelerated, spinning the plane around for takeoff. The tail came around quickly and hit a two-foot rock jutting from the side of the road, wrenching the tail wheel away from the fuselage. The pilot powered up the big radial engine and began rolling down the road, sparks lighting up the ground as the plane screeched and howled forward. Garret shouted to Manolo over the roar of the DeHavilland's engine. Manolo, cat-like, dove into the van just as a bullet shattered the Plexiglass windshield of the DeHavilland. The pilot's head rolled against the side window smearing a trail of blood across the glass. The plane continued to gather speed, and one hundred yards down the road spun off onto the shoulder, caught a wheel in the loose sand, and flipped onto its nose, finally settling on its back in a cloud of dust.

Manolo had jumped out of the driver's side of the van and was running toward us just ahead of a volley of bullets screeching off the metal of the half-full van. Garret fired a few shots toward the muzzle flashes, covering Manolo, while his men raced up the culvert returning fire. Manolo landed next to me with a thud, and then the sky lit up with the silver burn of a flare. With rock chips flying in my face from ricocheting bullets, I could see the plane, a dead cockroach lying on its back in a fog of dust. I could see the shapes of men running behind the rocks on the other side of the road. I could see the blood staining through Manolo's sleeve at his shoulder where he had taken a bullet.

"*Diego y Esteban, muerto,*" Manolo said to Garret during a lull in the shooting.

I peaked around the edge of the rock long enough to see the bodies of Diego and Esteban lying next to the van before Garret yanked me back. His face was as hard as the rock I now had my back pressed against.

"That bastard isn't finished yet," he said with a coolness that defied the bullets that had been flying around us. He slipped another clip into the .45 and pulled the strap of an Uzi over his head. "But we're getting the fuck out of here." He rattled off some Spanish to Manolo who then sent it out over the handheld. Within seconds, while taking fire from automatic weapons, Garret's remaining men had thrown the bodies of Diego and Esteban into the van and were now speeding back toward the fire road, bullets sparking off the bumper and side panels.

"I told you once that a bullet would be a shitty way to die," I shouted, "but I'll be damned if I'm going to die out here like some animal. Give me that damn gun!"

Garret slid a banana clip into one of the Uzi's and handed it to me along with another clip. "Push the button on the rear of the grip to free the trigger. Keep firing until I get to the Jeep. And don't hit me!"

Garret bolted out of the ditch toward the Jeep twenty feet away. Manolo and I started firing short bursts at the muzzle fire across the road as incoming bullets thunked into the fenders and whined off the wheel rims of the Jeep. I found the clip release on the Uzi and fed another clip into the grip. Garret had the Jeep in first gear and was heading down the road toward the overturned DeHavilland when he signaled for us to jump in. We ran along the gully side of the Jeep, firing into the rocks and knolls at the unseen intruders, keeping them silent for the moment. Manolo, with only his good right arm, easily pulled himself into the back of the Jeep. I grabbed the panic bar and hauled myself into the front seat just as we passed the DeHavilland.

"*Incendelo,* Manolo!" Garret yelled, but Manolo had already dug something out of the duffel and had tossed it toward the plane. I heard a few bullets hit the Jeep's steel bumper and then there was nothing until I heard the explosion and saw the plane burning in dull orange flames a half mile behind us.

I still had a tight grip on the gun, its barrel warm against the skin of my thigh below my shorts, not believing that something so abhorrent to me five minutes ago had suddenly become my savior. It wasn't until we were two miles down the highway, away from the chaos of the last few minutes that I felt the pain in my right calf. "Shit!" I growled swiping my palm across a three-inch laceration to clear the blood running down to my ankle.

Garret looked straight ahead, expressionless in his intent to jump the Jeep off the highway onto a dirt road that headed back into the mountains. Manolo, meanwhile, had reached over my shoulder, yanked the gun from my hand and slipped it into the duffel bag beside him.

"Someone's going to die for this," Garret said with his usual calculated calmness, carefully winding his way up the weed and shrub covered road until we were in the protective cover of the stands of banana trees higher up the mountain. With the headlights off, it was slow going. "We were set up, Skipper." He looked at my leg and snickered. "Caught one, eh?"

The adrenalin in my system was firing its own bullets. It took a few seconds to slow enough until I could find my voice. "I don't give a damn what happened, Garret," I railed. "I didn't sign up for this." I could feel the mass of Manolo's body stirring behind me.

"Grow up, Skipper," Garret said. "This isn't Vallarta and umbrella drinks or an after- game party. You just experienced an occupational hazard. This is an anomaly, and you're still alive to write about it. You handled yourself pretty well down there. You've got more *huevos* than I figured you for."

He stopped the Jeep behind a thicket of heleconias, grabbed a pair of binoculars from the duffel, and motioned me to follow him. We walked to a rise overlooking the highway. In the distance, I could see the still burning airplane under the waning glow of the flare. I could see movement on the road. I could feel the pain in my leg.

My laugh still had remnants of the adrenaline I had felt earlier. "You think that was guts back there? That was fear of dying. You think I would have chosen to do that?"

"Didn't you?" He focused the binoculars on the wreckage down the highway. "Don't worry. I've a good guess who's responsible for this. I'll flush the bastard out."

Panama was looking better all the time, I thought. Staying with friends that weren't going to kill or be killed was an impressive option. And the five hundred dollars Garret had slipped into my pocket would get me through a couple of months. I could leave as soon as I could get back to the city, collect my things and get on the three o'clock bus. I looked back to where Manolo was still chattering into his handheld radio and saw his blood soaked shirt, his left arm limp at his side.

"Guess I'm spending the night at the Hotel Garret," I said, my calf throbbing a nasty beat; the blood still flowing.

CHAPTER
ELEVEN

Manolo and I were propped up next to each other on the dining room table. I was cleaning the surface wound on my leg with alcohol and taping a gauze bandage on it as Esperanza cut away Manolo's shirt and washed the blood from his shoulder. I could now see that the bullet had just missed his collarbone and taken out a chunk of skin and muscle in his shoulder, leaving a two-inch strip of red running between his upper arm and neck. I could also see the concern on Garret's face as Esperanza tenderly applied pressure to stop the bleeding. *What would he do without Manolo?*

"He loses blood but is not serious," Esperanza stated. She pressed gauze to Manolo's wound, taping it over his shoulder, then handed him a clean shirt she had brought out earlier. "I know he cannot rest, Mr. Garret. He has always been that way." She gently touched the side of Manolo's face with her fingertips. Manolo's guard came down for an instant. I couldn't miss the small, boyish grin that came over his face. "You have things to do," she said, patting his cheek. "But rest would be best."

Manolo hopped off the table. Both he and Garret hur-

85

ried out into the early morning darkness, leaving me with Esperanza. Garret shouted orders as they ran along the tiled floor of the portico and down the road to the armory.

"Esperanza." It was Garret on his handheld from somewhere below. "Take care of Skip. We don't have time to babysit him. We're going to the bushes."

"Take care of Skip" didn't sound right to me. I had seen too many gangster movies where those words meant someone was going to die. Neither did having to have a babysitter ring with much confidence in my mind. I shrugged at Esperanza.

"Fate is not to tempt, Mr. Reid," Esperanza said. "Is better to be *preparado*. Stay here. I come back quickly." She dashed into an adjacent room and came back with two .45s and a short-barreled automatic rifle. After handing me a .45, she said, "It's crazy! These boys make me crazy! You can use this, no?" She chambered a round into the rifle she was holding and went to stand next to the door. "Is *precaución*, Mr. Reid. Maybe no more tonight. Is finished. But we protect the house."

"What are they doing out there?" I asked, staring at the .45 that Esperanza had insisted I keep in my hand. My memory was still fresh with images of tracer rounds, flares, an exploding plane, and the chaos of just trying to survive in a battle where only bullets could be the ultimate winners. I was hoping it was only precautionary and that it was over.

"Mr. Garret will make sure they do not come to the house. They kill them before they kill us. Is only *precaución*, but chances we cannot take."

Esperanza flipped the lights off and we stood in the dark room for forty-five minutes, waiting for the sounds of gunfire down the hill. I didn't know what Esperanza was capable of and wasn't sure what message Garret had given her regarding me. She could have had the barrel of her rifle pointed at my heart for all I knew waiting for a signal to "Take care of Skip" if Garret decided I was a liability. When she had said, "We are prepared," I saw, like so many times before with Garret, Manolo, and the men I had met in the compound, that commitment to die for a cause burning in her eyes. From maid to nurse and now to a woman who knew how to handle a gun, she had become the very definition of enigma.

A half hour later with the sun stealing its first look at the new day and no further incidents with bullets flying, I watched Garret bark some orders to Manolo, who was clearing the van of the remaining kilos of dope and storing them in the outbuilding. They then headed up the hill toward the house.

"Why are you here?" I asked Esperanza while keeping an eye on the rifle she was now holding at her side. "Is there something keeping you here?"

"Mr. Garret, he is good to me," Esperanza said. "I take your gun now, *por favor.*"

The gun had become such a part of my anatomy that I had forgotten I was holding it. With her words, though, the weight and feel of it reminded me that I hated guns. I handed it to her, glad to be rid of it.

"You could die here," I said.

Esperanza moved toward the adjacent room. "Is good place to die, no? *Muy Hermoso.*"

Granted, it was a beautiful place, but as she had said earlier, why tempt fate? A raid on the compound could shorten her life dramatically. "Esperanza?" I called to her. "How did you get this work?"

She stopped in mid stride, bringing one of the .45s up

to her waist. "Why you ask that question?"

"I want to know why you work for Garret and if you are free to go," I said in my best broken Spanish.

"I do not work for Mr. Garret. *Este es mi casa.* I can go when I wish, but where do I go? Family is here. Money is here. My home is here. Mr. Garret is *un bueno gente.* He pays the crazy boys with much money. He pays for my son at *Universidad.* My son will be a *veterinario.*"

"Talking about Jorge?" It was Garret. He had stormed through the open door pulling his sweatshirt off, tossing it on the sofa. Esperanza wandered off into the adjacent room as Garret snapped the caps off two bottles of Dos XX, handing one to me. Garret finished half of his before he continued. "That kid's bright. Has a lot of sense. Knew what he wanted and Manolo and I are helping him get it. He's a little too proud, but we're working through that."

Adrenaline was still pumping through me from the tension of the night. The beer helped steady me. "I'm having a hard time believing you're a selfless humanitarian, Garret."

"In hard times, people need a break. When I was eighteen, the same age as Jorge, I was a trained killer, thanks to Uncle Sam. At the time, I knew that was what I wanted; but that obsession turned into something ugly. I had a short future and there was nowhere to go. Jorge has made a better decision. For his mother's sake, I'm going to see that he gets what he wants."

"Honorable intentions." I saluted him with a wave of my Dos XX.

"Fuck you. I'm not that honorable. Technically, Esperanza owns this property. It's been in her family for a hundred years. It's in her name because non-residents can't own property here unless a resident cosigns. I'm buying it from her."

"Why does she hang around here? You, no doubt, have made her a wealthy woman. She could live anywhere she wants, away from all this."

"She loves the land, she loves the house. She has a history here. Five thousand acres, Skipper, with a river."

"Is it worth dying for?" I asked.

"She was shooting cattle rustlers before you were born, Skipper. She knows her way around."

"It would just make more sense to me for her to go and live with her son, out of danger."

"She does. Manolo is, also, her son."

That statement hit me like a high stick to the head. "Holy shit, Garret! She must be torn apart inside. How can you allow that?"

"Everyone makes their own choices, Skipper. And they live or die with them." He swallowed the rest of his beer, then quickly turned and threw the bottle across the room. It shattered against the far wall, narrowly missing a ceramic figurine, sending shards of brown glass out across the dining room.

"Fuck!" he went on, his voice sounding calm beneath his anger. "Somebody's ass is deep in dog shit."

My pulse upped its ante when he stared hard at me. I was suddenly back in the third grade, where Sister Mary Elizabeth was flying down the row of desks toward me, her black habit flowing behind her like a strong wind from hell. It wasn't me she was after, but I could feel the shock wave as she reached for the boy behind me. Garret's stare had passed over me as quickly as that ill wind had at age eight. "I'm on your side," I finally said.

"Don't worry. You're not on my hit list."

That wind from hell had passed by me again and I

breathed a little easier. "So, catch any bad guys out there?" I asked this with my usual flippancy.

Garret opened another bottle of Dos XX. "The compound's secure. Manolo's on patrol. The 'bad guys' seem to have left the area. Whoever it was didn't want the load. Left it burning on the highway. They weren't after the damn weed, and that's what worries me."

"So this is a vendetta?" I asked. "Maybe Interpol trying to shut you down? No idea who?"

"Shit, Skipper, everyone's after me. But that wasn't an Interpol hit. It was too sloppy. Interpol works from the inside out. But if it's who I think it is, he wants me alive. He needs me alive."

The sun was now casting a brassy glow over the valley, and the compound began to heat up. Esperanza had made huevos rancheros for the entire cadre and was busily putting plates on the dining room table for the first shift of ten men when Manolo rushed into the room breathing hard. He spat some words to Garret and immediately the men at the table began shoving pieces of egg into their mouths as they rushed from the room in a flurry of quick, angry Spanish.

"We've been breeched, Skipper" Garret stated. "It may be nothing. It may be everything. We have to take a look. Let's go."

"No babysitter?" I said, trying to make light of the situation.

Garret wasn't buying it. "Get in the fucking Jeep, wise ass. That was for your own good."

Manolo had already brought the Jeep up the hill to the house and parked it next to the fountain in the courtyard. The familiar duffel full of guns and ammunition lay in the back behind Garret's seat.

"I know you're good with an Uzi," Garret said jokingly as he rummaged through the bag and handed me the butt of a .45. "Always the possibility of trouble. Ever use one of these?"

"My father was a hunter," I said. "Taught me how to kill tin cans. Never cared for guns." I handed the pistol to Manolo who shrugged and put it into his belt. "I'll take my chances that whatever you're getting me into will go smoothly." The thought of Garret's gun in my forehead yesterday on the lake and firing the Uzi at unknown targets last night had made me feel even more accountable for other people's lives, how valuable they are, and how vulnerable we all are. I was never a cowboy with a six-shooter mentality. Life has always been too precious.

"I'll do what I can to keep you out of trouble," Garret said.

Familiarity had touched the edges of the jungle road and rocky creek beds as Garret maneuvered the Jeep over the mountains to an area of lush, green plants hidden under the canopies of large-leaved banana trees, hazelnut, and pines. I watched as several men and women hacked at the marijuana plants with their machetes and threw the branches onto a waiting trailer hitched to an old Ford tractor. One of the men told Garret that he had seen three horse riders cutting across the property on a ridge that followed the river, but he knew them as neighbors and they were not a problem.

"Twenty acres that no one can find," Garret said. "Gives you a rush seeing all that sitting out there doesn't it, Skipper?" He didn't wait for an answer. Instead, he headed back toward the ranch, taking a circuitous route through the mountains.

Garret's guards waved us through with their guns and

a shake of the head, indicating they had seen nothing, and then faded into the foliage beside the dark arch of tree branches shadowing the road. Even though I had stepped outside of the tight, limited perspective of yesterday and the sudden immersion into something potentially dangerous, I still felt the hot expectant breath of Manolo at my back, his radio crackling with broken sentences like a cheap stereo speaker. His presence kept me alert to the wild chattering of the parrots in the trees and the scattering of varmints in the underbrush, bringing out the soul of the back country. His method was simple: stay quiet, look cherubic, and hurt people. He was easy to like with his big ranch-boy body and easy smile. I could like him. I could respect him as I would a sleeping pit-trained dog. I also felt sorry for him.

I couldn't allow myself too much freedom around this kind of thinking. The arrogance of familiarity could get me killed. But I felt more relaxed now, bouncing in my seat next to Garret, as he ground through the lower gears, working the Jeep over the last mile back to the ranch. I knew from my experience with Coleen that with familiarity comes a very untrustworthy friend: complacency. I had become too complacent with her, took her too much for granted. I had dropped my guard and got burned. *Not this time*, I thought. Too much at stake. Complacency could be that weak step on a shaky ladder, the one that finally proves fatalism could be dangerous to one's health.

I was feeling a lot less nervous knowing that whoever had started the firefight last night had left the area, and I was beginning to relax as we headed down a winding dirt road toward the open area of the compound. I could see the old colonial house sitting on the knoll overlooking the small valley where the outbuildings sat in unpretentious disarray. I was making mental notes of the area when, suddenly, about a quarter mile from the compound, Manolo's radio began to squawk with short, garbled shouts and exclamations.

"Shit!" Garret yelled as he stood on the brakes, the tires kicking up dust clouds that chased us down, overrunning us in airless, gagging swirls. His sudden loss of control sent a flash of hot lightning through my body. My concern over familiarity and complacency disappeared quickly into the dust surrounding the Jeep. The message had clearly shaken him. If he was afraid, I had a lot to consider.

"You want a goddamn story?" he snorted and looked above the tree canopies surrounding us, jabbing his index finger into the air several times. "It's fuckin' coming out of the sky."

Manolo had already dug into the duffel and was slamming magazines into the .45's. He tossed one to Garret and then grabbed one of the thirty-round clips and jammed it into the short-barreled automatic he was holding. Garret then eased the Jeep down the hill to the armory and cut the engine.

"Stay with Manolo," Garret ordered, then with that bravado that only fear can bring out, he said, "Sure you don't want this?" He offered me his .45.

"No thanks," I said with the same bravado. "I have Manolo."

Manolo nudged me into the bushes at the corner of the armory wall. I could hear the helicopter's rotors thudding up over the mountains then as light as a bird the chopper settled onto the open ground near the outbuildings. It was unmarked military, drab green, and menacing.

When the rear door slid open, two men in green military uniforms jumped from the bay holding small automatic weapons. After surveying the area, one of the men nodded toward the helicopter, and I saw a silver-tipped cowboy boot swing out over the deck.

"What the hell?" I nearly choked on the words. "That's Carlos Huerta."

"We go back a ways," Garret said. "It wasn't a picnic." He cocked his .45 and sized up Huerta and the two men walking out from under the blades of the chopper. "Manolo?" he whispered, "*¿Qué pasa?*"

Manolo shrugged his huge shoulders, pulled me farther into the bushes, and said calmly in Spanish, "I don't know. I paid Victor on Monday." He looked at one of the guards I assumed was Victor. "*Le pregunta.*"

"Damn straight I'll ask him," Garret sighed heavily, angrily. "I need some answers. Somebody's fucking with me." He waited until the three men had spread out in front of the helicopter, Victor to the left of Huerta, the other to the right, each fanning the air with their short-barreled rifle. Huerta had a pistol in his hand. "They haven't cut the engine," Garret said. "It's going to be quick and dirty." He chambered a bullet then walked out to meet Huerta.

Manolo took only a few steps out of the bushes we were hiding behind, his menacing bulk in view of the three men. His rifle had "ready" written all over it.

High-risk confrontation has a double underscore in my dictionary of survival and scribbled boldly in the margin next to it are the words *find a door!* Even with Manolo so near, I felt the cold bite of vincibility sinking its razor teeth into my rising hackles.

Huerta stepped forward, systematically moving his pistol over Garret's body. His smile was a gash in concrete, cold, hard. It would have been a pleasure to rip it off his sweaty, pockmarked face. As he settled his aim, I saw a dark smudge on his right forearm that looked to be the same tattoo I had seen on Garret and Kopek.

Who are these guys?

Garret held his ground, his gun aimed at Huerta's chest.

"Garret, my friend," Huerta said above the roar of the engine. "We'll speak English. Too much information to subordinates can ruin great careers." He held his gun steady at Garret's head. "Tell me, do I have to kill you?"

Manolo came to attention next to me, jerking his rifle into firing position.

"Not the best idea you've had," Garret said. "You'd play hell getting out of here. I think you know that."

Huerta seemed to consider this, and momentarily dropped his insidious smile. He kept his eyes on Garret, jerking his head quickly toward the man on his left. "Victor tells me you missed a payment. You know we can't protect you if we aren't paid. This is just business, my friend."

"It would be foolish of me to miss a payment, amigo," Garret said. "That would not benefit either of us. A few thousand dollars is not worth terminating our business relationship."

"Money is our relationship," Huerta said harshly. "Don't confuse our business relationship with friendship loyalty. Money is the only thing that keeps you from dying. We're forgetting you exist because of what you pay us. And the money did not arrive."

Garret came back hard, determined. "Manolo paid your man, Victor, Monday afternoon. Has he misplaced it, or forgotten to deposit it? Was that little episode last night a reminder? A mistake? I lost two good men out there."

"I have only heard about that. It may have been some-one's mistake, but we had nothing to do with it. We can't afford to lose you as a source of income."

"Then it wasn't political," Garret stated. "But I can't help thinking that the incident with Victor and the money failed to filter down to the ground troops."

"Nothing's political any more," Huerta said. "Money has bypassed politics as the decision maker. Could have been any band of wannabes with a few guns and hunger pangs. We don't know who it was. It could also have been a warning."

Garret stared hard at Huerta. "I pay you to know these things. Where is my protection?"

"Be assured that we will find out who set you up," Huerta said. "It will not happen again." He then took a quick look at Victor. "He will tell me the truth about where the money went."

"And I trust Manolo," Garret said. "Ask Victor. Ask him where the money is. He knows. Ask him quick. He's getting nervous. You don't want him going off on us, and I don't want to put a bullet in him. Ask him!"

I didn't see what they saw in Victor's eyes, but there was no confusing his body language. He swayed from side to side and his head bobbled around on his neck like a loose spring. Huerta gave the order. The second guard fired one round into Victor's chest. Victor crumpled to the ground.

Garret and Huerta lowered their guns, slack coming back into their bodies, as Huerta's remaining guard prodded and pushed on Victor's body with the barrel of his rifle.

"Such a horrible business," Huerta said smugly, his ironic grin returning. "He was suspected for months. I needed you to flush him out. You gave me the reason to dispose of him."

"You son-of-a-bitch!" Garret yelled, raising his gun.

"There are twenty men surrounding you. If that bullet had been meant for anyone other than Victor, you'd all be dead."

Huerta snickered and waved his guard off. "It would never have come to that, my friend. You and I give the orders."

"So where's the money?" Garret asked.

Huerta wiped his brow of sweat. Not even a hint of conscience found its way to the surface of his skin. He smiled widely. "Consider it a favor paid in full."

Victor lay in the dirt like a lumpy sack of mangos as Huerta and his guard headed for the helicopter. The blades rustled the trees, sucked up dust and blew it across the compound as the helicopter rose.

Manolo shouted into the compound. Four men came out of the bushes near where Victor's body lay and dragged him off into the jungle.

"I'd have introduced you, Skipper, but you've already met." Garret laughed as he made his way back to where Manolo and I were waiting. He must have noticed my concern and added, "Don't think about it, Skipper. You start to think, and you die." The gun was still in his right hand, still ready with its undelivered message. "They'll bury him somewhere. Maybe just dump him at his mother's front door."

"Let's go," Garret said after Manolo had gone for the Jeep and stowed the weapons in the armory. "Get you back to your hotel. Hope you took good notes."

As Garret guided the Jeep down the hill and out of the compound, the tightness in my throat began to loosen. We were headed away from the field of blood, from another bull being killed in the ring, which, like the smoke from the gun that killed Victor, seemed to be suspended in a

ghoulish dream above my head. What in the hell was I doing in a Jeep in the mountains of western Mexico with a
drug dealer and his bodyguard? Was any amount of money worth being a part of what I had witnessed in the last
twenty-four hours? Sure, it would make a fantastic story,
but so would biographies of worldclass surfers and hockey
players. As fast as I could pack my bag and get to the bus
depot, I could be headed south and out of this mess. I
sensed Garret was giving me that option.

Manolo, hovering in the back seat, was triggering his
radio, heating up the airways in rapid Spanish. He was
praising the men in the compound.

"Think very big," Garret said to me over Manolo's
squawking radio. "Think Government. When you get to
the top, stop and back off one. Huerta works for him."

"Huerta works for the Vice-President of Mexico?" My
voice rattled as I spat out the words.

Garret was taking in the scenery, seemingly relaxed
behind the wheel. "Don't act so surprised. Consider where
you are. Huerta is his skip chaser, pimp, and collection
agent."

I was trying to be conversant, but I could already feel
the seat back of the air-conditioned Pan American bus
cuddling me all the way to Panama City. "What about his
role with the museum?" I asked. Before he could answer,
a quick jolt of electricity shot through me. *Was Itzla one of
Huerta's girls?* That possibility unnerved me. *Did she know
that Huerta was in business with Garret? If not, did she even know
what Huerta was capable of?*

"His job's legitimate," Garret said, "and it's a good
front for his other activities. It allows him freedom to
move in and out of the country. Diplomatic immunity."

As we bumped our way down the periphery road on

the outskirts of Teuchitlán, I thought I saw Itzla's Toyota a good distance away parked in front of her aunt and uncle's store. There seemed to be a lot of hurried activity in the town. While I was distracted looking for Itzla, I said, "So he really is looking for the missing artifact?"

Garret downshifted and made the turn onto Highway 15, heading us back toward Guadalajara. He adjusted his sunglasses. "Among other things. But I imagine that would be his priority at the moment."

I was still thinking about Itzla and what might be happening in the town when I said, "So he does have a soft spot for history."

Garret shook his head. "Skipper, wake *up*," he hissed. "Sometimes you can be pretty fucking stupid."

"So educate me," I said. "Details, remember?"

"Details," Garret said with a quick laugh. "Huerta wouldn't be giving it a second thought if there wasn't a profit in it somewhere. His commitment depends on the fullness of his safe deposit box."

"Garret," I said. "This is just speculation, but I'm guessing you know where that artifact is."

"No, I don't, but I have a good idea where it might be."

CHAPTER
TWELVE

I'll see you at the *fonda,* per our agreement," Garret said as I climbed out of the Jeep in front of my hotel. "We'll look for more details." And then as though reading my thoughts, he added, "Where would you go where I couldn't find you?"

"Kiss my ass, Garret," I said and got a nasty glare from Manolo.

The haunting images of Victor's murder clung to the surfaces of my brain like flaking paint on a rotting plaster wall. And Huerta was pulling the strings. Everything was telling me to get out.

Not caring that Garret would consider my leaving a matter of discretion, I decided to take the chance. After peeling the gauze from my leg wound and seeing that it had stopped bleeding, I changed into a cleaner pair of shorts. I pulled on an Hawaiian T-shirt with palm trees and a surfer printed on the front. Garret's five bills slid nicely into my pocket. It was a start. After stuffing my duffel with the few clothes and toiletry items that remained after my hasty exit from the States, I re-checked the bus schedule to Panama that I had picked up earlier in the week. There was the three o'clock bus, and if I hurried, I could be on it and away from the mayhem of Guadalajara. A fast exit would be too slow. I threw the duffel over my shoulder and hurried down the unsteady staircase, not knowing if Garret thought I knew too much and would send one of his "crazy boys," as Esperanza had called them, to track me down.

With that thought in my head, I tried to slip by Armando; but he was quickly on his feet behind the desk, once again giving me an undeserved grin. As I headed for the bus depot, I wished I could have been Armando's idea of a hero.

Lino's dirt-caked bus looked almost whimsical sitting in its usual place against the fence away from the other buses. I now noticed that its cabin sat a few degrees off center. Its front bumper was curled at one end, giving it a small, twisted, metallic smile. It looked like a large Tonka toy that had been kicked around by children in someone's back yard. It was 2:45 and I saw no sign of Lino. On my trip to Teuchitlán, the bus was packed so tightly even the sweat had no place to go; but now there were only a few people milling about the old bus, carrying their unsold wares in boxes, baskets, and tied blankets. These few people seemed to be waiting for Lino to welcome them on board and take them on up the highway toward Teuchitlán. *But why so few passengers? And why so early?*

I bought my ticket and was looking forward to the comfort of padded seats and a long, comfortable ride to Panama. At this point, long meant farther—the farther the better. It was the first time in two days that my nerves weren't rattling around in my body like BBs in a boxcar. After I found my seat and threw what belongings I had into the overhead, I turned for a last look at the smiling dog of a bus sitting across the lot. After thirty-six hours of little sleep, I was looking forward to the comfort of a reclining seat and the consistent hum of rolling tires.

It was then I saw Itzla step out of her uncle's bus, looking serious and agitated. She spoke to the small group of men and women for several seconds; they then gathered their goods for sale and walked out the gate. Even as she stood straight and tall in her Tabachine-colored slacks and blouse, I could tell she was distressed.

With fifteen minutes to kill before my bus left, and after watching Itzla climb back into the old bus, I suddenly felt like I could surrender the luxury of air conditioning and velour seat coverings for a few minutes of conversation with the *Azteca*.

She was sitting in Lino's seat, turned toward the back of the bus when I came aboard. "Is everything alright, Itzla?" I asked. "Where is Lino?" She had been crying. I reached out and touched her shoulder, the only comforting gesture I could think of in that moment. She leaned into me for an instant, surprising me.

"Mr. Reid." She sniffed and wiped her eyes with a tissue she had pulled from her slack's pocket. "I didn't think I'd see you again. Thought you were just passing through."

"I am," I said, pointing across the lot. "I'm on that bus to Panama. This city's a little too rabid for me. What's going on?"

Itzla straightened up in the seat, dabbing her eyes. "My uncle has disappeared. No one has seen him since he came in yesterday morning. The bus you were on, Mr. Reid."

So that's what all the commotion was about in Teuchitlan earlier. "There were a lot of people on his bus," I said sharply. "Are you accusing me of something?" It wasn't my intention to agitate her more than she already was, but the accusation and the coldness of her words went right to the core of my dignity. *Where do you start with this woman?*

She sighed and turned toward where I was standing on the second step into the bus. "*Lo siento.* I'm sorry," she said. "Of course not. I thought it was a coincidence, that's all."

"Coincidence that I happened to be on the last bus he drove into town? Coincidence that I happen to be leaving for Panama right now?" I looked over at the sleek Pan American bus that was filling rapidly. "I know what you're thinking, Itzla. Come on, you can do better than that. You're thinking I had something to do with his disappearance."

Itzla stood, rising like a life-like icon of the Aztec goddess *Xochiquetzal*, her head nearly touching the roof of the cabin. "I've been thinking of everything, Mr. Reid. I'm asking everyone. I can't discount anything. And now you're leaving for Panama. What am I to think?"

"Think what you want. I don't know anything about Lino's whereabouts, and I have a bus to catch. If there's anything I can help you with in the next five minutes, I'd be glad to do it." I looked again toward the doorway of the luxury coach, idling across the way. I could almost smell the sweet fragrance of the breeze from the air conditioner blowing across my face. "Has this happened before?" I asked.

"No," Itzla said. "He sometimes has an occasional *cerveza* with his friends. But they have not seen him either. This is not like him. He is always where he is supposed to be."

"Have you talked to the police?"

"Of course. They are looking. He has been gone for twenty-six hours. Nailea is frantic, as we all are. Mr. Reid, you were one of the last ones to see him yesterday when you came in on the bus. Did he say anything or talk to you at all?"

I shrugged and said, "We had a short conversation on the bus."

"About what?"

"It's really not important," I said, trying to keep her name out of the conversation. It could prove to be embarrassing.

"Anything could be important, Mr. Reid," Itzla snapped. "This is serious." She suddenly seemed twenty years older and could have been wearing a black habit. Sister Mary Elizabeth reincarnated. "My uncle has disappeared, and you were one of the last people to see him."

I nearly pulled myself to attention. "We talked about you, if you must know. Nothing more."

"Me?" She turned those dark eyes toward me, and I faltered a bit. I could feel the warmth that Lino had spoken of building behind them. "You probably learned little," she said. "There really isn't much to talk about." Then, as quickly as it came, that Aztec fire went to ashes. "What did you do after you left the bus?" she quickly added.

"I went back to my hotel for a nap, and then I met Garret and Manolo at the central market." I had to chuckle at her tenacity. "You do suspect me, don't you?"

"I suspect everyone, Mr. Reid. What do you know about those two men? You seem to be hanging around with them a lot."

"You think they had something to do with all this?" I said while trying to figure out what and how much to tell her. "Garret is buying a ranch back in the mountains. Manolo works for him," I began.

"We know that, and we know they grow cannabis," Itzla interjected. "It's a small community, Skip. You were seen with them at the restaurant on Lake Chapala and also riding with them into the mountains yesterday afternoon. I need to know more about them."

"You seem to know more about them than I do," I said, not wanting to give anything away. Even though Manolo was miles away, I could still sense his hot breath on the back of my neck. "I don't know any more than that," I lied, reminding myself that Garret's last words to me were a strong reminder that details were only meant for the book he wanted written. Discretion, I thought, was a better proposition than having to look over my shoulder for the rest of who knew how long. "We had lunch on the island, and he gave me a tour of his ranch," I said. "Why the interrogation? And if you knew all of this, why did you pretend to not know them yesterday?"

Ignoring this, she said, "It's my uncle, Mr. Reid. I have to find him. And I need the truth. He may be in danger."

"In danger?" I asked, adding a grin at the thought and saying, "I can't imagine Lino being wanted for anything more than an overloaded bus. What possible danger could that affable old man be in? He's probably off having a good time somewhere."

Itzla was not laughing. "Mr. Reid, you do not understand what his disappearance could mean."

"Then maybe you'd better start telling *me* the truth, Itzla. Why would anyone want your uncle to disappear? Why do you think he's in danger?"

"I can't tell you that."

"So this is some kind of game we're playing, Itzla? I have to get on that bus in about two minutes. I can't help you if you won't talk to me."

"I haven't asked for your help, Mr. Reid. But if you're willing to tell me what you know, I'll explain everything to you. It's complicated though and will take more than the two minutes you have left."

Shit! I thought as I stared into the fire of her eyes. At that moment, I could have taken her hand and led her on a few turns around the *Plaza de los Mariachis*, playfully discovering each other's secrets until the first rays of sunlight struck the twin spires of *La Catedral Metropolitana*. Maybe there was still a chance to make that happen. Maybe I could help her find her uncle. I could use my ticket to Panama after we had settled Lino back into his bus and brought everyone's life back to normal. The police would surely find him before the day was over, and I'd have a little time to spend with Itzla.

"I'll get my duffel bag off the bus," I said.

* * *

Itzla led me to a small, quiet café near the museum. We sat on worn Naugahyde, metal-legged chairs at a tiled table that had an energetic, unpredictable wobble, and stared at each other. I ordered coffee for both of us hoping it would keep me awake and alert and possibly comfort her, melt some of the ice.

After an awkward moment of sipping silence, Itzla said, "Everyone is looking for him, Mr. Reid. I am only following up on leads. I saw you at the station. If you had not come to me, I would have come to you."

I smiled across at her. "But you haven't even packed," I said, trying to break through to any sense of humor she might have hidden beneath her chilly façade. "If you're worried about getting your toothbrush, don't, I have an extra."

"I have no intentions of going anywhere, Mr. Reid." She was sitting as straight as the back of her chair. Small strands of hair had pulled away from her barrette and were blowing around her cheeks from the warm air of the electric fan swiveling on the counter next to us.

"Please, Itzla, it's Skip," I said, irritated with her insistent formality. Impatience grows like crabgrass in me when I'm tired. "We're having coffee. You can cut the decorum."

"It sounds like you *need* coffee," she said curtly.

"I haven't had much sleep," I said. "It wears on me." An angry twinge of pain shot up from my wound. I shifted in my chair, straightening my leg out into the aisle.

She was looking at the coagulated blood that had accumulated on the strip of sliced skin where the bullet had grazed me. "And that nasty looking cut on your leg is a result of sleeplessness?" she asked. "It looks like it could use some attention."

"Are you volunteering?" I said hopefully.

She gave me a look that was somewhere between you-need-help and I'd-love-to. She wet her napkin in the water of the oversized, glass pitcher sitting at her elbow, then reached over the end of the table and gently patted the wound. "It seems to be healing, and I don't see any signs of infection," she said as she inspected the fading pink smear on the napkin. "It should be alright. Looks worse than it is."

"Maybe if you continued the treatment, Doc, it would heal even faster," I said with a quick grin.

Itzla set the napkin next to the pitcher of water and then slid both to the edge of the table. "I see you haven't lost your arrogance. You must have had a good night, even without sleep."

It's all relative, mi amiga.

The momentary delight of her touch fled like a house full of illegal immigrants with INS breaking down their door. I leaned back and asked casually, "Pino, Pino?"

"You noticed that?" she asked. "It's a term of endearment Lino used when I was a small girl. He would yell, 'Pino! Pino!' and drop to his knee. I'd run into his arms, and we'd hold each other. I'd love to hear that from him right now."

She closed her eyes for a moment, giving me time to wonder if that magic would work for me. I kicked out of that reverie when I suddenly remembered why I was sitting with this woman and not on a bus to Panama. I asked, "What's this 'everything' you said you were going to explain?"

Itzla hesitated looking warily around the nearly empty café. "It's not as simple as you might think," she stated. "As you know, Carlos Huerta and I have been trying to locate the missing warrior chieftain. You already know of its intrinsic value, but there is more to it." She moved her coffee cup around in small circles in front of her looking at the tiny maelstrom forming inside.

"And just when I think I have all the answers." I gave her another smile as she looked up at me.

"You know that Lino and Nailea raised me after my mother and father died," she said after completely ignoring my remark.

"Carlos did mention that briefly at the ruins," I said, thinking it rather ironic that death and dying should come up at the same time Carlos Huerta's name popped up. "Do you mind if I ask you how they died?"

She studied me for a moment. Her lips tightened. I was almost certain she would keep that a secret, but surprisingly, she said, "Not at all. Lino and Nailea have told me the story many times. I was only four years old and don't remember many details. It was a fire that killed my parents.

Perhaps you saw the ruins next to the cantina?"

"I remember seeing a pile of ashes and the scorched walls of an old adobe."

"That is it. The town has left it as a reminder of a good family. That was almost twenty-five years ago."

I could see that this was not easy for her. Both parents gone and now Lino missing. She had earned a few tears. "What happened?" I said, pulling a stubborn paper napkin out of its broken metal dispenser and handing it to her. "How did you survive it?"

Itzla's chest rose as she drew in a deep breath. She released the air with a petite sigh and said, "It was a fast fire and my parents were trapped in their bedroom. They were taken quickly. I remember the flames roaring into my room and Lino pulling me out my window. Lino says it was a cinder from the cooking stove that started it. And the house was very small, as you may have noticed. It didn't take much to burn it down."

I reached to the center of the table and took her hand. It was cool even with the heat of the day. "I'm sorry, Itzla," I said.

She waited for what seemed to be an appropriate amount of time then pulled her hand back to her coffee cup. "Thank you," she said. "That was a long time ago. That part is over. But I remember and celebrate their spirit on *El Día de los Muertos*."

I took two swallows of coffee, trying to keep the fog of sleeplessness from taking over my brain. "Do the other people in town, Benito, Vincencio, Luz, ever talk to you about it?"

"*Sí*, but they all tell me the same story." She paused when a group of rowdy Americans passed our table and plopped down in a corner booth. When the noise level dropped, she began again. "When I began asking," she said, "they told me that my parents were now with God in Heaven and I must try and forget the accident. That I must be strong. I've never been able to get any details from anyone."

"Funny how when people don't want to talk about the details of something, there are usually secrets involved," I said. It was my cynical nature kicking in.

Itzla jerked her head toward me as though she had caught me with my hand in the till. "What's that supposed to mean?" she said.

"Nothing, I suppose. It's just speculation. It's the reporter in me. You must miss them, your parents."

She eyed me carefully. "I really didn't remember them. I often think about how it might have been had they lived. But they are not here. That is why Lino is so important to me. He's been like a father."

I had to ask the question. "What would make you think he might be in danger?"

She went quiet for a moment. She shifted in her chair, crossing her long legs under the table. Her knee brushed against mine. I felt a spark, a lightheadedness that distracted me for a moment. "I don't know for certain, but I think he knows something about the missing artifact," she said.

I straightened up quickly, stunned. "In the theft?"

She leaned forward, fanning her fingers on the table, the stiffness leaving her back. "My uncle is not a thief, Mr. Reid."

"Then what are you suggesting?" I asked. "Has he talked to you about the Warrior?"

"Only that he, my father, and Carlos used to search the *Guachimontone*, finding pre-Columbian artifacts that they would then donate to the local museums. They were all born in Teuchitlan. They were in their early twenties at that time and wanted to help preserve local culture."

"Huerta was a friend of your father's?" I asked.

She gave me a quizzical look. "Yes," she said. "The three of them found the pair of warrior chieftains in an isolated shaft tomb on the upper plateau you and I visited the other day."

"So your uncle and Carlos have a history with artifacts," I said.

"So who is doing the interrogating now, Skip?" After her short hesitation with my name, that hint of a smile returned to her lips. "That's all that Lino has told me. But I know that something happened after they found the Warriors, after they gave them to the museum. They no longer spoke much to each other. Carlos left Teuchitlán shortly after that, got his Ph.D. in Cultural Anthropology and is now the cultural liaison to the vice president of Mexico."

And a helluva lot more than that. Jesus Christ! "What else has Lino told you?"

"Nothing more," she said. "He doesn't speak of it much, and I've never had any reason to question him."

"When we find him, maybe we should," I said, not actually believing that I had put the two of us together in one sentence. But if Lino was in trouble and if Huerta was responsible for his disappearance, then Itzla could also be in danger. Even though she was quite savvy and astute, she did have an innocence about her that cried out for protection. I didn't know how this all would play out, but I wasn't willing to have anything happen to her. Fortunately, Huerta hadn't seen me when he had Victor killed. I could use that to my advantage. And, of course, telling Itzla any of this was out of the question. "Lino may know more than you think," I said.

She was staring out the window, probably looking for her uncle. "Why do you think he would hold anything back from me?" she asked in frustration.

"Again, it's just speculation, Itzla," I said. "If it were me and my parents had died a mysterious death, I'd start asking questions. I'd want to know as much as everyone else knows."

"I've asked many times, and there's no mystery that I can see," she said.

"Maybe you're not asking the right questions. Maybe you have to break the loop, ask the hard ones."

She sat quietly, staring into her coffee. "It was an accident," she said in a near whisper. "You have just put some very strange thoughts into my head, Mr. Reid, and I'm not sure I want to go there."

I reached over and put my hand on her forearm. She didn't pull away. "I'm sorry, Itzla, I get a little carried away with my scenarios sometimes. What do you know about Huerta?"

She lifted her cup, realized that the coffee had gone cold, and set it down on the end of the table next to the pitcher. My little spell was broken, again. "Carlos?" she said. "Carlos has always been helpful and a good friend to me. As I mentioned, he and my father grew up together."

"Do you think Huerta might have something to do with Lino's disappearance?" I asked.

She began drumming her slender fingers on the table. "Just because they went their own ways, Mr. Reid, doesn't mean there were any ill feelings between them. What reason would Carlos have for doing something like that?"

"Doesn't it seem strange that your uncle would disappear within a few days of the warrior chieftain being stolen from the museum? More coincidence?" I reminded her.

"And that Lino and Huerta haven't spoken to each other for twenty-five years, possibly because of the Warrior?"

"But that was so long ago. Why would this happen now?" Again, the drumming of fingernails. Then as though a flood light had gone off inside her head, Itzla stood up quickly, banging her chair against the wall behind her. "Mr....., Skip, what are you suggesting?"

"My older brother died mysteriously from a fall in the mountains when he was twenty-one," I said. "No one who had witnessed it could explain it, and my parents immediately removed all memories of him from the house and their minds. Took all his pictures, trophies, and clothes out of the house. It took me five years to get to the truth of his death. To find out that it was not an accident."

Itzla's eyes narrowed in anger. "Are you suggesting that my parents were killed? That doesn't make any sense at all."

Neither do all the unimaginable things that had happened in the last few days with Huerta and Garret, I thought. "Anything is possible," I said.

"Why would it be anything other than an accident, and who would have wanted to...kill my parents?" She sat down again, thinking hard, her eyes burning into mine.

"I'll give you one greenback dollar for what you're thinking right now," I said.

"I'm thinking that we need to take a ride."

I smiled again. This time it worked. A slight flush came over her face. "Coffee can do wonders, no?" I said. "Where to?"

"We need a trip to Teuchitlán. Now."

CHAPTER
THIRTEEN

Highway 15 was rapidly becoming as familiar as my surname. The highway, along with the rolling tumbleweeds and dust clouds kicked up by the wind of Itzla's Toyota, seemed to carry with it a conspicuous smell of trouble. First Lino in his comical commuter bus, then Garret in his well-tuned Jeep. *Did I need to keep my eye on Itzla? Was she in danger, or a danger? Or both?*

Itzla drove the little red Toyota hard, but it was up to the task of getting us to Teuchitlan. She stopped several places along Lino's route to ask locals if they had seen her uncle. What she got were shakes of the head, a few comforting hugs, and a growing surety that Lino had actually been kidnapped. No one had seen him.

She roared off the highway onto the dirt road leading up the hill to her village, easily outpacing the roiling clouds of dust that chased us with a vengeance. She slid the car to a stop in front of her aunt and uncle's store and jumped out. A panicked Nailea ran out of the store, followed by Luz, Vincencio, and Benito, who was wearing a bandolier of bullets over an ancient leather vest and a not-so-ancient, wide-brimmed charro.

"I have to know more about my parents' death," she said harshly as the four gathered around her. "Lino has disappeared because of something that happened back then. And I think all of you know more than what you've made me believe." Nailea reached out to her. Itzla shook her off and glared at the people who had helped raise her. "If we're going to find him, you have to tell me everything you know." She turned to me and shrugged. "You're in the mix, too, Skip."

I had made my way to the right front fender, away from the action. Discretion. "At your service," I said, coming to attention.

Nailea again stepped forward, her brown face a tangled web of lines and wrinkles from too many years in the sun. "*Itzlaita, querida,*" she said, nervously. "We never thought it would happen again. We thought it was over."

Itzla looked at all of them, a combination of contempt and confusion spreading across her face. "What's not over? What haven't you been telling me?" she demanded.

Vincencio walked to her, gently taking hold of her arms. "Come inside," he said. "There is much that needs to be explained."

I followed Benito through the confines of the small store, checking out his worn leather vest, bandolier buckled over his shoulder with rifle bullets in a neat row, and wondered if he was still waiting for another call from Pancho Villa. "Why the outfit?" I asked as he pulled aside a colorful blanket and led me into the living quarters behind the store. The others had already gathered around a large rectangular oak table in what appeared to be the living room.

Benito tenderly patted his bandolier. He shifted the charro into a more strategic position on his head. "There is evil in the air, Mr. Reid; and I am prepared to defend the ones I love."

"Evil?" I asked with a half laugh. He then shot me a look that practically turned me to stone. "What kind of evil would we be talking about, Benito?"

He pulled me to the corner of the room away from the chatter at the table. We stood next to a rifle propped against the wall. I assumed it was his. "The evil is a *gabacho*," he whispered, his left eyebrow arching high onto his forehead.

I immediately thought of Garret. He may be evil in his own way; but as he had told me, he doesn't hurt innocent people. Maybe Benito thought it was me. Cringing, I asked, "Who is this evil *gringo*, Benito?"

His right hand traveled to the long barrel of the rifle. "I do not know his name, but he has been asking questions in the village."

My eyes followed his hand as he began stroking the barrel. He was an old man, but his reflexes and strength were still working for him. "What kind of questions?" I asked.

"If we have artifacts for sale here. Where he might find authentic pottery."

"Maybe he was a tourist looking for deals," I suggested.

Benito straightened against the wall. "He was not a tourist," he retorted in a low whisper. "Tourists do not carry guns."

Just what I needed. Another crazy gringo with a gun.

"He tried to hide it," he continued. "It was small, but I saw the handle under his shirt."

"When was he here?"

I waited while Benito clicked back the clock of his memory. "He came about three o'clock," he eventually said, "asked his questions and was gone in thirty minutes."

"Do you remember what he looked like?"

"I have seen many men like him," Benito said, fingering the tip of one of the many bullets that were spread across his chest. "Your height, muscular, jeans, running shoes and a silly khaki pullover shirt that made him look like Popeye. His eyes were evil. The eyes of a killer. That is why I am prepared, no? There is danger coming, *amigo*." His quick eyes gestured toward the table. "The others see it only one way," he said. "My eyes are clearer than theirs." Even though most of Benito's front teeth were missing, his smile was still engaging.

With his description, the man could only have been Kopek. What was his interest in artifacts? What was it that he and Garret were arguing about in front of the central market that day? Kopek had told Garret that Garret owed him something. What was the debt?

After nudging Benito playfully, I scooted back to the group at the table and slid onto the wooden bench across from Itzla, my eyes tracing the curves of her long arms and swan-like neck, trying to make sense out of the last few days. She had undone her hair from the barrette, and it was now cascading over her shoulders, down to her breasts. She had suddenly softened, her face glowing from the mixture of tears and perspiration. If I could have put her on a plane to Los Angeles at that moment, sent her away, away from the danger, and into the comfort of a house on the Strand in Manhattan Beach, I would have; but right now that was not in the cards. She needed to be kept safe here.

"Remember how for so long we have told you how your parents died in the fire?" It was Vincencio. He was holding Itzla's hand from across the table.

Nailea and Luz jerked their heads up. "Vincencio, *por*

117

favor," Nailea begged.

Vincencio put his hand up. "Nailea, this has got to stop right now. Itzla has a right to know the truth."

Benito scooted his chair out quickly. "I'll get my rifle," he said as though he had done it a thousand times before. The sound of old leather creaked as he took three healthy strides across the room. "We're going to need it."

"Pay no attention to the old man," Luz whispered to me. She circled the side of her head with an index finger. "He still has dreams of the revolution."

With all that was happening around me, I suspected that Benito may be the only sane one in the bunch.

"What is this secret?" Itzla suddenly wailed, wrenching her hands away from Vincencio and shrugging off Luz's and Nailea's attempts to comfort her. "I need to know! Was it an accident, or were they killed?"

Except for the sound of Benito tapping the butt of his rifle onto the dirt floor, the room was silent. After a few seconds, even he stopped. My guesses and speculations earlier that afternoon had been nothing more than worse case scenarios for a bad screenplay. Now all that supposition seemed to be taking on a life of its own, exploding into a full-blown crisis. My curiosity and naivety had somehow picked up another hitchhiker – stupidity. Not a very handsome trio for a long life.

Vincencio, with a toughness that caught me off guard, broke the silence. "Itzla," he said, "you are everyone's daughter, and we will do everything necessary to protect you. No one is going to harm you as long as we are breathing."

Nailea went white. "We can't," she grimaced.

What the hell! Who would want to hurt this woman?

Itzla looked quickly at each person. Fear had replaced

the shine in her eyes. "Protect me!" she exclaimed. "Why do I need protection? From what?"

"Itzla," Vincencio said softly, "After your parents died in the fire, the town had no other choice than to consider it an accident. It was for your protection that we had to keep the real reason a secret from you."

"What reason? Are you telling me they were actually… killed?" she said, choking out the words.

Nailea stood up and fretfully paced around the room, her face consumed with worry, both for her husband and now for Itzla. Neither she nor Vincencio had to say a word.

"Why would anyone want to kill them?" Itzla finally said. She was breathing hard, and the words sputtered and stalled as she spoke.

"I think it is for the same reason that Lino has disappeared," Benito declared. He was looking down the sights on the top of the barrel aiming at something outside the window. "It's that damn clay. The piece of crap you've been looking for these last few days. The goddamn thing won't leave us alone."

"You mean my parents were killed because of the missing warrior?" Itzla stated.

"Because of the artifact, yes," Vincencio said. "Listen to me," he pleaded as Itzla began to squirm in her chair. "Back then, just after the three of them had found the two warriors, Huerta had connected with an American who promised to make them all rich. All they had to do was smuggle the twin artifacts into the United States. Lino and your father wanted to give the pieces to the Museum in Guadalajara."

"Carlos is a pig!" Nailea had stopped pacing long enough to exclaim. "All he ever thought about was money."

Vincencio glared at Nailea. The frustration in his eyes

seemed to sadden him. "They argued for weeks over this," he said. "They decided to store the pieces in your parents' house until they could agree on what to do with them. But Carlos couldn't wait. He went to your parent's house to steal the pieces, telling them that if he couldn't have them no one could. When his attempt at bullying them to give the Warriors up failed, there was a terrible fight; and your father was badly hurt. Later that night Carlos went back to the house, planning on destroying the artifacts. All of you were in the house when he started the fire."

"Carlos killed my parents?" she said, unbelieving. "Carlos Huerta?" She was quiet for a moment, looking at her friends confirming the truth. Then she exploded, sending her chair scudding across the hard-packed dirt. She stood with her palms flat on the tabletop, her piercing stare first flicking to Vincencio, then to Nailea, and finally to Luz. "You knew, and you did nothing?" she raved. "You knew this man had intentionally killed my parents, and you just let him go! Why isn't he in prison? Why didn't you do something?"

"Our hands were tied," Luz said. "What Huerta didn't know was that your father had given the pieces to Lino earlier that day for safekeeping. Days later when Huerta found out they hadn't been destroyed in the fire and that Lino had them, he was furious. Carlos went after Lino and the artifacts, but Lino had already turned them in to the museum."

"We couldn't tell you, Itzla," Nailea said. "It was for your own protection. Huerta told Lino that he would kill you, too, if anyone mentioned his involvement in the fire."

Vincencio closed his eyes, maybe to block the tears. "And he left only silent witnesses," he scowled. "We have been living with this for twenty-five years. I'm sorry you had to find out this way."

"Now one of them has been stolen," Benito said. "What does that rat of a man want this time?"

I caught up with Itzla outside the store. She had stormed into the narrow street in a rage and circled the Toyota with her long strides, pounding the hood with her fist with each pass. Her head swiveled from side to side, first to her aunt and uncle's store, and then to the blistered walls of her parents' charred house.

She pounded the hood one last time, hard, laid both palms on the hood and stared out over the roof of the car. "I trusted that man," she said. "He sent me money for my education. He found my position at the museum. My life was so good, and now I find out that he killed my mother and father. What kind of monster is he? What does he want? I want to strangle him! Impale him on a saquaro cactus!"

I wanted to tell her what I knew about the killing ways of Señor Huerta; but for her safety, I kept quiet. I couldn't be of much use to her if I had to keep an eye on Garret and Manolo for giving their little secret away, and I didn't know how entwined they were with Huerta's illicit activities. As much as it hurt to see Itzla in this kind of pain, disclosing what I knew might only make it worse. This, along with Lino's disappearance and the secrets it held, was flipping my life into an ordeal of mystery, mayhem and murder. I thought about the bus to Panama as I fingered the ticket in my pants' pocket; but when I looked at Itzla, it hit me. I wasn't going anywhere.

Itzla pushed herself away from the car, turned toward me, and surprisingly, wound her arms around me, weeping uncontrollably. "I'm all mixed up," she stammered. "I'm so mad and sad at the same time. I feel so lost and cheated."

She melted into my chest, pressing her body to mine. I held her as though she were actually mine, feeling the softness of her shoulders, the firmness of her breasts, the tears spreading across my chest as she nuzzled into my neck. She was a delicate, ruffled feather in my arms. It was what I had longed for since I first saw her walk out of her office at the Museum. And now we were clinging to each other, she in desperation, I in an odd combination of selfishness and high-mindedness. For the moment, selfishness was the odds-on favorite, and I stood there absorbing all the warmth she wanted to give me.

That gentle moment ended when Benito marched out of the store, his toothless, little-boy grin spread all over his face. Itzla pulled away from me just as quickly as she had rushed into my arms as Benito raised his rifle above his head and shouted, "*Triunfo!*" as if he had just been victorious at the battle for Chihuahua. "*No más secretos!*" He then tapped me on the shoulder with the barrel of his rifle and strutted off across the street and into the cantina.

"I need to apologize, Itzla," I said after she had once again brought herself under control. "Back in the city, there in the café, I had no idea what I was saying. It was mind-wandering chatter. Speculation. I had no idea it would turn out like this."

She was breathing easier now, her crying being reduced

to a slight whimper. She seemed to have found some relief in the family's disclosure. "But you were right," she said softly, "and I had fallen victim to a betrayal."

"They were only trying to keep you alive," I said. "I'd consider that a rather benevolent betrayal."

She pushed herself away from the car, slapping it as she did so, and said with renewed anger, "They are good people, but my life being suddenly turned upside down isn't my idea of protection. They hurt me. And all this secrecy over an ancient piece of Tabachine sculpture? What other secrets are they keeping from me?" She paused, then looked me square in the eyes. "Do you have any secrets, Mr. Reid? We might as well get them all out on the table. Pain is pain."

"We all have dirty little secrets, Itzla," I declared. "But this isn't the time or place to be airing my dirty laundry, even though my dirty laundry could use a good washing. What we need to do is figure out why Lino has disappeared, who, if anyone, would want to kidnap him, and why?"

She began pacing again, small circles in front of me. "Is that all?" she said frivolously. "Where do we begin?"

I looked out over the Guachimonton, trying to get a better feel for the area and said, "As far as beginning, you've already made a damn good start by breaking through the silence your family has kept for twenty-five years. Is the shaft tomb where the warriors were originally found out there?" I nodded toward the open land beyond the town.

"Yes," she said, "but several miles up the hill, on the upper plateau. We'd have to drive there."

"Then let's drive."

"But I don't see—"

"I'll explain later. We've only got a little sunlight left. Let's go. We need to do a little speculating."

We followed the road up the hill for about a mile until we reached a small junction. My stomach turned when I recognized the road that came up from behind the town, the one Garret used to take me back to his ranch. To my relief, she opted for the other fork which she said would take us to the upper ruins of the Guachimonton.

After another mile at a pace that would make a tortoise laugh, the road ran out. "We have to walk from here," Itzla stated, pulling a small flashlight from the glove box and sliding it into her slacks' pocket. "It's on a knoll in a small valley overlooking the major ruins. No roads to it. We'd like to keep it that way, at least until we've completed the archeological studies and excavated it. There are still treasures out here, Skip." She paused, looking out over the ruins beneath us and to the town where she had grown up in the shadow of secrecy. "I never thought I would not love this place," she said. "It hurts me deeply to be up here now."

I knew that pushing through hurt was like trying to haul a Zamboni ice machine up a muddy hill: It's impossible without a lot of help. "It's a good starting point," I said. "This seems to be where this fiasco began. Besides, at least for the moment, I wanted to get you away from the pain your family is putting you through."

She gave me a cautious, sideways glance. "This way," she said, and started us down a narrow, hard-packed animal path that split the horse grass flowing along its sides. I noticed some recent footprints and figured that some of the children from the town had come up to play their games in the ruins. Itzla continued gloomily, saying, "The old axiom, 'The truth hurts,' can't compare with the pain of being lied to."

"We're on the same wave, Itzla." Her statement had brought up old memories and the rage I felt toward Coleen with her instant decision to blindside me with the lie of her long-term affair.

"Excuse me?" Itzla asked. Her face wriggled slightly into what looked like stunned curiosity.

"I know how you must feel," I said. "One of the reasons I'm down here is because of a lie."

She guided me over a small rise where the hills flattened out into a narrow plain. I could see the shadows darkening the waters of the crescent-shaped lake below us. "Deceit seems to be swarming like mosquitoes today," she said. "Attacking when you least expect it. What lie are you running from?"

I hadn't thought that I was running from a lie. The situation with Coleen had stripped me of all my plans and dreams, but that was mostly because of the pain caused by her lie. "Mine was a girl, my fiancée," I said quickly, not wanting to belabor the fact. "I know that doesn't equate to the way you lost your parents, or to Huerta's unconscionable behavior. I just wanted you to know that you're not alone in what you feel. It's the loss compounded by the betrayal that hurts so much." The explanation of my affair with the U.S. government would have to wait.

She gently brushed my shoulder with her fingertips. "Maybe we are on the same wave," she said, her smile betraying a little of the coldness she had been harboring. "You said *one* of the reasons you were here. There are others?"

"Yes, there are. Someone told me surfing was good at Punta de Mita, north of Puerto Vallarta."

Itzla's laugh was quiet, breathy. "And was it?" she asked.

"Bitchin'," I said, shuffling my sandals in the sand, walking the nose of a make believe surfboard.

"Unless you want to tell me, I won't ask you again, Skip."

"There's more," I said, and proceeded to tell her about the job I had quit, and more about Coleen, yet still avoiding mention of my overrated fugitive-from-justice status. She listened, but her mind was elsewhere.

"Right now, I don't want any of those people in my life," she said abruptly. "Not Nailea, not Vincencio. I've got to think this through. I can't believe that Carlos killed my parents and was using me as a hostage to blackmail the entire town. It sounds like a cheap paperback novel."

Her touch lingered with me for a moment, addling my wits. *What was I, twelve years old again, enamored with the first girl that would even want to talk to me?* I temporarily shelved that feeling and said, "Vincencio doesn't seem to be the type to lie about something as serious as that."

"Now you're scaring me, Mr. Reid. As long as I'm alive, they're safe. If something should happen to me...."

I could feel the air tightening around us. "This is only speculation, Itzla, but he'd most likely find another way to keep his secret. It would be to his advantage to keep you alive."

"Keep me alive! Mr. Reid, do you know more than what you're telling me?"

"Only what logic and intuition tell me. And they're telling me that there's more here than we know."

Itzla looked at me with a cold, insistent stare. "Then I suggest we start investigating. Do you think Carlos has anything to do with my uncle's disappearance?"

Knowing what I knew about Huerta, I would have to guess that he was probably involved. "If Carlos does have him," I said, "you can bet it has something to do with the Warrior."

Itzla slowed her walk, then said thoughtfully, "Carlos could steal it any time he wanted, why now?"

"Maybe the opportunity of following up on an old idea of selling it somewhere has poked its head up again." I wasn't buying that and I could tell neither was Itzla.

"Why would he need Lino for that? With his connections, he could simply steal it and smuggle it out on a government plane."

"Revenge?" I said unconvincingly. "For an old debt maybe?" Some of the pieces were working themselves into the puzzle, hovering around in my head, looking to match up. Revenge or past debt didn't seem to add up. "Itzla," I said after the realization hit me, "Carlos may not have the Warrior."

Itzla stopped abruptly as if she had run head on into one of the stone walls of the ruins we were now walking through. Her eyes widened. "After what we've just discovered?" she said. "Who else could have it?"

"Again, this is only speculation."

"So far your record is pretty good. Go on."

"If it isn't Carlos, your uncle may be mixed up in something more serious than any of you know. Whoever has Lino must think he knows where the Warrior is."

"My uncle hasn't seen that piece since he and my father took it to the museum twenty-five years ago. I doubt he even remembers what it looks like. He's a bus driver. How would he begin to know where a thief would hide something that valuable?"

"He may not know. That's why we have to find him. I'd hate to see him suffer for something he knows nothing about. Now show me this shaft tomb where they found these troublemaking twins."

* * *

Itzla led me around several mounds of unexcavated ruins to a clearing on a narrow plateau overlooking the Guachimonton. We stood in the shadow of the mountain at our backs looking out over the rich earth of the Tequila valley and the luster of the blue agave fields fanning out beneath us.

"I do still love this land," she said. "I used to walk up here as a girl, dreaming of possibilities. There were so many. They were endless. You can understand why the Tabachine people would have wanted to live and die here, no?"

"Just between you and me, I prefer ashes and an urn." I laughed; but my heart wasn't in it, nor, I could see, was Itzla's. I quickly recanted, "It's a beautiful place, yes."

She was quiet for a moment. And then in a sudden rush of pain, she lifted her head and screamed, a primal scream that echoed among the spirits of the Guachimonton and into the valley below. She put her hands to her face and said in a tearful, choking whisper, "I feel like I have been raped, Skip. Stripped naked and violated. Who can I trust?"

I knew her anger. Could feel it in my bones. Coleen and her Kiwi, unraveling the threads of my plans, pulling me apart until there was…..*Ah. Knock it off, Skipper. That kind of thinking won't help either one of us.*

I took the three steps separating us and pulled her to me. She again softened into me. "Vincencio, Nailea, and Lino," I said. "They're your roots. You have to trust them. Huerta can go to hell."

She rocked herself away from me. "Carlos," she said with a disgust that would have made anyone else spit into the dirt. "I can understand why my family wanted to protect me from him, and maybe it's not them that I should be angry with. But there have been so many secrets. Right now I'm so angry, I don't want to see any of them. I can't go back there, Skip."

"You may see things differently once we find Lino," I said. "I have a feeling things will sort themselves out once he's back in the nest."

The mention of her uncle brought more tears. She brushed them away from her cheeks with her fingertips. "Guess I'm not as strong as I talk," she said with a wistful laugh. "But I still don't want to see them for awhile."

"Okay," I said. "So what do we do? Hang out in a shaft tomb until you make up your mind?" I was looking up the sharp slope of the mountain toward Garret's place where a few rock outcroppings stuck out against the line of dense jungle about three hundred yards away. "Where is this reprobate hole we're looking for, Itzla? Not up there, I hope," indicating the rocks.

She looked at me as though I were the reprobate. "We've been standing on it for the last five minutes. The entrance is behind that sage bush." She flicked her hand toward a single, spindly sage ten feet away.

Behind the bush was an old wooden ladder, its arms poking out three feet above the shaft. The ladder, Itzla explained, was the original one that her father, Lino, and Carlos Huerta had built to search for artifacts. I shook its arms, felt the sway, and heard the creaking sounds of loosened nails. It was a straight shaft tomb, the mouth about six feet in diameter. The shaft itself, as Itzla pointed out, was dug to a depth of about twenty-five feet with five chambers eight feet long and five feet wide dug off the main shaft at the bottom, much like the arms of a sea star.

Itzla leaned out over the shaft and looked down into the semi-darkness. "The warriors were posted as guards on each side of the main chamber. We suspect a chieftain might have been buried here. Warriors were often used to signify royalty and...."

"Hand me your flashlight, Doc," I said. "I'm going in. You coming?"

She backed away, giving me a quick, cynical smile that made her look younger. "I know what's down there," she said, "I'll sit up here and watch the last light over the valley. If you need help, I'll come down."

The makeshift ladder quivered like a small California earthquake. Before I could bring the wobble back under control, the sixth rung snapped from my weight, and I dropped like a quarter in a pay phone to the sandy bottom, scraping my hands along the rails of the ladder, collecting splinters on my way down.

"Are you all right?" Itzla said. I could see her looking down at me, her face beautiful in the growing shadows of the early evening. "I heard the wood snap and your groan. I should have warned you."

"Other than a few splinters and an awkward recovery from a butt bounce, I seem to be fine," I said, then added, "These tombs seem to be having their way with me." I held the flashlight between my teeth and leaned against the cool wall of the shaft while picking at a half- inch sliver of wood that had embedded itself in the palm of my hand. "There's room for two down here," I mumbled. "Looks like a good starter house."

Itzla turned her head quickly to the side, distracted by something apparently moving up the hill. When she turned back, she said, "You seem to be doing just fine by yourself, Mr. Reid."

"Skip!" I retorted. "It's Skip! Coffee, remember?" I heard a quick chuckle as she backed away from the opening.

After squatting at the entrance of each of the low-ceilinged chambers and running the light over the floors and walls, I still had no idea what I was looking for. What clues to a nearly three-decade old mystery would still be here? I flicked the light off, saying, "Except for the smell of must, this place has been cleaned out."

"About ten years ago," Itzla stated. "What anyone other than a paleontologist would want with ancient skeletons and pottery shards is beyond what I know. Other than the looting being a travesty, it just doesn't make sense."

"Dollars and cents for someone, I would imagine."

The pun bounced off the limestone walls up to Itzla. "Do you ever take anything seriously?" she asked.

I held the light under my chin, flicking it on and off, and grinned up at her. "Ten-foot waves, Baby. That's serious."

"The chamber directly behind you is where they discovered the warriors," Itzla said, ignoring the seriousness of my seriousness.

Turning and flooding the area with as much illumination as the compact light would emit, I crouched and crawled through the low, narrow entrance of the main chamber. Squatting in the center, I tried to make sense out of the nothingness surrounding me. All I could glean from inside the darkness was the musty, dry air, the coolness of the walls, and the fine dirt beneath my sandals. All I saw of any consequence were two stone bases near the entrance, where I assumed the Warriors had been stationed to protect the honorable occupant. After several minutes of inspection, I decided that the shaft tomb was nothing more than a dead end for any clues leading to Lino's whereabouts.

Okay, so I'm not Phillip Marlowe. If I were, what would I be looking for? The Maltese Falcon? The thought had crossed my mind. *The Teuchitlán Warrior? You've seen too many movies, Skipper.*

While I was scooting out of the chamber, the light flashed over what looked to be tiny letters pressed into the loose dirt next to one of the warrior platforms. A closer look told me it was the brand name of a major running shoe company.

"Itzla," I shouted, "do you know anyone who wears Reebok running shoes?"

Itzla peeked her head over the top. "No, it's all cowboy boots and huraches around here. Why?"

"I need you down here, Itzla. I think you need to see this."

She was as graceful and quiet as a cat's shadow as she floated down the ladder. When she reached the missing sixth rung, I held her waist, feeling the lightness of her body as she made the leap into the sand. We were inches away, facing each other in the semi-darkness of the narrow shaft, my hands still resting lightly at her waist. I hadn't been this close to my feelings since Coleen; and after she betrayed me, I had vowed to never again give them away. There was too much pain in the giving. But Itzla was a twist in the fabric of that vow. She held my state as the seconds passed, up to the moment of decision. As much as I wanted her, I could not take advantage of her vulnerability. I shook my head slowly and slid my hands from her waist.

"What do you make of this?" I said, dropping into a crouch, shining the light off the chamber walls and onto the tread marks of the Reebok Man. We were kneeling elbow to elbow in the limited space of the chamber looking at the letters, her cool arm pressing against mine as we leaned in for a closer look.

"Can't be tourists," Itzla stated. "They don't make it up this far. They get as far as the town and walk the lower Guachimonton. Very few people know of this place."

I told Itzla about the fresh shoe prints I had seen on the trail coming up. "They match," I said.

"Great," Itzla said playfully. "We've got a matching pair of shoe treads. Ten pesos say you can't tell me the color of the laces. This isn't much to go on, Skip."

"You're probably right. Maybe they don't mean anything, but it does seem a little suspicious, don't you think?"

I shined the light on her face. She pushed it away and sat back on her heels. "Stop it," she said. "That's embarrassing."

It wasn't easy in the tight space, but I managed to rest my back against the wall, pull my knees up to my chin, and throw a handful of dirt off to my side.

"Are you having another one of your speculative moments, Skip?"

I was dead tired, and if I didn't keep talking or moving, I could easily fall asleep in one of the five chambers, become someone's souvenir on the Day of the Dead. "Try this on for size," I said. "Benito told me that another *gringo* was hanging around Teuchitlán earlier today. He said the man reminded him of Popeye, muscles and all, and that he was wearing running shoes."

Itzla shifted her weight, rolled off her heels, and sat cross-legged across from me. "What does that prove?" she said. "One footprint that may or may not be related to my uncle's disappearance isn't much."

"That this guy is one step ahead of us?" I could feel Itzla's eyes burning into me. "Alright, alright, sorry," I said. "But if it's the same man, I saw him the day I met Garret and Manolo. The three were in a heated argument about something Popeye thought belonged to him."

Itzla's eyes widened. "Do you know what that 'something' is?"

"No, I wasn't close enough to hear that part."

"Why would this Popeye man come to Teuchitlán?" Itzla was thinking out loud. "What could he possibly want?"

I told her what Benito had told me about the man's interest in early Tabachine pottery and about the gun he had stuffed in the waistband of his jeans. When I mentioned Benito's description of his eyes, like those of a killer, Itzla froze.

"We have to get out of here," she said. I flicked the light to her face again. She pushed it away. "I don't feel safe in here or anywhere else right now. All this talk of killing and killers is pushing me over the edge." She took a deep breath. I assumed she was considering cutting bait and running, but instead she said with muscle in the words, "Let's go. We have business to take care of."

Without having a clue as to what would come next, I nudged her toward the ladder. "One step at a time," I said, and grabbed the side rails, steadying the unforgiving ladder as Itzla began her cat-like ascent.

She had reached the top and had one foot on the ground when I heard the gunshot. In an explosion of splintered wood, the bullet shattered the right arm of the ladder a few inches above the tomb's rim, breaking Itzla's handhold. She scrambled back down the ladder, below the rim of the tomb, clinging desperately to the second rung, when a second shot rang out. The bullet ripped the other arm to shreds, sending a shower of wood chips down into the shaft and ricocheting off a rock next to my left ear.

Seeing Itzla hanging from the top rung of the ladder,

struggling to maintain her footing on the weakened rungs beneath her, my stomach turned over and my blood began to boil. "Itzla! Jesus!" I yelled, taking a chance the ladder would hold together long enough for me to clamber up to where she had frozen her grip on the rung. "Hang on." From what I could see in the shadows, it looked like the bullets had missed her. I was halfway up the ladder when I heard myself grumble, "If these assholes are after you, they're going to have to get through me first."

Itzla held fast to the rung, trembling. "I think I'm okay," she said. "What's happening, Skip?"

"I don't know," I said, "but I'm sick of this shit." I scrambled up beneath her, put my shoulder under her hips, and kept it there until she found better footing on the ladder, until she loosened her grip and we worked our way back down into the tomb.

Itzla took hold of both my arms staring intently into my eyes. I could feel the fear in her touch, see it in her expression. I knew what was going on inside her. It didn't take much to scramble your insides when you're being shot at. "We are not going to die in here," she said with conviction.

"You're right. Not if I can help it," I said in an attempt to reassure her. I pushed her back into the main chamber, fearing more bullets ricocheting off the tomb walls, and searched the ground for anything that could be used as a weapon. Other than fragments of pottery, a few bone remnants, and some stones scattered around the chamber, there was nothing that would even come close to fending off a large caliber rifle shell. I sneered as I picked up a useless, palm-sized rock. *Rocks,* I thought. *Now I know how the Lakota Sioux felt at Wounded Knee.*

After seeing that Itzla wasn't hurt, I peeked out from

under the chamber entrance and up into the darkening sky. The dusk, like the tomb, had a quietness about it. Only the shattered ladder, now leaning precariously just below the lip of the shaft, bleakly reminded me that silence was not always a friend.

Itzla must have felt the same thing. She had picked up a few palm-sized rocks, her body taut with determination. "It's too quiet. It's not over," she whispered.

"We're stuck down here until somebody makes a move," I said. "Hopefully, he feels he's made his point."

It was then I heard someone scuffing over the sand at the mouth of the shaft, kicking rocks down into the chamber.

"Listen," I whispered. She must have heard it, too, for she was suddenly more attentive.

"Who the hell are you and what do you want?" I yelled, and chanced another peek up to the rim. I had no sooner stuck my head out of the chamber when I saw the barrel of a rifle appear from over the lip. I ducked back into the chamber, diving onto Itzla, just as the first of four bullets pounded into the shaft floor. Then two more shots rang out, the bullets hissing like agitated snakes across the small valley above the tomb. Then it was quiet. I could hear the shooter moving quickly away.

"Those last two sounded like they came from a different gun," I said. "Different sound. And they didn't seem to be aimed at the tomb." I hesitated, unsure as to who else might be tracking us then said with an uncertain optimism, "We may have a friend out there."

She was now hunched over next to me in the warrior chief's low-ceilinged chamber, looking up into the dim light of the opening. "I don't have any friends who shoot at people," she said curtly. "Do you?" Her stare was long, cold, and painful, fixed firmly to a promise of *adios, amigo, para siempre. Goodbye, friend, forever.*

After considering her question, I decided that our lives were more important than any secrets I was holding; and if I wasn't telling Itzla everything, she'd have no chance to sort out what she needed to do for herself. "They're not on my A list of most intimate friends, Itzla," I said, "but yes, I have run into people who do that sort of thing."

"And is one of them out there now?" she scoffed, standing and pacing the limited confines of the chamber.

"I don't know who's out there, Itzla," I retorted. "Whoever it is, he's a damn good shot. Those ladder rails were blown off intentionally. The shots were too accurate. If he had wanted you dead, he wouldn't have missed you. Someone is trying to scare the hell out of you."

"They're succeeding," she said, realizing that she may be the target. She sidled up to me and grabbed my hand, holding it tightly. I could feel the fear pulsing from her. "I don't know who to trust. I have to know that I can trust you, at least."

"The last time someone told me that, a bullet cracked by my ear," I said. I could still hear the sound from Garret's .45 ringing in my head. "Trust is a helluva lot more than words, Itzla."

"But why would someone want to shoot at me?" she said in a half whisper, shaking her head, still in disbelief.

"You tell me. Are you holding something back?"

"Holding back?" She shook her hand loose from mine and spun away. "I've told you all I know!"

"I believe you," I said, my frustration rising. "But if he, or maybe it was a she, wanted you dead, he wouldn't have missed. Those were warning shots, Itzla. Someone must think you know something about the warrior. You work at the museum, Lino is your uncle, who has a history with the artifact, and there's Huerta. I don't know how he would fit into it, but he is capable of…, well, you know what he's capable of. Think, Itzla. What are we missing?"

Itzla started slowly, choosing her words carefully. "The chieftain was taken between three and four a.m. The rear service door had been pried open."

"What about security?" I asked. "A system? Guards?"

"The museum has a very sophisticated security system. We test it repeatedly, and it has yet to fail. Except for that night. It was working when I left the museum, but it failed during the time of the theft. It was functioning fine when I came in the next morning and found the Warrior gone. So you think it was someone who works at the museum?"

"That's possible. I don't know what I'm trying to say, Itzla. I'm just working through things. What about the security system? Who has access to it?"

"The guard, the curator, my secretary, and… Carlos," she said, her voice trailing away into the dankness of the tomb as she uttered Huerta's name. "Damn it, Carlos!" She slapped the wall, her face suddenly contorted and flushing with anger.

"Everything appears to be heading toward our infamous Mr. Huerta," I muttered.

Itzla sprang toward the ladder. She had jumped to the third rung and started up. "Are you crazy?" I yelled, grabbing her leg and finally hooking my arms around her waist to pull her back into the chamber. "Someone is out there taking shots at you."

"Maybe it is you they are after," she wailed, fighting wildly to free herself from my grip, her fists pounding into my chest. "I have to get out of here! Ever since you've been here, there's been nothing but trouble. Are you a part of this, you and your friends who kill people?"

I grabbed her wrists just as she began to spin around, but her long legs had already found the wall of the chamber and she pushed off, sending us both sprawling into the dirt toward the far wall of the tomb. With an unexpected quickness she was on her feet again, rushing toward me and to the entrance I was blocking. I couldn't let her get to the ladder and topside without knowing that it was safe.

After dodging a few blows and taking a pretty good slap on the cheek, I grabbed her upper arms and pulled her into a bear hug, keeping her arms pinned against her sides. She was stronger than I anticipated. When she broke free I expected her to run for the ladder, to attempt an escape, but she continued pounding my chest. The punches quickly turned into harmless taps, and then she began to sob deeply. My hands found her waist, and I pulled her to me. She came willingly, her arms tenderly wrapping around my waist, her body shaking violently as the tears rolled down her cheeks. I held her tight, smelling the musky fragrance of her skin. When she pulled back, only inches away, I brushed a few wet strands of matted hair from her face; and for an instant, as we looked into each others eyes, I saw what everyone who knew her saw: a tenderness, a warmth that could take the chill out of a cold night. Her trembling had slowed; and at that moment, my body was telling me that I had to have her. I wanted to feel her body, her skin next to mine. I wanted to make love to her on the sandy floor of the tomb. I wanted her here and now. She shifted her weight and leaned into me. Her body slackened against mine. I could feel the softness of her breasts against my chest. My hands moved to the top of the delicate curves of her hips. She looked up at me, and for a few seconds I was lost in the softness of her full lips, her kiss.

At the sound of horse hooves scuffing up to the rim of the shaft, she pulled away. "Itzla, *Señor* Skip, are you down there?" It was undeniably the guttural Spanish of Benito. "You are both not hurt?"

"Benito!" Itzla cried out. She bolted from my arms and the security of the chamber and leaped for the ladder. "What are you doing here? It isn't safe."

Benito was leaning over the edge of the shaft, his face hidden beneath the shadow of his *charro*. The long barrel of his rifle stood like a flagpole in his hand. "It is safe now," he said, looking toward the outcropping of rocks where I assumed the shooter had been hiding. "I sniffed something evil in the air, so I followed you. My bullets have driven the *baboso* away. *Pinche cabrón*. Pardon my swearing, Itzla."

Itzla had made it to the top and started toward the old man. When she reached him and threw her arms around him, he smiled timidly and backed away, playing with the reins of the large, chestnut horse that was pawing at the ground next to him. With her towering height, Itzla made the hero of the revolution look like one of the children dressed up for the Day of the Dead.

"Am I glad to see you, *mi amigo*," I said after crawling over the lip of the tomb. "So that was your rifle we heard."

"Two shots, and he ran like the *cobarde* he is." He smiled and gave the butt of his rifle two sharp taps. His face could have been cut from the same worn leather of the bandolier that rolled over his shoulder to his waist.

"Could you see who this coward was?" Itzla asked.

"No, my bullets chased him into the rocks." He mounted his horse and pointed his rifle at the outcropping. "I only saw him leave in a hurry. My eyes are not so good in the dark, but my rifle shoots straight."

Benito, sitting straight and tall in the saddle on the chestnut stallion, his rifle crossed over his arms, seemed a rather dubious sentry as he and his horse hastened us back towards Itzla's Toyota. The wiry old man had guts, I had to admit, then realized I had been thinking out loud.

"You've been mumbling since we left the tomb," Itzla said. "You're even answering yourself. Come up with anything that will help us?"

I shook my head, more in an attempt to rattle the sleeplessness loose than to negate any significant revelations. It had been a fairly inauspicious, and tiring, last three days. "Other than a hammock and waiters on the beach, nothing much," I said. It was obvious she thought my statement held about as much weight as a basket full of chicken feathers.

"There's more," she said. "I can see it in your eyes. Are you angry with me?"

"You? Hell no! I'm damn pissed off with Garret and what he's gotten us into. I told him I'd write his story, but I sure as hell didn't count on two other warped minds coming into the mix."

I was at the point of wanting to tell her everything. I needed to tell her of the last few days. The secrets were eating at me, and I needed a confidante. *But how much of everything could I safely disclose? She was already on emotional overdrive and giving her details of having a .45 pressed into my forehead in the middle of the largest lake in Mexico, being caught in an ambush by crazy drug-running idiots, shot at, seeing a cold-blooded murder, and currently caught in the middle of a damn conspiracy to find an uncle who has apparently been kidnapped for the secret of the whereabouts of a goddamn stolen artifact, might put her over the edge. Not discounting the fact that someone was now trying very hard to frighten her off. Maybe even kill her. All that information would have to wait.*

"This Kopek man and Carlos?" she asked.

"All three of them, Kopek, Huerta, and Garret were together in Vietnam," I said. "Something must have happened over there to create some bad blood between them, and now they're calling in their I.O.U.s." I decided that too much information would be too risky. It wasn't worth the price of losing Itzla. "I'm sorry I dragged you into this. Let's get you back to your aunt's. You'll be safer there than with me."

"I can't go back there," she said. "Not just yet. They have betrayed my trust in them."

"Then we'll go to Guadalajara. I'll drive," I said when we reached the Toyota. "You're not in any shape to get us out of here, Itzla."

She slid into the passenger seat, her fingers drumming the dashboard. Benito had reined in the stallion next to her door. "Do not go through the town," he warned, his watchful eye panning the terrain around us. "That *cabrone* is still out there. You won't be safe." He raised his rifle high in the air. "I will do my little part here."

I fired up the Toyota and flipped on the headlights, the anger I felt toward Garret warming to a boil. Maybe it was an omen, of what kind I wasn't certain, but Credence Clearwater Revival was blasting out Bad Moon Rising on the radio. I switched it off as I nosed the car around potholes and rocks until we reached the fork in the road leading up to Garret's ranch and down to the village. The secondary road skirting the town was directly in front of me, the road that would take Itzla safely into the city.

Benito, with his purposeful watch, had been galloping the big chestnut next to us. "*Vayan con Dios*," he yelled as I accelerated up the mountain toward Garret's ranch.

"Where are you taking me?" Itzla said, her voice quaking.

"I'm going to kick the shit out of that asshole! Then get you the hell out of here. I've taken all the crap I'm going to from him."

C H A P T E R
FIFTEEN

We had gone about a mile in the dark. With my adrenaline still pumping with the thought of taking down Garret, I recklessly wound our way through the hills and creek beds toward Garret's compound. His guards, hopefully recognizing me, would call ahead, and we'd be passed through.

Several hundred yards from where I knew the guards were stationed, the headlights flashed on something moving ahead of us along the side of the road.

Itzla had seen it, too, and braced herself against the dashboard as a man stumbled out of the undergrowth and slowly slumped to the ground in front of us. In the luminous glow of the headlights, I could see that he had a firm grip on a burlap bag and was holding it tightly to his chest. I could, also, see that his hands, arms, and clothing were covered with blood.

Itzla grabbed my arm and let out a shriek that could have frozen the night air. "Oh God. No," she howled, leaning into the windshield, "It's not—"

"It's not Lino," I reassured her. Her other hand found the door handle. She was halfway out of the car when I pulled her back inside. We were close enough now to see he was a young man, possibly in his late teens. He raised his bloody right hand, palm out, as though trying to deflect more punishment. Grimacing in pain, he then fell over onto his side, clutching the bag.

We were spitting distance to Garret's territory, and his men probably had their rifle sights zeroed in on both Itzla and me waiting for us to trespass the boundaries of the ranch. Maybe this man had crossed the line and been shot for his trouble.

"Stay in the car," I said. "I don't think you want to see this. Looks pretty messy."

"Better than being in this car alone," she said, and was out her door and standing next to me, as close as a shadow could be in the light of the moon. I could feel her breath as she clung to my arm, shivering.

The man was as still as a sack of stored rice. I checked his pulse. He was alive but barely breathing. I leaned toward his mouth and heard the rattle of his whisper. "Garret," he said. "He will know what to do."

Itzla kneeled next to him and pried the bag from his hands exposing an oozing bullet wound in his abdomen. Another ring of blood leeched from the middle of his chest. She turned away, gagging. "We have to get him help," she said. "The closest hospital is in Guadalajara."

I looked again at his wounds, listened to the wheeze of his breathing. "He won't make it that far," I said. "And you know we can't go down the hill."

"We can't leave him here," Itzla said. "We've got to do something."

"Throw that bag in the trunk, and open the back door," I said, cradling the man in my arms as I walked to the car. "He's coming with us."

Even in Garret's Jeep it had been a hard ride, and now

I was asking a lot of the Toyota as I worked it up the bone-hard ruts and ankle-high rocks of the road. Spread out in front of the headlights in strobe-like splashes of umber, the road took on the appearance of an out take from Dante's Inferno. At a point where the road began to narrow and grow steeper, I could just make out the dark shadows of the pine trees that hid Garret's guards, the foliage full and heavy, their branches arching over the road. I moved forward at a crawl as the Toyota twisted and jolted, its tires spitting gravel and dirt as the jungle closed in around us, limbs whacking at the windows.

Itzla had been nervously keeping an eye on the man in the back seat. "Still breathing," she said.

"Just over this rise," I responded, nodding toward the summit of the little hill. Thinking back on Garret's orders to shoot intruders, I could only hope that the guards would remember me, and, more importantly, that they were in an agreeable mood.

Their sudden appearance from the bushes felt like a quick dunk in a vat of ice water, the chill lingering long after the shiver had dissipated. Itzla had put a vice grip on my forearm as the men stood in the light of the high beams, their guns ready at their sides, the barrels at our eye level fifteen feet from the windshield. Their fatigues were the color of the night. If they hadn't moved, I would never have seen them. Garret was right, trespassers would never know how they died. I stood on the brakes and felt the car slip to the right. There was a quick thump as the drive wheel fell off into a pothole deep enough to keep the Toyota from moving. We weren't going anywhere. I recognized Elidio, the guard who had helped Manolo switch the hubs of the Jeep into four-wheel drive. His mustache and scraggly beard looked even more menacing in the light of the slight moon. The other had been at the compound helping Manolo load the van for the ill-fated drug run. They called him Chuey. He had a dark bandanna tied around his forehead and appeared to be looking for a reason to shoot us.

"Garret! Garret!" I hollered, my anger toward the man dissipating with the need for his help. "I need Garret's help! It's me, Elidio, Skip. Remember. *Recuerda*? Someone has been shot."

After a long moment of heated discussion, they lowered their weapons and Chuey pinched out the joint he was smoking. The sweet smell of cannabis wafted into the car as Elidio switched on a powerful flashlight and shoved it toward my open window. They were both high.

"*¿Qué pasa*, Skip?" Elidio said. I could just make out a smile beneath the mustache.

Chuey had made his way to Itzla's door and was lightly tapping his rifle barrel on the glass, the light of his flashlight following every curve on her body. Itzla slid over, huddling against me, her legs pressed hard into the center console.

I had just begun to explain the happenings of the last few hours when Elidio flicked his light behind me, running the beam over the wrapped bundle of the man lying in the back seat. He moved the light to the man's face. "*Madre Dios*," he said softly, recoiling from the sight of what I thought was the blood and mess that lay behind us. He stood frozen for a moment in the darkness and then exploded with an extended string of expletives. Chuey, shaken by the urgency in Elidio's voice, looked to see what the fuss was about. When he saw the man, he crossed himself and backed away. Elidio, in a fit of rage, yanked open my door, grabbed me by the hair, and dragged me from the car. I felt the cold barrel of his gun shaking under my chin as he threw me face first against the car.

Elidio triggered his radio, his voice quaking with forced words as Manolo listened quietly. Then as Manolo's slow, cold voice came on strong through the static, Elidio broke into a sweat.

Sometime during the exchange, Elidio had released the pressure from under my chin; and Chuey had hauled Itzla out of her seat. Chuey prodded her along with little jabs of his gun until they were both standing next to the right front fender.

"What's he telling him, Itzla?" My Spanish had suddenly crash dived into a mountain of mush.

"That we're asking for Garret's help. That someone is trying to kill us."

"What else? Who is this guy we've got? He sure as hell set something off."

"Elidio doesn't want to tell him."

"I can hear that in his voice," I said keeping an eye on Chuey slowly moving the barrel of his rifle across Itzla's stomach and up to her breasts. He began to finger the sleeve of her blouse. Itzla batted his hand away. Good girl. "You touch her, and it'll be the last thing you do," I declared, starting my move toward Chuey, but the pressure of the rifle barrel returned.

Chuey laughed and reached for Itzla's arm. Itzla, with a quick knee to Chuey's groin, sent him sprawling to the ground, writhing in a tight ball. He was gasping for breath as he lay paralyzed in the light of the high beams. She then edged her way around the car to me. "There is one more thing he told him," she said. "The person we have in the car is this man Manolo's brother."

Jorge? The veterinary student? What could he possibly have done to warrant two bullets in his body? I kicked that abstraction

149

around in my head for half a Mexican minute, until I heard Elidio say in a shaky treble voice, "Manolo, *ya viene*." He lowered the rifle and went to help Chuey. Once on his feet, Chuey wobbled a bit, found his balance, and shot a look at Itzla that could have stopped a train. "*Manolo dice les protegamos*," Elidio told him. "*Calma*."

The way things were going, I took small comfort in knowing that Manolo was on his way. Even though he had told his guards to make sure no harm came to us, the air was still thick with unfinished business. I quickly rolled across the hood to Itzla standing next to the two men and hammered my fist into Chuey's jaw. He went down like a bag of sand in the light of the headlights. Elidio brought the barrel of his rifle up my chest, thought twice about firing, just long enough for me to parry the barrel and slam the butt of the gun into his forehead.

While the guards slowly recovered, I slid the clips out of the rifles and tossed them into the bushes. Weaponless, the guards began pacing the dirt on either side of the car, their voices rising until they again ignited into the heat of an argument. The squawking radio call to Manolo had obviously done something to set them off, and their knowing he was on the road made it very clear that they were worried.

"Nothing more to worry about, Itzla." I said this as calmly as my anger would allow; but I could see her nerves were frayed, and I wasn't certain my words held much juice for her. "I think they're more worried about being stoned and facing Manolo than about the kid in the back seat." I saw her glaring at Chuey remembering how she had taken him down. "And, Itzla, please remind me not to piss *you* off."

She took my hand. "I only knew I didn't want his hands on me."

* * *

The Jeep's headlights bounced erratically down the last half mile from the compound. I heard the roar of its big engine then saw the dark shape of Manolo's bulk behind the wheel. Even in the dark, there was little mystery as to what was coming at us. One thing I knew was that I didn't want to share a small space with a psychotic gorilla. I had to give him all the room he needed.

When he slid the Jeep to a stop next to the Toyota, he was out of his seat before the engine could sputter and shut down. He took two long strides toward the Toyota; and before Elidio could get out of his way, Manolo grabbed him by the neck and threw him into the rocks on the side of the road. He looked at Chuey cowering on the other side of the car, then at me, then Itzla. There was no way I could protect her should he decide to take his rage out on her. I had thrown the rifle clips away, and both Itzla and I were holding lifeless weapons. If he came after me, I might get lucky with one punch. I wouldn't concede death and hoped he would honor that. Any way I looked at the situation, someone was in trouble; and at this point it wasn't clear as to whom. In all my encounters with Manolo, nothing was ever clear, until he acted. Only then did things take on meaning.

But he quietly walked to the Toyota, stood with his hands fanned out on the roof above the rear window, fingers drumming, blood seeping through his shirt from his shoulder wound, his head slightly bowed, silently looking through the window at his brother, at the blood leaching through the blanket.

Not sure of Manolo's state of mind, I backed away, moving Itzla along with me, waiting for another explosion.

I didn't have to wait long. He began pummeling the roof, his big fists putting baseball-sized dents into the metal. He stepped back and drove his right fist into the window, shocking the glass into a fine spider web. The second blow sent chunks of glass popping, sliding down into the back seat at his brother's feet.

The pressure of Itzla's hand on my arm when Manolo turned away from the car and glared at us was all I needed to know. There was no possibility of stopping him, but I could at least slow him down if he had any intentions with her. I stepped in front of her.

"Elidio! Chuey!" he ordered without moving his eyes from us. His face was hard and that boyish expression of his wasn't fooling anyone. "Get Jorge into the Jeep. And you know what careful means." He then stalked to the front of the car, stopping just short of us, looking me over with an unreadable expression which could have meant I was either going to die or that I had suddenly become his best friend.

"Garret wants to see you two, now," he said after a moment, his tone tipping the scales toward us living another day. "In the Jeep, *por favor.*"

As I climbed into the jump seat behind Itzla, my feet arching across Jorge who lay in a cocoon of blankets stretched lengthwise in the bay of the Jeep, his head resting on a pillow of sacked rice against the back panel, I remembered the bag that Jorge had been so tightly clinging to. "He had a bag with him," I said. "It's in the trunk."

On a signal from Manolo, Chuey popped the trunk open and retrieved the bag tossing it onto the jump seat behind Manolo.

Manolo's silence was unnerving as he carefully hurried through the vastness of the empty night. I could only guess what was seething beneath the surface of his quietness and hoped that whatever it was the lid would keep tight. His tacit anger had me on edge. Once in a while that silence was broken by the grinding of gears as he downshifted watchfully threading the Jeep over strings of ruts and narrow creek beds on his way back to the ranch. I had little confidence that Manolo's powder keg was used up; and I wasn't going to be the one to start a mundane, "Nice night, huh, big guy" conversation with him. He could easily reach back and flick me out of his life like a pesky gnat.

Garret and Esperanza were waiting on the walkway under the portico when Manolo brought the Jeep through the gate and slid it to a halt on the cobblestones next to them. Garret, Manolo, and I carried Jorge into the living room as Esperanza kicked the chairs out from underneath the dining room table sending them spinning and crashing into the walls. She then cleared the table with one sweep of her arm. She spread a few blankets, and we gently placed Jorge on the table. Itzla grabbed a pillow from the couch and tucked it under his head.

Esperanza had already brought out all the medical supplies she thought she would need and had them ready on the buffet table next to where Jorge lay. Jorge looked through half-opened eyes at his mother. Even the blood and dirt that caked his face couldn't mask his sadness.

"*Por Dios*," Esperanza wailed after seeing the extent of her son's wounds. "*¿Por qué Jorge?*"

Jorge labored at lifting his hand. Esperanza seized it immediately. "I wanted to do good, to make you money," he whispered. "Now there is nothing. Am I going to die?"

"No, you're not going to die," Esperanza said. Releasing his hand, she feverishly began the work of removing the bullets from his stomach and chest. Jorge had little strength to struggle, and it was becoming obvious that he wasn't going to make it. Still, Esperanza poked and dug into her son's wounds, searching for the bullets, chanting small prayers as she worked. Esperanza was living up to her name. She had hope.

Garret and I stood at the end of the table, above Jorge's head, Garret keeping an eye on Manolo who was pacing the room. "Who did this to you, Jorge?" Garret asked.

Jorge was going in and out of consciousness. "He said he would give a lot of money for little work," he murmured, then slipped away for a moment.

"Who?" Garret repeated.

Jorge groaned and turned his head toward Esperanza. "I wanted to help mother."

"God damn it!" It was Manolo, pounding on the other end of the table. "Who was it, Jorge? Who the hell shot you?"

Garret straightened up and took a long look at his lieutenant. "Manolo," he said sharply, "settle down or take it outside. We'll sort this out later."

Manolo, still enraged, stood seething over his brother. Then, in a moment of deep affection, he rested his head on Jorge's blood soaked chest and said softly, "*Te quiero, hermano.*"

"It was only for a few hours," Jorge said, more air than words. "...guard was paid, had key to security system... Crowbar to make it look like a break in. I took the warrior to Guachimonton to give it to him and collect my money. He said no witnesses, and I ran. He shot me, and I fell into a ravine where he couldn't find me. But you found me. I am happy for that. I brought the Warrior to you. I'm sorry."

Esperanza clasped hands with her two sons. There was nothing more to be done. "*Tu perdono, mi hijo,*" she said. "I forgive you. Tell me who did this to you."

Jorge hesitated, probably pulling his thoughts together. Even with the trauma of his wounds, tears rolled from his eyes. "He said he would hurt you."

Esperanza leaned over her son, kissed him on the lips, and said, "I have seen much pain, *hijo*. It no longer hurts me."

He sucked a breath of air and mumbled, "Carlos Huerta."

I was standing close enough to see the light go out of Jorge's eyes. He was gone. And how he lasted as long as he did was another question for the gods. Esperanza wailed over him, slapping his face, shaking him, trying to break the pattern of death, and realizing that he was not coming back, finally embraced him, rocking him as though she herself was putting her son to sleep.

Itzla, too, had been standing over Jorge and heard those last words. "I want him in jail," Itzla said with a bite. "I want to see his ugly face behind bars." She then ran from the room. I thought it too much for her to take, the death and dying she had seen and heard so much about. But she returned holding the bag that Jorge had been clutching to his chest when we found him on the road. She set it on the table next to Jorge's body.

Manolo, hearing his mother's cries and watching her as they both held his brother, suddenly exploded. The fuse had burned to the keg. "Not in jail!" he yelled with such force that the walls would have blown out had they not been made with two feet of concrete. "He will be in pieces spread over Mexico!" He threw one of the heavy dining room chairs shattering it against the far wall of the living room above the sofa. "He is as dead as my brother already." The hutch was next, and it came down hard onto the floor next to Itzla and me. His cries of pain were deafening as he destroyed the room piece by piece, leaving only the table his brother lay on intact.

I moved Itzla toward the door, attempting to keep her out of harm's way, and thinking Garret would put a stop to Manolo's tirade; but he stood silent next to Esperanza with a calmness that told me he knew what he was doing.

Garret saw my look and said, "We have to give him this, otherwise he'll be of little use. I need him calm." He then raised his .45 to the ceiling and fired one shot.

Manolo stopped immediately, slumped against the wall, and began weeping. I pulled Itzla outside under the portico. Manolo needed to be with his family, and I felt like an intruder. Garret followed us out and motioned to two men who had run up to the building to remove Jorge's body from the table. We watched as Esperanza followed the men into the adjoining room.

"Huerta will get his bullet," Garret said under the dim light of the covered porch. "It's been coming at him for a long time. But we have to stay calm. Carlos isn't easily suckered into anything."

Itzla stormed back into the room. She took a long breath. "He has to pay! I will kill him myself!"

"He's pretty well insulated," Garret said as he and I hustled after her. "He's been allied with the government for as long as I've known him. But I think the time has come to put him in his place."

"Whatever value this piece has for Carlos," she said, pulling the Warrior from its bag and tossing it onto the table, "is nothing compared to the value of the lives he has taken. What is so important about this that he has to kill for it?" She raised it over her head. "It should be smashed into a million pieces."

"Itzla! No!" I shouted. "It's not the Warrior! It's Huerta. Don't do it!"

"This is what has been causing all the misery for the last twenty-five years. And that *malvado* Carlos has killed three people, maybe more, to get it. Neither of them belongs in this world."

I wasn't quick enough. Before I could reach her, she threw the Warrior against the stone mantel piece above the fireplace, shattering the Warrior, and scattering hundreds of glittering diamonds onto the dining room floor.

S o that's what this shit's all about," Garret said
after we had recovered from the shock of seeing
such amazing wealth explode from the Warrior.
He raked his hand across the smooth surface of the well-
worn oak mantelpiece, collecting a handful of diamonds.
"That son of a bitch," he said with a grin and stirred the
stones in the palm of his hand.

Seeing so many stones scattered about on the polished
tile floor hit me like an aftershock of a major California
earthquake. There had been enough rumblings ahead of
all this to dull the edge of my enthusiasm. Or maybe I
just couldn't see the reality of a tile floor covered with diamonds. Until the reality actually hit me, those little gems
seemed no more significant than a shattered glass vase.

Itzla, after realizing what she had done, was on her
knees frantically sorting through the rubble Manolo had
created earlier picking out shards of the Warrior from
amongst the gems surrounding them, trying to piece the
Warrior back together. "First the Warrior, and now a fortune in diamonds," she said, frustrated at her attempts to
round up all the pieces. "And they were hidden inside the
Warrior. Right in front of me! Carlos is a son-of-a-bastard!"

Garret laughed, a false laugh that never reached his eyes. It was a joke he was sharing with someone who wasn't in the room. "So that's what that asshole was doing with them," he said as he rolled the stones out onto the blood-stained table, where Jorge had lain just a few moments before. "Diamonds were his deal. I bailed at the trade in Johannesburg. Until now, I didn't know what had happened to them. Didn't care. Still don't. I wasn't a part of that."

To discover that Garret was somehow involved wasn't much of a surprise, though I was now counting on him as an ally, hoping the riches that now lay on the floor wouldn't turn him against me. And there was probably more in this rabbit hole than I would ever know, maybe didn't want to know; but it seemed that the inquisition was at hand, and I had drawn the short sword.

"You knew about this?" I said coarsely. "You knew Huerta had these diamonds?"

"I wasn't a part of that," Garret repeated kicking aside one of the broken chairs.

"What were you a part of?" Itzla snapped. "The kidnapping of my uncle?" She was back on her feet, sorting through the shards she had collected and placed on the table away from the blood stains drying quickly in the hot, still air.

By the look on Garret's face it was obvious he didn't know about Lino's disappearance. "Why would anyone want to kidnap a bus driver?" he said, his face giving way to a comical expression.

After Itzla and I explained what we knew about Huerta's relationship with her uncle and the long ago murder of her parents, Garret said, "That would be Huerta's M.O.. When? When did your uncle disappear?"

"The morning after the Warrior was stolen from the museum," Itzla said then added fiercely, "Where is he? Who has him?"

Garret considered this, then countered, "I have a pretty good idea who might have him; but as to where, that's anybody's guess."

"What about this Kopek?" I said, watching in amazement as Garret carelessly walked over the millions of dollars of diamonds to straighten an unharmed artifact in an open-fronted cabinet near the door. I could hear diamonds scraping on the tile floor from the stones caught in the rubber souls of his Nikes.

"What about him?" he said casually.

"What have you got going with him?" I asked. It was difficult keeping a lid on my anger, but I needed answers. "Who is he? And what do you have that he wants? He was even up at the ruins nosing around about old pottery. I think he's the one who was shooting at us. And Huerta. You're in business with him. Tell me you're not a part of this conspiracy."

Itzla moved away from me, dodging the overturned hutch, to the end of the table, obviously angered. She flicked her hand at me. "You're just full of secrets aren't you, Skip," she said. "How do you know all this? Next you're going to tell me you're in partnership with this man, I suppose."

"Stop!" Garret ordered. "We need to clarify a few things right now." He then proceeded to tell Itzla how I came to be involved with him and what my role actually was – a reluctant writer he had "hired" to document his life in Mexico. He washed over the incident of the blown drug deal and of Huerta's surprise visit to the ranch.

There were still too many unanswered questions

though. I dropped to one knee and scooped up a handful of the stones, almost certain that it would be the only time I would ever hold so much wealth in my hands, and said, "What does Itzla's uncle's disappearance and her being shot at have to do with South Africa and diamonds?"

"I'll give you an overview," Garret said. "You don't need to know all of it." He seemed to be picking at his thoughts as he sorted the stones he had tossed onto the table into various sized piles. "Kopek and I had a business venture together in 'Nam," he began. "We were bringing opium out of Laos to CIA assets who had opened a cluster of heroin laboratories in the Golden Triangle, the tri-border area of Burma, Thailand, and Laos. We flew it in from Laos, and the CIA's Air America and Vietnamese First Air Transport Group were the mules. We were providing 99% pure, No. 4 heroin to army camps and sidewalk cigarette stands throughout downtown Saigon."

"You were killing American soldiers!" Itzla snapped.

Garret ignored her comment. "The CIA facilitated the transport logistics of the opium trade among its allies as part of its mission in its efforts to support the U.S. invasion of Vietnam. We were, in effect, being sponsored by the CIA. Our little enterprise was silently being overlooked by the CIA's Inspector General who had people convinced that the war was the overriding priority. We knew that, and we took advantage of it." He stopped shuffling the stones for a moment, looking up at us with a humorless grin. "Hell, we had Hmong officers loading opium on Air America, and the Lao Army's commander opened a heroin laboratory to supply U.S. troops in 'Nam."

"How'd you get it into the country, past customs?" I asked.

"Itzla, did I mention he was naïve?"

"Hell, Garret, I'm a surfer who likes big waves and margaritas! If you don't want a hockey puck up your ass, you'll tell us. How would I know how you did it? Enlighten me."

"Yes, enlighten us both," Itzla said, straightening a chair and sitting down. She glared at Garret. "Enlighten us as to how you were helping the war effort by supplying drugs to American soldiers."

Garret met her stare. "That's a philosophical conversation we're not going to have right now, sweetheart," he said. "When all this other crap is done with, maybe the three of us can sit on a beach somewhere and suck up margaritas and discuss ethics and morality; but right now we've got more important business to tend to."

Itzla leaned into the table looking ready for battle. "I'm not your sweetheart," she said. "And I don't appreciate being patronized. And furthermore, I don't plan on getting into a philosophical discussion with someone who has the ethics of a snake. Let's get down to business."

They kept their eyes fixed on each other for a few more seconds then Itzla flicked her wrist in the air and turned away, disgusted with Garret's arrogance.

"So, how did you get it past customs?" I asked again, this time hoping to diffuse the energy between them. "For the story, you know."

"The story gets better, Skipper," he said, his eyes brightening. "I hope you're taking good notes." He shuffled one of the piles of diamonds on the table, scooped up a few and rolled them around in his palm. "The secret police had a well-developed drug infrastructure with the Vietnamese air force providing most of the transit, bypassing customs and using air force bases as distribution hubs. And it didn't hurt that a South Vietnam Major General was one of the chief traffickers in the country. One of the largest shipments we brought out was on a mile long, 16-ton load carried over the mountains on a 300 pack horse caravan, guarded by 500 Laotian soldiers. And to our advantage, the State Department, which was then honoring Vietnam sovereignty, was concerned that any pressure on the drug traffickers might damage the war effort."

"So where do Carlos and the diamonds fit into this?" Itzla interjected.

"Good, we're talking again," Garret said. "We're all in this, so we all need the facts. Huerta was a mercenary in Vietnam cloaked by the Mexican government. Because he had diplomatic immunity, he was free to do just about anything he wanted. He was with us in Tiger Force. That's the tattoo you've been so curious about, Skipper."

"I knew he'd disappeared for a time while I was in the States," Itzla said, "but I didn't know he was involved in all this. Knowing what I know now, that's easy to believe."

"He was there for about a year when he approached me and Kopek with a deal that was hard to refuse. He had already set up a network with some Corsicans in South Africa who would basically trade diamonds for heroin. Huerta wanted us to use our resources in Vietnam to smuggle the heroin to his men in Johannesburg, who would then pay Huerta off with the stones. They would then send the heroin off to market in the U.S. and Europe. Huerta, with his immunity, would then smuggle the diamonds into Mexico to later be sold in the U.S. Kopek was his man. By that time, I'd seen enough wrongful death. That's when I took my cut and severed my relationship with them and the army."

"And Kopek is here for his cut in the diamonds?" I said.

"Up until a few days ago, I hadn't seen him since 'Nam. I assume that's part of his plan."

My mind seemed to be threading its way through the fog of sleeplessness. "I suspect he's after more than that," I said. "You owe him something."

Garret was not one to give much away, but I did notice the anger in his eyes. He shook his head and the anger disappeared. He said calmly, "I owe both him and Huerta a bullet in the head. They've broken the code. Kopek is trying to take over my business, and Huerta has killed one of our family."

Itzla was fidgeting with the shards of the Warrior, trying to conceal her worry. "And two of *my* family," she said. "Now maybe my uncle."

"I think your uncle is the trump card in this whole deal," Garret stated. He had walked around the table to the fireplace and was staring into the long-settled ashes.

Some of the pieces to the puzzle were slowly finding their way onto the table. The picture was getting clearer. "And Kopek and Huerta are working together in this," I said.

"It's not beneath Huerta to have Lino taken. Lino's a link to the artifact."

"That was twenty-five years ago," Itzla said. "Why now?"

"Call it insurance," I said. "Lino and the Warrior disappeared at about the same time. I think Lino was picked up because he would be the most obvious person to know where the artifact was."

"You think Jorge was taking it to Lino?" Itzla asked.

"This is just speculation," Garret said, "but I think when this whole thing fell apart for Carlos, he panicked and had Kopek pick Lino up."

"Of course." It was Itzla. Her head seemed a bit clearer than mine at the moment. "After Carlos shot Jorge at the ruins and escaped, Carlos thought Jorge would take the Warrior to my uncle. And with my uncle knowing the history, Carlos couldn't take any chances. Carlos had to kidnap him. Lino's a bargaining tool."

"Carlos can hold him for ransom until he gets the diamonds," I said.

Garret put his palms on the mantelpiece and leaned into it. "Shit!" he said, pulling away quickly. "And by now he knows the diamonds are here. That's trouble in itself. But Huerta has a bigger problem. He made the mistake of doing his own dirty work."

"Why didn't he have Kopek go after Jorge?" I said.

Garret was now nervously pacing the room. "Kopek and some hired mercenaries were too busy sabotaging my drug run. The timing on the theft and the payoff had to happen in a hurry, and Kopek wasn't available. Carlos probably had Kopek pick up Lino and fire a few warning shots at you two."

"Why would he shoot at us?" Itzla asked.

"Maybe he thought you knew something and was trying to scare you off. With Kopek, you never know. He was the craziest of all of us."

"Let's just give him the diamonds, get my uncle back, and forget the whole thing."

Garret turned quickly toward Itzla. "You really don't know Huerta, do you?" he cautioned. "If it was that simple, I would. I don't give a damn about these things," he said and scuffed a handful of stones onto the floor with his forearm. "But if you haven't learned by now, Carlos doesn't want any trails leading back to him. He's going to come after this. He'll want to make a trade, Lino for the diamonds, then he'll try to take us all out. That's his style."

"He'd kill all of us?" Itzla said, visibly shaken by the thought.

"He'd shoot his mother if there was profit in it," Garret said. "But he'll probably pay Kopek to do it."

"Then we wait him out, here." My words sounded like a line from a spaghetti western, but without the certainty of success.

"He won't come up here," Garret said. "It wouldn't be to his advantage. He'll want to meet in a neutral place. We'll be safe here. My men now have orders to shoot anything that moves."

I grimaced, thinking how ineffective Chuey and Elidio had been with me and Itzla.

"Why do men always have to settle things with bullets?" Itzla protested. She had moved next to me again.

I leaned into her and slid my arm around her waist. "I think gunpowder makes up a good part of our DNA," I said with a smugness that was smothered by the thick air of the room.

Garret's lips tightened. He glared at both of us then zeroed in on Itzla. He pulled the .45 from his waistband and slammed it down into the drying blood on the table, scattering several piles of diamonds. "Sweetheart," he said, "this may be the only thing that keeps you alive." He eased up a bit and said to me, "Get some sleep, Skipper. You look like shit. You could use some too, Itzla."

"Sleep? Are you crazy?" Itzla wailed. "You may not want to do anything, but I can't wait around for killers to show up. I have to do something." She stomped out into the night, stopping under the portico, her slim silhouette backlit by the light of the fountain. Even in her rage, she was beautiful. She turned slowly and headed back into the room trying hard to hold back her tears. "I want my uncle back unharmed. What are we going to do?"

"We're going to get Huerta," I said. "And we're going to bring Lino home."

"How?" Itzla said.

"There is a way," I said. "It's just speculation, but I suspect Huerta's belly isn't as tough as he thinks it is. We need to find his weakness. We need to know everything about him, Garret."

"You will," Garret stated, "but right now I have a burial to tend to and a bodyguard that's having a psychotic breakdown with the delusion of bringing back body parts. There's nothing you two can do. I'll have these stones swept up and put into a container for the trade when it comes. Go get some sleep." He indicated several rooms that opened on to the walkway under the portico. "Take your pick. Esperanza will get you anything you need. I'll catch you up on things in the morning."

Itzla stood her ground. "That may be too late," she said brusquely.

I could see an impatience growing in Garret. I gently took Itzla's hand and began to lead her out the door. "Maybe," Garret said, "but knowing Huerta, he'll want to negotiate. I suspect we'll be hearing from him soon."

I walked Itzla to her room down the outside hallway, passing several armed guards who were now on high alert. I was feeling closer to Itzla than I had felt toward anyone since Coleen. Maybe it was the pressure, or stress of the circumstances; but it seemed she felt the same way toward me. I sensed a desire in her to be close. It was something I had wanted since the afternoon I had seen her walk out of her office at the museum.

The iron knocker on the heavy oak door thudded lightly when I swung her door open. We stood in the dim light of the corridor. She met my eyes with a combination of anxiety, warmth, and desperation.

"I don't know what to do now," she said. "So much has happened. I'm scared, not just for me but for the innocent people of my family."

"I'm working on options," I said as we held hands in the doorway, "and as long as I'm around, no one is going to touch you or your family." I felt a bit like Jimmy Stewart in a role made for Sean Connery.

The last thing I wanted to do was let go of her hands, but I felt the need to search her room, to make sure she would be safe. Checking the premises and its windows, I noticed that the door had no lock, only a small metal latch on the inside and a sturdy pull chain on the outside. Except for the guards nearby, room security was nil.

The answers seemed to be buried deep inside us, working their way out through our bodies to that place where lovers meet for the first time. Yet, the danger and exhaustion of the day's events, added to the grime and sweat on our bodies, was beginning to take its toll. Neither of us knew how to handle the next move. Our fleeting connection died as she pulled away, kissing me quickly on the cheek, stepping inside, and closing the door behind her.

The short twenty feet from Itzla and her bed to my room next door felt more like a mile of heavy walking than winged feet. It seemed the closer the distance between the two of us the harder it was to get next to her. If I couldn't touch her, the fantasy would be the same no matter what the distance. I was fighting back the temptation to break through her door and take her to bed when I realized that both our worlds had been flipped upside down, and we both had a lot to think about. I closed the door of my room trying to convince myself that it was a far nobler thing that she sit alone with her thoughts. But it was obvious my body had other ideas of its own—it was aching for her.

This room was a leap upward from Armando's seedy hovel of a hotel. Garret, it seemed was good to his guests, much better than the mirror over the sink was to me. I hardly recognized the person staring back at me from the glass. I was used to sand and grit, having slept in the back of surf wagons up and down the west coast in search of the perfect wave. But the thick layers of dirt and grime that now covered my face and neck, that couldn't quite conceal the three days of beard growth and a mess of matted, freestyle hair, took me by surprise. I looked like a street urchin out of a Dickens novel. The bullet wound on my leg had stopped bleeding; but I noticed a few new cuts on my left ear, a result of the ricocheting bullet in the shaft tomb, not to mention a nettling of splinters in the palms of my hands.

I had turned the shower on when I came in. The steam was now roiling out into the bathroom, covering the mirror. Even in the heat of the night, a warm shower would be just what I needed. As I stood under the showerhead washing off the last of my three-day grunge and watching it swirl down the drain, I snapped to the fact that Huerta and Kopek, if they had their way, would probably kill us. It was a game they loved, and it was the thrill of the hunt that kept their blood hot. I also realized that Garret wasn't the only one who could get us out of this mess alive. I wasn't going to die here and neither was Itzla. I would have to find a way out of this nightmare.

After shaving, brushing my teeth, and wrapping a fresh towel around my waist, I felt renewed and a little higher on the food chain than a cave-dwelling troglodyte. My clothes still smelled of dirt and sweat so I tossed them into the sink for a quick washing. The folded wad of money Garret had given me two days earlier fell out of the shirt pocket. I stared at the bills for a long time, long enough to realize their irrelevance when faced with the choice of living or dying. My face in the mirror then said it all. Even cleaned up, I was looking at someone who no longer looked like the easy-going hockey jock I used to know.

This close up look at myself was interrupted by the click of the door latch. When I turned around, Itzla was standing in the doorway, her hair wet, looking as fresh as the day I met her at the museum. She had changed into a low cut, mid-thigh shift, most likely a gift from Esperanza.

From the light behind her, it was obvious that that was all she was wearing. Her nipples pressed hard against the soft cotton of the shift, her breasts rising and falling with each breath she took. She didn't seem to notice, or care, that I was wearing only a towel. I was hoping my sudden interest in her thinly clad appearance didn't show too noticeably.

"I don't want to be alone, Skip," she said with a softness that beat the edges off the heat of the evening. It was the same voice and body language I had seen her use with her family and with the children at the ruins. What I was looking at and hearing was the core of Itzla.

"You don't have to be," I said, and walked the few steps to her. We held each other in the middle of the room for what seemed an eternity. The comfort of holding each other, began to calm the angst of the last tenuous hours we had spent together. I began stroking her lightly, familiarizing myself with the contours of her body.

A minute went by, maybe two. She looked up, her face close to mine. "I'm afraid," she said, nuzzling her cheek into my neck. "There are so many terrible things happening, and I don't want this to be one of those things," her fingers lightly moving over my chest.

"I could never hurt you, and I won't let anyone else," I said, shifting my head slightly, noticing the gentle curls drying around her face. I felt her breath on my cheek, could smell the clean, exotic fragrance of her hair. As I slid my hand over the softness of her hip, I became increasingly aware of the sound of her breathing, the feel of her skin. My languid sense of the danger we were in, and our place in it, began to fade.

"If you want me to stop, tell me now," I offered.

With her few seconds of silence I thought I may be losing her, but then she raised her face to mine. Our lips brushed lightly. I kissed her cheeks and eyes, all of the features of her face I had wanted to touch since the first time we had met. She ran her hand gently over my back, exploring my shoulders and the scoop of my lower back. Our lips met again, hers moist and soft, playing against the heat of my skin. Our kisses quickly turned to flame and sent a flare of heat and blood to my groin. I was ready and wanted her more than anyone I had ever wanted.

"God, I want you," I exclaimed, pulling her even tighter. "I have since the day I first saw you."

She wrapped her arms around my waist. "Don't let go," she urged.

I gently took a handful of her soft, straight hair, tipped her head back and looked into her eyes. Even in the dim light of the room she glowed, her eyes fox fire reflecting her longing. The heat from her touch radiated through my flesh like a swelling wave. I wanted all of her.

I held her up against my body as we moved across the room toward the bed, locked in a deep, hungry kiss. I slid her shift off of her shoulders, watching as it fell over her breasts and hips and drop to the floor next to where my towel had fallen. There were no secrets between us now. Our desires were obvious. For a single instant of truth, we stood face to face, my eyes running over the delicate curves of her body, her fingers lightly caressing my chest. My hand slowly rolled down over her erect nipples and cupped one of her breasts, massaging it gently. I ran my other hand down the small of her back, pulling her even closer, feeling the long lines of her body, the curving slope of her waist and hip. Holding her firm, round buttocks, I pressed her body harder into mine. We fell into a tangle of lust and tumbled onto the bed. Her back arched up. She moaned as I kissed her breasts, her belly, running my tongue down to the apex of her thighs. The smoldering fragrance and touch of her skin drove me to even harder readiness.

"Now. I want you now," she gasped as I moved up, parting her legs with my knee as she opened herself to me.

I felt the heat of her thighs wrapping around my hips and the rush of satiny wetness between her legs as I entered her, as I buried myself completely inside of her. I wanted to take her swiftly enough to forget ourselves. Moving as one, thrusting our hips against each other, the sensation sending sparks from my head to my groin and back again until I couldn't tell where she ended and I began. I took her wrists in one hand, pulled them up over her head, and held them there against the pillow. Her body arched again and she cried out, "Now, come to me now." I felt a massive wave building between us and in us like storm surf, ready to crash on the beach. I held her hands tighter as I plunged deeper into her, bringing us again and again to higher peaks of sensation in all the places we were joined. We trembled with roiling after waves, one after another, leaving us panting and shuddering in each other's arms.

The sight of Itzla's innocent, beautiful smile, and the peach-sweet scent of her skin after we made love, made me want her even more. Slipping away in the early morning cool-down after anxious, desperate sex as I had so many times before with sand-brained beach girls was not even close to a thought. I didn't want to get back into my pants and bolt for the door. I wanted to hang them up in a closet next to hers. Where we would finally end up seemed not so much a mystery but a direction.

"You're making me forget how tired I am," I whispered, again trailing my fingers along the curves of her body. I wanted to see her, to take her in, in all her vulnerability, and hold her, feel the softness of her flesh. I knew that while she was in my arms, I could protect her, help her feel safe. There was comfort and shelter in our embrace, a passionate, euphoric willingness that brought our flesh together. I wanted her and she wanted me. The past two days faded to black as we explored each other's body again, shutting out the world around us, giving us the night.

CHAPTER
EIGHTEEN

The clock on the nightstand read 4 a.m. I was lying naked on the bed watching Itzla wiggle back into her shift, mesmerized by the glow of her skin as she paced the floor in the soft light of the moon passing by the window. She was talking hatefully of Huerta and how he had betrayed her, how he had used his influence to cover up all his contemptuous actions. Her disgust with the fact that he had used blood money to support her while she earned her degrees in the states had fired her own blood.

She paced for a while longer, then realizing the futility of her anger slid onto the bed and sat facing me, her arms folded across her breasts. She sighed. "What kind of conscience does that man have, Skip?"

I leaned over and gently rubbed her bare thigh. "That word is not in his dictionary, Itzla. He's tasted blood and money. That's where conscience stops. He has none."

She heaved another sigh and rolled onto her side. "I have been back from the States for one year, and already I feel my life is falling apart."

"Why did you come back?" I asked. "You could have named your price up there."

"The job offers were good," she said, "but I love my people. Even with the hurt they caused trying to protect me, they're still the only family I know."

"There's more, isn't there?" I could see it in her eyes. "Something happened."

Itzla sat up, crossing her legs Indian style, her hands in her lap, eyes cast downward. She hesitated for a moment then said wistfully, "Have you ever been in love, Skip?"

My heart leaped. *Was that ever the right question!* She had asked the question with such innocence that my mind had a hard time catching up with the meaning. I was hoping she was referring to us, but I felt it had more to do with her past than our future together. My mind raced from Itzla back to Coleen and then back again to Itzla.

"Yes," I said, yet wanted to say more, to include Itzla in the mix. "Her name was Coleen. She's definitely past tense, Itzla."

"There is no past tense, *querido.*" She ran her cool fingers along my cheek. "Memories of love never die."

I was about to add, nor do memories of betrayal, but decided against it. We were in the middle of enough treachery, and I didn't want this conversation to slide into morbidity. "What happened to you in the states?" I asked. "I'm thinking a boyfriend took a hike on you. How close am I?"

"I had a boyfriend," she said with a hint of sadness in her eyes. "He was killed in what you call 'The line of duty.' You're the first person I've told. Nobody here would understand."

"I'm sorry," I said and tried to wipe away some wetness from her cheeks with my thumb. She brushed my hand away. The memory of him was still too close. I understood. It now made sense as to why she had been so unapproachable, and why Lino had said that she had to be certain of someone's trust before she could love freely.

"It's still difficult, Skip."

"It's a nasty affair. The scars go deep," I admitted. "There's no disguising the pain of lost love. He was police?"

"Interpol," she said in a whisper. "He was shot rounding up drug dealers in Panajachel, Guatemala. He used to take me to the shooting range in the basement of their offices in L.A. He wanted me to be 'gun savvy' he used to say. I also went through their self-defense course, always hoping I never had to use it. Then he went undercover for six months in Antigua and Panajachel. He never came back. Some say there was foul play."

"Jesus, Itzla!"

At that moment the heavy metal knocker slammed against the bedroom door. I jumped off the bed and raced to where Itzla was standing, putting myself between her and the door.

"What is it?" I called out and made for the door keeping Itzla blocked from view.

Manolo suddenly charged into the room, as serious as a bull entering the *corrido de toros*. His right hand was wrapped around the handle of the .45 holstered at his waist, his left was stretched out in front of him in an attempt to calm us.

"Garret wants you both in the dining room," he said in his gravelly Spanish, his voice and face giving away nothing but urgency as he scanned the room. If anything, he looked tired and determined – not a good combination for someone who had just lost his brother to a bullet. How he was controlling his rage must have something to do with those mysteries borne of the Mexican back country, either that or a punitive slap down from Garret. "*De prisa!*" he ordered.

"Hurry?" Itzla said, locking eyes with the big Mexican. Then as if suddenly realizing the exigencies of Manolo's words, she started quickly toward the door. "What's happened? Have you found my uncle?"

He turned to me, looking me over, a scarcely detectable smile spreading across his face. "Garret has received some information," he said. "*Vamonos!*"

I wasn't sure if he was snickering at my luck with Itzla, or thinking that my virility didn't measure up to some obscure Mexican rule of *machismo*. It didn't matter. Itzla had shared *my* bed.

I pulled on my half-dried clothes, slid into my sandals, and made haste after Manolo and Itzla down the outside corridor to the dining room. Manolo broke away from us and trotted out near the fountain in the center of the compound where a dozen armed guards were efficiently snapping magazines into their weapons. He then began dispersing them, directing them off to corners of the compound, and out through the gates into the jungle that surrounded us.

"The puck is in play," I said to Itzla as we hurried into the dining room where Garret was sitting at the table in the low light of a candle, his forearms spread wide on the table. He was still wearing the same dirty shirt and jeans from the night before. The room had been cleaned; and in the dim light, there was no sign of the mess from the spilled diamonds, the blood stains on the table, or Manolo's fit of rage.

The embers of a half-smoked joint glowed red as Garret took a hit. His .45, lying on its side at his right elbow, loomed large and ready. With the slight breeze that had picked up and cut some of the heat, the weapon appeared to pulse in the flickering light of the candle.

"What the hell's going on?" I snapped. "You've got a damn army out there."

A quick squawk came from the radio on his hip. As he turned down the volume, I noticed the hunting knife hanging from his belt. I remembered him slicing his fish lunch at the Mercado with it, stabbing it into the wooden table top. "Sleep well?" he asked, ignoring my question and eyeing Itzla in her thin, cotton shift. He exhaled a cloud of smoke and popped a grape into his mouth from a platter of fruit that sat next to a serving bowl full of *huevos rancheros* in the middle of the table. He didn't wait for an answer. "We've lost power. Happens all the time here. I've got men checking it out."

"And the army?" I said again.

He appeared to be preoccupied with the diamonds that had been picked up and placed in a glass bowl on the mantelpiece where they glowed ominously in the shimmering flames of a candle set on either side of the bowl. Even though my nerves jumped a level, I had to keep faith that his interest in the diamonds wouldn't cause him to sell us out.

"Precautionary," he said. "Probably nothing."

Itzla had made her way over to a basket sitting on the middle shelf of the cabinet Garret had walked to the night before over hundreds of diamonds. She pulled out a shard of the broken Warrior, considered it for a moment, and then flipped it back into the basket.

"Is there anything else I can lose?" she said with a satirical laugh.

The room went quiet. It was a short silence then she mumbled, "*Teotl*," and laughed again.

"What?" I asked, thinking I hadn't heard her right.

"It's the god of everything," she said sullenly. "Carried

over from the Aztecs. We blame it for every bad thing that happens."

I remembered reading about *Teotl* during some research I had done before my trip south. It was an Aztec belief that the world is constantly shifting with the ever-changing *Teotl*. Morality is focused on finding the path to a balanced life, which would provide stability in the shifting world. It looked like Itzla and I were both off track in finding any stability in the way our world had shifted. If she couldn't figure it out, I wasn't going to leave it to the gods.

"Teotl, or no Teotl," I said. "I know what my options are and I'm not waiting for anyone to dictate them to me."

Garret suddenly stood up and nervously walked to the window, gun in hand, giving away his fake calmness about the blackout. "We have a meeting with Huerta in two hours," Garret interrupted, still with his back to us. "And I doubt seriously that he's interested in Aztec philosophy." He flicked the joint out the window, turned, and walked back to the table. A stubborn diamond stuck in the sole of his left Nike rasped the floor with each step. "Got a call from Kopek setting it up. Lino for the diamonds."

Itzla straightened to her full height. There was worry and warning in her posture. "Is he alright? My uncle? Is he hurt? What did they say?"

"If he was hurt or dead, this exchange wouldn't be happening," Garret stated.

"It could be a set up," I said, falling back on old Bogart movies and Chandler novels where someone was always being set up for something. And there was always a girl involved. "It seems obvious to me with Huerta's and Kopek's history."

Garret was again looking at the diamonds. "Kopek maybe. He's a wild card; but as long as he's on Huerta's payroll, he'll do as he's ordered. Huerta doesn't want his political reputation tarnished so he'll probably play this one safe."

"Hell, Huerta shot Jorge and had Victor killed!" I exclaimed. "I think we have two wild cards. What would keep either one of them from trying to take us out after the exchange?"

There was another cat out of the bag, and Itzla didn't miss it. She gave me a quick look, her face twisting into a mix of curiosity and irritation. "Who the hell is Victor?" she said.

So many things had happened in so short a time that it was difficult to keep track of who knew what. And even though Huerta had given the order to kill one of his bodyguards in the compound only yesterday, it seemed like ages ago that it took place.

"There's business beyond the diamonds," Garret stated, "but the possibility of being 'taken out' before it's resolved is always a factor."

"Who is Victor?" Itzla insisted.

"I'm sorry I mentioned it," I said. "I didn't think it was something you'd want to know. You've been through enough already."

"Didn't want to know?" she parroted, and then began to chuckle. She raised her arms and ran her fingers through the tangles in her hair then pulled the bulk of it into a knot in the back, her shift rising well above her knees. Even though her eyes were seriously darting back and forth between Garret and me, I felt a sudden urge to whisk her back into the bedroom. "I think by now I've earned a membership in your disreputable boys' club," she said, mockingly. "Why shouldn't I know? I couldn't be hurt any more than I have been by all the secrecy and surprises."

Garret had been deep in thought, studying the bowl of diamonds. He turned suddenly to Itzla and said in a coolly unconcerned way, "Huerta shot Victor yesterday. Skip was a witness; he wasn't involved. Let it go." Then he got serious. "We're going down the hill. I convinced Kopek to have Huerta meet us in the Mercado where there are plenty of people who know him. He won't try anything funny there. He'll bring Lino, and it will be a simple exchange."

I had stabbed a forkful of *huevos rancheros* and was waving it around, cooling it down, encouraged a bit by Garret's optimism, yet keeping the memory of a 'simple' marijuana pickup in the front of my mind. "Let's go. When do we leave?" I said.

"You don't," Garret stated. "Itzla, Manolo, and I are going; you're staying."

It took a few seconds for that stinger to sink in. "Itzla?" I exclaimed. "No way! You're not exposing her to that shooting gallery, Garret. She's not going anywhere."

"Huerta won't hurt her," Garret stated, "and she's the only one who knows what Lino looks like."

"*I* know what Lino looks like," I retorted. "I'll go. She stays here."

Garret was adamant. "The deal is to bring the diamonds. I had to convince Kopek that someone needed to be there to identify Lino. The girl was his choice. We can't go in force, Skipper."

"I'll go instead of Manolo." It was a stupid statement, but I meant it.

Even in the low light of the room, I could see Garret's dark eyes glaring at me, and when he reached out and pinched my cheek, the inanity of my statement was confirmed. "I don't think so," he said, "and if you're worried that Manolo will go off on Carlos, he won't. There's a time for everything."

"Skip, it's alright." It was Itzla. She had walked over and put her hand on my shoulder. "This is not your problem. I'll go with them. I have to see Carlos for what he really is."

Petulantly, I brushed her hand off and grabbed her by the shoulders. "Are you crazy, Itzla? Do you know how dangerous that is? Besides, it *is* my problem, and you're not going without me." I was about to tell her that it had become my problem when I first saw her walk out of her office at the museum last week when Manolo suddenly trooped into the dining room.

"*Estamos preparado*, Garret," Manolo declared.

Garret nodded approval of his bodyguard's efficiency in preparing to meet Huerta then said, "Get the Jeep ready. We're leaving in half an hour."

"*Estaremos listos*," I said quickly, thinking that by switching to Spanish I might create some empathy for my going. All I got was a hard look from Garret and a snickering laugh from Manolo as he spun and left the room.

If Garret decided to keep me at the compound, I would be of little help to anyone, especially Itzla. I could feel sweat forming in my armpits, nervous sweat. I decided to try another tactic. "I'll jump out of the Jeep before you get to the Mercado. I'll set myself up, away from the meeting place, but in view of the exchange. I'll be there just in case things go haywire."

"You're staying," Garret said slowly, his patience waning as he shoved his .45 into his waistband. "You're free to use the compound, but I suggest you keep to your room. I wouldn't want one of my guards thinking you're one of the bad guys and putting a bullet in you. *¿Si comprende?*" With that, Garret pulled the radio off his hip, keyed it, and barked several commands. A few seconds later, two guards rushed into the room. "Take Mr. Reid to his room," Garret ordered, "and make sure he stays there."

CHAPTER
NINETEEN

I wasn't in the most advantageous bargaining position to argue with Garret; and the barrels of the two carbines poking at my back, herding me along to my room, overrode all the conciliation skills I had ever learned. When I was nudged into the room and heard the knocker bang against the door as it slammed shut, I knew the rules had changed. I also knew that I could play their game, and I had thirty minutes to get Itzla out of danger. I was not going to sit like a midwife, waiting, while Garret and Manolo played with Itzla's life.

Yes, she had volunteered to go, and, yes, she had said she needed to face Huerta. It was a dangerous thing to do even under the protection of Garret and Manolo, even in the openness of the Mercado. And Kopek was out there somewhere freewheeling with a cache of ordnance, supposedly taking orders from Huerta. I had seen enough betrayal in the last few days to know that greed and profit can trump allegiance as fast as a trigger pull, and I didn't want Itzla to be caught in the rifle scopes of a bunch of trained killers. *What could she possibly do against those odds?*

Besides, Huerta seemed to have Garret in his pocket. *And what about Kopek? How tight were these three?* The story seemed bigger than what Garret was giving up, and with Itzla out there on her own I needed to be in a position to protect her. And who knew if Lino was still alive?

I lifted the latch and quickly opened the door, more in an attempt to test the water and bring the guards to attention, if, indeed, they had hung around, than to make an escape. I was greeted with a startled smile from the two guards and the business end of their carbines, both determined to keep me in my place. Had I got to one of them, the other would surely take me down.

"*Paz*, Kahuna." I grinned and flashed them the peace sign. Their smiles disappeared, and I closed the door. I was again back in Sister Mary Elizabeth's fourth grade class getting my knuckles rapped for having the temerity to ask her what a French kiss was. Like her, the guards were simply going to hurt me enough to keep me in line.

Pacing had never been my style. But now I was nearly carving furrows in the limestone tile floor as I paced from one end of the room to the other pulling my wits together. Itzla's presence still filled the room, her scent permeating the tangled sheets and pillows. Even the air smelled of her. Thinking of her in danger only drove me harder.

In my mind I saw her, frightened and determined, climbing into the Jeep with Garret and Manolo. I pictured them heading down the hill to confront Huerta. My stomach turned over. A few foggy thoughts later, my rational mind kicked in. Wasn't Itzla's Toyota sitting on the side of the road less than a mile from the compound? If Garret hadn't had it removed, or shoved over the side, it should still be there. And if I could get to it before Garret left the compound, I could get off the hill before he knew I was missing. I could beat him to the Mercado. Set up my own surveillance.

It was a plan I could live with. Or die with. Getting out of the room would be a challenge in itself, not to mention moving through the compound without being spotted, or worse, having a nervous guard empty his banana clip in my direction. I had a vivid recall of Garret's ever so subtle message suggesting that I could be dodging a few rounds if I strayed too far. I didn't think Garret would have his men shoot me intentionally, but it was still dark and hadn't he told me that his guards had orders to shoot anything that moved? Shoot to kill or not, I had to get out of that room and down the hill to Itzla's car.

The only way out of the room was through the window. The wooden shutters were opened fully and from the window I could see it was close to a fifteen-foot drop to a dry, narrow creek bed that ran along the side of the house. A combination of tall, broad-leaved plants and pinions followed the creek to the front of the house which would give me a small amount of cover. If I didn't break an ankle on impact, I could be at Itzla's car in ten minutes.

I spun my legs over the sill and sat on the ledge, ready to drop into the cobbles of the creek bed. It was then I saw the beam of a guard's flashlight searching through the shadows of the pinions on the other side of the creek beyond the trees. I quickly retreated into the darkness of the room.

Shit!

I watched him walk to the back corner of the house, turn the corner, and disappear. *Go now, Skip. Could be your only chance.*

I slid onto the sill again, turning to hang by my fingers until I found my balance, then I dropped the remaining seven feet onto the stones of the creek bed. There was little light, just the glow of a sliver of moon filtering through the trees and bushes. The power failure had knocked out the floodlights around the entire compound, and the generators had not kicked in yet, giving me the edge I needed to move along the wall undetected. If ever there was a god of electricity, at that moment, he, or she, had gained a new devotee.

When I reached the corner of the building I dropped to my stomach and looked over the darkened compound. I craned my neck to see if the guard was returning. It was clear. A few other guards were flicking their flashlights off the walls of the arsenal building at the foot of the knoll; a few more had slowly disappeared into the foliage across the open area where Huerta had landed in an attempt to collect his *mordida*. Two more were headed down the road, following the beams of the flashlights. From their silhouettes, I could tell they were Elidio and Chuey. Manolo had pulled the Jeep up to the arsenal, and in the reflection of the Jeep's headlights on the wall I watched him toss a large duffel bag onto the jump seat. He then turned the Jeep around and drove it quickly up into the compound. Time was running out.

From what I could see, the closest distance to the road was straight across the field. Going that way would either leave me dead or put me back in the corner of my room wearing a dunce cap. The road, however, did swing by the arsenal before starting its climb up to the house. I knew from a few days ago that there was plenty of cover on the other side of it. I had watched Huerta give the nod to kill Victor from behind those bushes.

I waited a few minutes, and then under cover of a passing cloud made my way down the hill past the guards who were occupied with nervous chattering inside the arsenal. Once on the other side, I slid into the bushes and started down the hill, paralleling the road, keeping to the undergrowth, while maintaining a fifty-yard safety zone between myself and Elidio and Chuey. And maybe it was a stupid consideration, but I figured they'd be looking for people coming up the hill towards them, not following them down.

After battling branches and brush and my own sweat, I was off the road and twenty feet into the jungle. In the dark, my foot slid under a root and into a snare of leggy vines. Even with no light, I knew there was blood involved. By the time I freed myself, Elidio and Chuey were disappearing over the rise of a hill where the road suddenly turned and dropped into a steep incline. I no longer had the luxury of following spots of light on the ground. From what I could remember of the road, they should have been about one hundred yards from Itzla's car. And hadn't they come out of the bushes just short of Itzla and me when they discovered Jorge dying in the back seat? The rise, it appeared, was their vantage point and they could see anyone or anything coming up the hill from that location. All I could see from where I was situated was the top of their heads. I had to get around them.

As I made my way toward the rise, I heard rustling in the branches to my right and I hit the ground, taking in a mouthful of dirt. Lying flat on my stomach, spitting grit, nervous as hell, thinking that some other guard might have been tracking me, I slowly moved my head to the sound of the noise and watched as a gray fox scurried through a tangle of brush. I silently chuckled, releasing a little of the nervousness. When I looked back at the road, Elidio and Chuey were gone. They had most likely posted themselves in their favorite bushes on either side of the road under the arching banana trees. I heard Manolo's voice squawking

189

something on their radios, and then silence.

Still on my hands and knees, I crawled the few remaining yards to the rise. I could see Itzla's car shining in the moonlight at the bottom of the hill. It had been moved to the side but was still facing uphill. I could also hear muted voices coming from near the car. Elidio and Chuey must have decided to situate themselves at the bottom of the hill instead of the top. I figured they had a good reason.

Out of the stillness, a radio screeched close to where I was hidden in the bushes. The surprise straightened me up, and I pounded my shoulder into the trunk of a pinion tree, sending a sharp pain through my upper back. The radio, I could see, was lying in the dirt on the side of the road twenty feet away from me.

"*Dime dónde estan, culos! ¿Qué pasa?*" Manolo's voice came through the air cursing.

I wanted to know where they were, too. It wouldn't be like Elidio or Chuey to abandon their radios. They didn't breathe without them attached to their hip. And now one of them was in the dirt. It took a few seconds for my mind to register the squawking of the second radio that was lying a few yards down the hill in the middle of the road, a few more seconds before a fearful jolt of realization hit me: it wasn't the muffled sounds of Elidio's and Chuey's voices I had heard earlier. The voices I had heard were speaking English.

I scanned the immediate area for the two guards. They seemed to have simply vaporized into the jungle. Not knowing who was down the hill, I continued my crawl to the closest radio. I was about to key it and tell Manolo that his guards had abandoned their posts when I thought better of it. I didn't want him racing down the hill in a rage after discovering I had outsmarted his guards at the compound. I also didn't want anyone storming up the hill should they hear me talking.

What I wanted was to know who was at the bottom of the hill.

Damn curiosity. Just go back up the hill, Skip. It seems I had my own form of *mordida*. My curiosity was being bought off with stupidity.

Leaving the radios behind may not have been the smartest thing to do, but I couldn't have them squawking an alarm as I made my way down the hill. If I turned them off, it may create suspicion. It was challenging enough avoiding snapping twigs and crunching dried branches on the slope of the rugged hillside in the dark, not to mention peeling spider webs off my face and arms. What I needed was stealth.

I rolled over into the underbrush, crouched, and started down. At one point, to check my position, I moved up the slope until I was eye level with the road. I reflexively looked up the hill, hoping I wouldn't see the headlights of the Jeep flickering with Manolo in a panic to see what had happened to his guards, or worse, Garret deciding to leave early with Itzla in tow. But there were no headlights. I figured I had about fifteen minutes if they were keeping to the schedule. But the schedule would change now that Manolo couldn't reach Chuey and Elidio.

Make haste slowly was my new mantra as I spun to look down the hill. Two dark figures had reached the bottom of the hill and then disappeared into the backdrop of vegetation, only to reappear next to a third figure hovering around Itzla's car. They began whispering and snickering, passing around what appeared to be a joint. I needed to move closer to hear what they found so amusing.

I was no more than fifty feet away from them when

I stumbled over a tangle of roots again. After regaining my balance and cursing my coordination, I tripped a third time, this time tumbling into a sage bush the size of a Volkswagen and landing squarely onto Elidio's chest. He was sprawled face up, nearly hidden in the sage lining the road. His throat had been sliced open. Blood was pulsing in a thin stream from his neck, covering his shirt and the Uzi that still hung from its strap on his shoulder.

I rolled into the bushes next to him and vomited. For a few long seconds I sat silent and immobilized, holding my breath, thinking my retching had given me away. Of all the places I could be, why was I here, fighting for my life, bargaining with a bunch of psychopaths bent on destroying themselves and everything around them. Of all the things I could be getting my mind around—surfing the warm waters of the Pacific, mind wrestling with beach girls, trying to get laid—I was stuck in a place that seemed to have my balls in a vice at every turn.

When I heard no break in the quick exchange of words at Itzla's car, I exhaled slowly and peeked over the edge of the road. They hadn't heard me. If they had, they weren't coming to check it out. Across the road I saw Chuey, his twisted, lifeless body laying face down on the shoulder. He was certainly dead, or dying, and there was nothing I could do. I froze, staring back and forth at the two bodies.

This isn't happening, I thought. Then I realized that I had been only a few yards behind them, tangled in tree roots when they were killed. *If I hadn't... doesn't matter.* My mind raced; and my body felt like I was swimming through a heavy kelp bed, struggling to stay afloat.

There was nowhere to go and the idea of confronting these killers had practically turned me to stone. I decided that the best of my bad options was to get my ass back up the hill and warn everyone before they became unsuspecting targets. It was a far better option than ending up next to Elidio bleeding out.

I took a hard look at the weapon resting on Elidio's chest. *What luck*, I thought rolling the guard onto his side and stripping the sticky, blood-soaked Uzi off his shoulder. My own haste and bravado was punching at me with such intensity that I hadn't noticed the clip was missing until I was a few yards back up the hill. I backtracked to Elidio and searched through the pouch he carried on his belt. The killers had been thorough. The pouch had been cleaned out of any extra clips. *Shit! Where was a banana clip when you needed one?*

I had just started my climb again when I heard a voice cut through the air. It was Kopek. The chill that swept through me was pure ice water.

"Let's toke to the kill," is what I heard as Kopek passed the joint around and leaned back against the front fender. The three then burst out in an ugly, snickering laugh that seemed to suck the soul out of the night.

After a moment of silence, Kopek said, "Garret's mine. I'm personally taking the son-of-a-bitch out. He got away from us the other night on the dope raid. He won't make it past the car this time. You two can dispose of his goon and the bitch any way you like."

One of the men loomed over Kopek taking a hit from the joint. His face lit up through the curling smoke and blood-red embers. He was wearing a bandana wrapped tightly around his forehead. His nose needed alignment. "You kill him, you'll never see the money, Sir."

"Fuck the money, Casey," Kopek said in exasperation. He pushed himself off the fender and faced the two men. "The stones are worth ten times that."

"One problem, Colonel," the other man said casually, "he still has the files. If he dies, we may never find them."

"You think I'm stupid, Nuñez?"

"I'm just reminding you of our directive, Sir."

"I'm aware of our directive, Sergeant," Kopek retorted. "Before I kill him, he'll tell me where they are. We get the files plus the bonus of two million in diamonds."

"What about Huerta?" Casey asked.

Kopek sneered. "He's as stupid as Garret. It was nice of him to tell me that Garret has the stones. We get it all in one mission and get out. Huerta's next on the list. No trail. Remember that."

"If it's as easy as getting past these two pissant guards, we'll be out of there in ten minutes," Nuñez said wryly. "Tam Ky all over again."

"This isn't a damn gook village, Nuñez," Kopek said. "Once they know Garret and Manolo have been compromised, his men will scatter all over these hills. No leader, no contest. If they want to hang around, we'll bring all the heat they can handle."

"We should have cut the phone line when we cut the power," Nuñez said. "Keep them isolated in their hole."

"That's why you were busted down to three stripes, Nuñez," Kopek said impatiently. "You don't think. We may need to negotiate at some point. At least we'll have the option."

Nuñez tensed then his body went slack. After a few seconds, he said with bitterness, "Why didn't we use the bitch's uncle for negotiation. To hell with Huerta. We could have walked right into the place and taken what we wanted."

"Straighten up, Nuñez," Kopek said sharply. "You're under orders. The uncle doesn't mean shit. I picked him up for Huerta in exchange for Garret's location. Huerta can do what he wants with the old man."

Casey laughed. "Anyone know who the joke of a dude in the Hawaiian shirt was with Garret the other night?"

Joke of a dude? I didn't have to look at my shirt to know I was the target, but I wasn't going to raise a debate over semantics after these guys had just killed two people, the bodies still warm and strewn across the road. Nuñez and Casey seemed to savor wiping the blood from their knives on their thighs, and I had no doubt they wouldn't hesitate to add more stains to the camouflage on their uniforms.

"He was hanging around outside the Market a couple of days ago," Kopek continued. "I didn't think he was connected to Garret. He looked like any other assbite *gringo* tourist. Then the other night he shows up with an Uzi. And when I saw him with that bitch at the ruins, I thought a couple rounds fired at him would send him packing. She must be a good fucking lay for him to stick around."

"Pussy fucks you up, man," Nuñez stated, "messes with your mind."

"Never mind that," Kopek said. He snuffed the joint with his fingertips then dropped it into his shirt pocket. "If that dude is here, make him disappear. We can't take any chances on him knowing anything."

Even though my body hadn't so much as twitched since I had crawled to where I could hear them talking, my blood seemed to be pounding its way through my veins, beating a drum solo in my ears. I had to move. I had to get back up the hill to warn Garret, to protect Itzla.

I stayed inside the tree line just beneath the shoulder of the road, hunched over, moving slowly and quietly through the thicket. It was a slug's pace, but the alternative was not an option. I couldn't outrun a bullet or a killer familiar with jungle warfare slashing his way toward me with an already bloodied knife.

As I worked my way through tangles of roots and hanging limbs, avoiding the patches of dry leaves underfoot, I could still hear the three men laughing. I straightened up and peeked over the shoulder of the knoll I had climbed. To my relief they were still huddling around the Toyota. The reprieve didn't last long. They were loading clips for what looked like pistol Uzi's with silencers.

"Shit!" I whispered and went back into my crouch. Without thinking, I moved too quickly and stepped through a dead branch, the snap scattering birds from the trees, and echoing through the jungle.

A quick look over the shoulder of the road made my blood freeze. Kopek had given a hand signal to Nuñez. Nuñez grinned, grabbed one of the Uzi's from the hood of the car, and started toward where they had heard the sound. I scrambled into the bushes and crouched behind the trunk of a large tree which wouldn't offer much protection if Nuñez spotted me. With the exception of a four-foot length of solid branch, it was all the protection I had.

I could see Nuñez through the thick brush that helped hide me. He was twenty feet away, squatting next to the branch I had stepped on. He raised his head as though sniffing the air for prey, slowly scanned the area, and headed toward where I was hiding.

"Show your face, asshole," he chided, his grin as arrogant as the Uzi in his hand. "I don't know who you are, but you're dead."

I put a tight hockey grip on the branch, stupidly thinking I could take him out with one swing. I could do more damage with a marshmallow. One insignificant branch against an automatic pistol and a very sharp knife. The odds were falling fast.

"Three seconds, asshole, or I light you up." He fired two nearly silent rounds into the tree trunk next to me then swung the pistol in my direction.

Don't think, I remember Garret saying. *It could get you killed.*

But before I could react, a commotion had started in the bushes behind Nuñez. A pack of coyotes began howling. They had made a kill and one of them was carrying a rabbit back into the jungle. Nuñez spun around just long enough for me to jump out into the clearing and high stick him in the forehead. He went down hard. I swung again, an adrenaline filled swing, this time smashing the branch into the back of his head. I stood over him, thinking him dead. *Don't think. Move.* I pulled the Uzi from his hand and started back up the hill. That's when I saw Kopek and Casey running to the top of the knoll. They were both armed with the automatic pistols. Being uphill from them and under cover of heavy undergrowth, I felt a little safer; but it was not the time to rejoice in small victories. I scooted onto my belly and waited for their next move. Kopek hand-signaled Casey, indicating that he had seen something in the bushes up the hill. They then split off in opposite directions, heading toward the undergrowth. If they got that far, they'd find me. I couldn't let that happen. The Uzi was my only way out. The weapon was heavy in my hands, but the weight seemed to calm my nerves, steady my hand. With a Hail Mary attitude, I squeezed the trigger, spraying bullets in and around Kopek and Casey. Casey went down in the brush on the other side of the road, and I saw Kopek fall into a thicket of sage off the knoll. After that, there was no sound, nor movement.

I hurriedly retraced my steps back up the hill, confident that the worst was over. Only Huerta remained to be dealt with. *The diamonds for Lino. A simple exchange.* After that I would get Itzla out of this hellhole and try to patch up our lives.

When I reached the outside perimeter at the tree line of the compound, Garret was revving the engine of the Jeep parked a few feet outside the gates of the courtyard. He switched on the lights as Manolo jumped into his place behind the passenger seat. I noticed Itzla had changed back into her pants and blouse and was now nervously settling into the seat next to Garret. Then I heard the grinding of gears as the Jeep lurched forward.

CHAPTER
TWENTY

Breathing hard from the climb, I staggered out into the compound and started to yell to Garret when a rifle butt slammed into my chest and laid me out in the dirt. Sprawled on my back, holding my chest and gasping for air, I felt the end of another rifle barrel push against my cheek. When my wits returned I saw the two guards, one on his radio to Manolo, the other continuing to drive the barrel into my face.

"Bring him up here," Manolo squawked through the radio. "Now!"

"What the fuck is he doing out here?" I heard Garret say through the static.

When the guards grabbed my arms and yanked me to my feet, I thought my chest might explode. The pain ran through my ribs, up to my neck, and down into my diaphragm. I still had trouble taking in air, and I hadn't wobbled this much since my first day on a surfboard. And I still had to contend with Garret.

The lights went out on the Jeep and Garret killed the engine as I staggered up to him ahead of my two no nonsense escorts. Itzla leaped out of her seat and rushed to me. I heard her gasp. She backed off to look me over.

Was I that broken?

"God damn it!" Garret growled as he spun out of his seat and stood facing me. He had drawn his hunting knife from the sheath on his belt and had the tip pressed lightly under my chin. Bent over from the blow to my chest, we were now nearly the same height, and nose to nose. Even in the early morning light and with my blurred vision I could see the same eyes that scared the shit out of me when Manolo had cut the engine in the boat at Lake Chapala. "I should have tied your fucking ass in a chair!" Garret's voice rasped with disdain.

"Listen," I whispered trying to get a breath, my words cracking, my ribs aching.

"If you ever try anything like this again," he said now with a calmness that chilled the air, "you can forget our deal. I told you to stay in your fucking room. What the hell did you think you could do out here anyway? My men could have killed you." He withdrew the knife and slid it back into its sheath.

"Listen," I repeated, my voice stronger now. "They're down the hill. Maybe dead. They were waiting."

With quiet concern, Garret looked toward Manolo who was now standing next to me. "Who's down the hill?" Garret asked, "And what the hell were you doing down there?"

I looked at Itzla standing tall and strong at my side. "Kopek," I said, "and two guys. You didn't think I was going to let her go alone with you and Manolo. I couldn't help her if I was locked up."

"You couldn't help anybody if you were dead," he snapped. "But forget that. Two others. Any names?"

"Nuñez and Casey is what I heard," I said, relieved that his interest in them seemed to be outweighing my interference.

"Fuck!" Garret pounded on the fender and Manolo snapped to attention.

"They were at Itzla's car." My breathing came harder as I tried to push out the words. "After some files. And the diamonds. They killed Elidio and Chuey. Huerta was on their list, too." Itzla touched my shoulder and then slid her hand into mine. "They want all of us dead," I said. "What the hell are you not telling us, Garret?"

"You said, 'were at Itzla's car.' Where are they now?"

"They were lying in the bushes when I ran back up here. I took Nuñez out with a tree branch. I don't know if he's dead. I used his gun to shoot at Kopek and Casey."

Garret looked stunned. "You tried to take all three of them out? You're probably the luckiest son of a bitch alive," he said almost respectfully. "But you're not the best shot and they've been trained to dodge incoming. My guess is they're alive and really pissed off. Did you check to see if they were dead?"

"Hell, No! I was getting my ass back up here; warning you."

"Manolo!" Garret ordered, ignoring my last statement and marching toward the gates. "Alert the guards and get the Jeep inside. I want guards on all the outbuildings and all non-essential personnel inside, now!" He whirled around, taking a hard look at me and Itzla. "That means you two. Move!"

Manolo keyed his radio, barked a few crisp orders, and hurried the Jeep back through the gates, sliding it to a stop next to the fountain. He grabbed the bag he had earlier tossed into the Jeep then disappeared into the dining room.

My legs were stronger now, but the stabbing pain in

my chest wouldn't let go. Itzla moved me along, her arm easily and comfortably wrapped around my waist. When we reached the dining room, Garret was pacing around the table. His lips were tight, his arms folded across his chest, the fingers of one hand lightly rubbing his chin. Manolo had already unzipped the bag he had taken from the Jeep and dumped several .38s and .45s, a few automatic weapons, and the short-barreled, pump action Mossberg shotgun on the table. A cloth bag followed the guns out, spilling a dozen or more diamonds next to the cache.

"Take care of him," Garret said to Esperanza as I dropped into one of the chairs and tried to get comfortable. She had been standing in the doorway to the kitchen, her small bag of medical supplies waiting for use on the buffet table next to her. She moved swiftly, and unbuttoning my shirt, she sighed. Itzla cringed.

I cranked my neck down far enough to see black and blue spreading out beyond a puck-sized lump on my chest. Esperanza lightly dug her fingers into my ribs and sternum. Even with her gentle touch, the pain shot me upright in my chair. Apparently feeling nothing broken, she pulled a small can of paste-like substance from her bag. "Only a bad bruise," she said, "nothing broken." She gave me a slight comforting smile as she dipped her fingers into the can and began rubbing the chocolate-scented balm onto my chest. "This will ease the pain. *Xocóatl*. An Aztec remedy. You can eat it if you choose to."

"Nuñez and Casey," Garret said abruptly. He stopped in mid stride and turned to me. "You're sure of those names?"

"Yes," I retorted trying to hold back my anger at being left out of the information loop. "And I was close enough to smell the blood on their hands. Who the hell are they?"

"You surprise me, Skipper," Garret said. "You have more balls than I figured you for. Those guys were under my command in 'Nam. You're lucky you still have your ears."

I looked up into Garret's eyes and for the first time really saw who he was. He was a man who had long ago crossed over the tenuous line between the passive arrogance of fantasy and the reality of instant action.

"Why are they here?" Itzla asked. She had come up behind me and was massaging my shoulders. I could feel the tenseness in her fingers.

Her question lit my fuse. "*I'll* tell you why," I exclaimed. "They want some damn files Garret has. They want some money Garret has. They want the diamonds Garret has. And they want to get rid of all of us. 'Leave no trail' is what Kopek said. So tell us Garret, or our deal *is* off!"

Garret gave me a look that refuted his otherwise cold demeanor. His eyes flickered brightly for an instant, and I thought I saw a smile start. "You could have gone AWOL Skipper. Headed down the hill and disappeared. Gotten yourself out of this shit. Why didn't you?"

I looked to Itzla and back to Garret, at Manolo standing watch over the weapons' cache, to Esperanza who had packed up her medical kit and was marching back into the kitchen. At that moment, I realized it wasn't only for Itzla that I had come back up the hill. It was the excitement, our short history of adventure, the adrenaline still coursing through my body that had brought me back. I was beginning to like these people, and I didn't want any of them hurt. I was on the crest of a wave and already committed.

"I'm in it for the whole ride," I said.

Garret tentatively punched my right arm. "I can trust you," he said after a few seconds. He dropped his hand and backed away, fingering the handle of his hunting knife. "Kopek, Nuñez, Casey, we were all part of Task Force Oregon. It was made up of numerous Army units including Tiger Force. Our commanding general at the time thought that the North Vietnamese would take control of the Central Highlands and cut South Vietnam in two. He sent us in as part of the 1st Battalion, 327th Infantry to clear out enemy troops and relocate civilians. I was a Captain under Kopek. Nuñez and Casey took their orders from me until they decided that heroin was more profitable than listening to their CO. The money went to their heads. They started using. Went maverick. That's when the sport killing started. When they began wasting civilians. Collecting body parts." He flicked at his ear and gestured to his groin. "They're crazy fuckers."

I cringed, shuffling in my seat at the image. "We know about the diamonds," I said. "Where does money play into this and the files they're so interested in?"

"I left 'Nam with a quarter million dollars of what Kopek thought was his cut of the last opium run. He fucked up on the paperwork getting the shit out of Laos. His cut paid for the bribes to get a thousand kilos of heroin to South Africa. That's the discussion you overheard at the Market the other day. He wants his money."

"He's willing to settle for the diamonds," I said.

Garret continued pacing. "Little consolation. He's got death on his mind. He's after the files."

Whatever Esperanza had rubbed on my chest was working. The pain was subsiding and I could breathe a little easier. "What are these files?" I asked, grimacing, shifting to a more comfortable position. "And what do they have to do with anything you're involved in? Nuñez had to straighten Kopek out on some directive about them. What's that all about?"

Itzla had moved to the end of the table where Manolo was drawing the weapons out of the bag and sorting them into neat rows. She pushed aside a few diamonds and picked up a small caliber handgun, a .38, felt its weight, and placed it back on the table. "If I have to use one of these to get my uncle back, I will," she said.

"That's noble," Garret said, "but I'm going to try to keep you out of this. Neither of you belong here. This is way over your heads."

There was no reason why I couldn't ride out what was coming next. I had made it through the first few waves that had been building behind me for the past several days. I only needed to keep my feet on the board. "The directive?" I asked again.

"I had to get out of 'Nam," Garret said. "I couldn't control Nuñez. Casey followed him around like a damn puppy. Kopek took Westmoreland's orders as gospel, even adding a few new lines to feed his own psychosis. They all wanted blood. And because of our directive, they felt they were entitled to kill everything in sight. The talk of courts-martial came up and they went nuclear. One of my other men heard talk of them fragging me. A day later, the grenade went off under my bunk. Fortunately, I was pissing in the jungle at the time."

"So you split," I said, straightening my shoulders, feeling the muscles stretch and cramp. "I'm through speculating, Garret. You bought your way out of there and came to Mexico. You used Kopek's money to set up your business. How does Huerta fit into this?"

I saw Itzla's eyes grow cold and her face harden at the mention of Huerta's name. Had I not been watching her, I wouldn't have seen the quick look she gave to the gun she was holding earlier.

"Huerta owed me," Garret said. "I saved his ass from Hmong warriors on one of our opium runs. The son of a bitch couldn't keep his pecker in his pants. He almost lost it and his head. He was on a rape and kill campaign of young girls throughout the Golden Triangle when he was caught with one of the Hmong girls. The men threw him in a small cage and kept him like an animal. Fortunately, Kopek and I had developed some trust with the Hmong leaders. That, some jade we'd been collecting, and a lot of U.S. dollars saved his life. When I wanted out, I called in my marker. Huerta used his political influence in Mexico to get me out. He's the one who set me up here. He's the one I pay to stay in business. We have an equal but volatile business relationship, as you saw when he brought his chopper in the other day, Skipper."

Itzla gave me a quick, sideways look that told me she knew I was holding back even more. I responded with a weak grin and forced myself to my feet. "Does Huerta have anything to do with these files you're not telling us about?" I asked.

Garret again ignored the question. "I knew Huerta and Kopek would catch up to me someday," he said. "I've been able to track them through some of my 'Nam buddies. After I left, I heard that Kopek had been recruited by the CIA, for obvious reasons. He took Nuñez and Casey with him."

I swallowed hard. "CIA assassins?" I asked.

"That's not speculation, Skipper. They've gone professional. And they want what I have."

"And that would be?"

"Before I left, I pillaged every bit of paperwork I could get my hands on related to the operation. I needed security. The files have all the receipts for shipments in and out of the area, including requisitions for Air America aircraft. They contain memos from the leaders of three different countries and photos of those leaders as key players in the operation. All that, plus dates, times, quantities shipped, and payoffs gave me the security I needed. As long as I had the files, no one was going to bother me. Now, from what you're telling me, the directive you heard Nuñez mention is to get the files and get rid of anyone remotely familiar with the operation."

"That's what I heard," I said. "But why now? All that happened five years ago in Viet-nam."

Garret walked to the end of the table and stood next to Manolo who was now leaning with his palms flat on the edge of the table, staring down at the weapons in front of him. Garret pulled the .38 Itzla had held earlier from the line up and, after examining it, nodded to her. "Pride dies hard in some people," he said. "I've been pretty well insulated here. Huerta was the only one who knew where I was." He stopped, his eyes thoughtfully searching the room as if for something he had overlooked. "Huerta," he said with a short snort.

"You two have a business relationship," I said, turning my body, trying to find a more comfortable position. "Why would he sell you out?"

"Mercenaries go where the money is," he continued. "That's all part of the game. And the CIA pays well. Huerta isn't CIA, but money talks and bullshit walks. I'm figuring Kopek was convincing enough to get the Pentagon to agree that the files needed to be recovered at all costs, that the country couldn't afford the negative payback if the information reached the public. The Pentagon boys most likely slid it under the door to the Spooks. Kopek gets the job. There are other files and photos of the atrocities that were committed. Kopek and the Pentagon definitely don't want those exposed. And Huerta, it seems, is their CIA asset."

"And Huerta was trying to smuggle the diamonds out of the country before all this exploded in his face," I declared, running my fingers over the barrel of a gun on the table then adding, "What are our chances?"

The question was never answered. At that moment, the telephone rang.

CHAPTER
TWENTY ONE

Carlos, *mi amigo*," Garret said slowly into the handset. Itzla and Manolo stiffened and came to attention, glaring at the telephone in Garret's hand. The anger in their eyes told me they were both ready to seize, strangle, and kill Carlos Huerta. Before they could speak, Garret waved them into silence with the palm of his hand. Manolo, in frustration, snapped up a handgun, aiming it quickly at the phone as though the bullet could pass through the line and enter Huerta's skull on the other end, then calmly pointed the barrel of the gun at his buttocks. There was no doubt about what he had in mind for Huerta. Itzla started for the phone; but Manolo quickly moved in front of her, wagging his finger, silently telling her "no."

My stomach didn't like hearing Huerta's name either, and told me so with a quick jolt as I struggled to my feet, tested my balance, and gave Itzla an optimistic grin. I leaned into the hutch next to Garret, surprised that Esperanza's balm had relieved most of the pain in my chest. Nothing left but tingling and a numbness that went deep into the muscles.

"I've been expecting your call," Garret said after a

slight pause. He was using that love/hate business voice that gave away nothing, yet the anger in his face belied the calmness in his voice. "What can I do for you?"

There was a moment of tense silence as Garret listened to Huerta ranting on the other end of the line. I edged closer to Garret and could hear Huerta's voice shrieking through the receiver.

"Kopek's in town," I heard Huerta say, his normally deep voice hollow with stress.

"No shit," Garret responded. "He thinks we're still in 'Nam. You know where he is?"

"Not at this moment, but be assured he's coming after you."

"Why would you care what happens to me?" Garret asked. "All our IOUs are paid in full."

"You might say I'm protecting my business interest," Huerta stated. "Kopek's after the files, that's all he wants. Turn them over to him, and we'll have a very prosperous future together."

"And you aren't interested in the files?" Garret asked, mocking Huerta. "Your ass could be thrown in jail for a long time. You looking to be put into another cage, Carlos?"

Huerta snorted a small chuckle. "This is Mexico, Garret. We play by different rules down here. The files are of no interest to me."

"I'll ask you again," Garret said, nursing the words. "What do you want?"

"I know you have the Warrior," Carlos said. "I know that little turd of Manolo's brother must have made it to your ranch. I should have put another bullet in him."

Wrong thing to say, Carlos. You'd pay in hell trying to justify that to Manolo.

"I thought he'd try to get it to Lino," Huerta continued. "When he didn't show there, I knew he must have gotten it up the hill to you."

"So it's the Warrior you're after," Garret said with a sardonic grin.

"It's not the fucking Warrior!" Carlos shouted into the receiver.

Hearing Huerta's voice for that instant, Itzla jerked forward, her hands tightening around a chair back, her fingers turning white from the pressure. Manolo, scary as he was normally, showed no expression as he briefly looked toward the phone, then methodically continued loading rounds into the magazines of the guns on the table.

"You know damn well what I'm talking about," Huerta continued his rant. After a few deep breaths, he said more rationally, "Here's our deal, Garret. The stones for Itzla's uncle and I'm gone, out of your life."

"You make it sound like it would be an easy exchange, Carlos."

"And what would get in the way?"

"You have some very pissed off people who would love to see you dead."

"Ah! They talk a lot. I'm not concerned about a few pissant townspeople."

"They may be a factor, Carlos," Garret said looking at Itzla who had abandoned the chair for a more serious display of her feelings, that of helping Manolo with the weapons. There was pause on both ends until Garret said, "Kopek knows about the diamonds, Carlos. It's not just the files he wants now. It seems he's getting greedy, too." There was a longer pause as the words sank into Huerta's brain.

"Then you have a serious problem," Huerta finally

said, a strain of uneasiness in his voice. "Kopek's here under directive from your government, but it now seems he has his own agenda. He's gone rogue. He's a CIA sanction, but a ghost in their eyes. And they have conveniently overlooked his psychotic behavior."

"And you just happened to be available when he blew into town?" Garret said rhetorically.

I heard a long sigh on the other end, then Huerta spoke, the hollowness in his voice had given way to his normal arrogance. "Garret, my friend, I just happened to give him a few side jobs. As I said, when Jorge didn't show up in Teuchitlan, I had Kopek pick Lino up."

Garret glanced to Manolo and Itzla, and seeing no evidence that they had overheard, said coldly to Huerta, "In exchange for my whereabouts."

"That and also for insurance, my friend," Huerta said. "It's business. Nothing personal. We have a good relationship." I pictured Huerta's sweaty, pockmarked face pressed against the receiver. It disgusted me. "Kopek would have found you eventually," he went on. "You know how tenacious he is. Sure, I helped him out a little."

"Still the *cobarde*, eh, Carlos?" Garret said. "I should have left you in the jungle in Laos to rot in that cage the Hmong put you in."

Carlos snorted again. "Let's not talk of cowards, Garret. What do you plan on doing about this problem? You seem to be having difficulty keeping friendships."

"This is not just my problem, Carlos," Garret countered. "We both know how Kopek operates, and with Casey and Nuñez out there with him, it will be nearly impossible to keep them from what they want. If Kopek gets to me, he gets the files and the diamonds. Then he comes after you. The bastards who used us in 'Nam get to walk, and you get nothing but a bullet, or a murder wrap for killing Jorge at the least. This problem belongs to both of us."

Carlos laughed. "You're telling me we should have another business arrangement?"

"I'm telling you nobody will win as long as Kopek is out there. We need to hurry the exchange."

Carlos went silent. I could hear him breathing on the other end as I pictured his face strained in thought, sorting his options. "Being in business with you is dangerous, my friend," he finally said.

"Cut the crap, Carlos," Garret snapped. "You want the diamonds, and we want Lino. Let's make the trade. We'll meet you at the upper ruins in Teuchitlan in one hour. Let's hope our buddies are a long way off. And Carlos? Save the bravado, leave the chopper at home. I want to see you coming up the hill."

"I play only as well as my competition," Carlos stated. "One hour." He hung up.

CHAPTER
TWENTY TWO

You get close to your friends and even closer to your enemies," Garret said when I asked him why he hadn't told Carlos about Kopek being at Itzla's car and how Kopek had tried to set Garret up with the bogus phone call. "You get so close you're in their skin. You know what triggers to pull to get them moving. We were brothers in battle. I know these guys. And they're having the same thoughts about me right now."

"Maybe they'll all run into each other down the hill, and the problem will take care of itself," I said halfheartedly. I shrugged, feeling the bite of a muscle pull across my chest.

"That would be the best thing that could happen," Garret said, "but it won't. If Carlos knew Kopek was waiting in the bushes, he might not show. If he did show, there's the possibility of them joining forces. As much as they despise each other, when it comes to riches, they are of one mind."

"I think they would kill each other before they split the diamonds," Itzla said, curling her lips with distaste, picking up the .38, looking it over as if it were a child's water pistol, and finally saying, "Give me a clip."

Manolo gently took the gun from Itzla's hand, laying it on the table next to the Mossberg. Itzla snatched it back to her chest, saying explicitly, "I'm a part of this. I do know how to use it."

A hint of a smile washed across Garret's face. He seemed pleased with Itzla's spunk. "So now I have another warrior," he said. "Maybe the Mossberg would be better for you. Not easy to miss with a shotgun." He then nodded to Manolo. "*Enseñarle!*"

Manolo pulled a nine-round magazine from the bag and took the .38 from Itzla. "*Mira,*" he said sliding the magazine into the bottom of the grip. He released the magazine and handed it and the gun back to Itzla who deftly shoved the magazine into the grip. Manolo quickly and delicately eased the gun out of her hand and set it down in front of him. He then began to show her the details of the Mossberg.

"My uncle taught me how to use a shotgun when I was seven years old," Itzla said, irritated by Manolo's insistence. "I have killed a lot of quail and coyotes. I don't need a lesson."

Manolo, seeming a bit humbled, began loading each of the weapons on the table.

"They probably would kill each other," Garret said, chuckling at her readiness to leap into battle. "But they have to get the stones first. That's why we can't put all of them together. It'll be nasty enough dealing with Huerta by himself. Fortunately, thanks to Skipper going AWOL and Carlos' phone call, we have the advantage of knowing where they are."

"They sure as hell know where *we* are," I said. "They'll suspect something if you don't head down the hill."

"Hell," Garret growled, "You don't think they're going

to wait, do you? Not their style. They're already on their way up."

With a quick shake of his head, Garret gave Manolo one of his silent orders. Manolo didn't need to be prompted. He had already swept the weapons into the bag and was zipping it up when Esperanza appeared at the kitchen door holding a rifle and a .45. She was wearing jeans, a long-sleeved shirt, lace-up boots. A radio hung from her hip.

"And have four of the men meet us at the ruins," Garret oredered Manolo. "Have them do nothing until I give the order."

Manolo silently hoisted the duffel off the table, walked to his mother, kissed her on each cheek, and hurried out the door into the courtyard.

"We can't stay here," Garret said, his voice calm, unruffled. "We have to go, now." He and Esperanza exchanged nods then he said, "You know what to do. We'll be back when it's over." With a flick of his hand, he shooed me and Itzla toward the door.

Esperanza raised her rifle in acknowledgement and then crossed herself. The irony threw me for a second. There was something about giving a blessing while holding a .45 in one hand and a rifle in the other that wobbled into moral territory. But I didn't have time to think about why it didn't fit because at that moment Manolo skidded the Jeep to a dusty stop in front of us at the curb of the portico. He jumped into the back when Garret climbed behind the wheel, Manolo's legs protectively covering the duffel.

"What are you two waiting for?" Garret said, tapping out his nervousness on the steering wheel. "This isn't a goddamn Disneyland ride! Get the hell in!"

"Mr. Toad's Wild Ride if anything," I mumbled to Itzla

and crawled over the fender to sit across from Manolo.

Itzla had barely swung herself into the passenger seat when Garret stomped the accelerator and headed out of the compound toward an outbuilding half hidden by dense overgrowth. It was the building I had wondered about the first time I had been to the complex, the one Garret had said was on a need-to-know basis.

"Head-to-head would be suicide, Garret," I said above the whine of the Jeep's big engine.

Garret stopped the Jeep in front of the heavy, metal door, jumped out, and blew the lock off with his .45. He swung the door open and said as he rushed inside, "We're going around them. You don't go face-to-face with these guys. That shot was for diversion."

Thirty seconds later, he climbed back into the Jeep, carrying a leather courier pouch bulging with what I suspected to be the incriminating evidence of his in-country days. He tossed it to Manolo who set it next to the duffel under his feet, ground the Jeep into first gear, and aimed it toward the armory building, toward the main road.

Garret stopped to say a few quick words to one of the guards at the armory. After verifying with Manolo that the guard had understood his instruction, he started the Jeep up the hill where only a few days ago Manolo had protected me from Huerta and his two bodyguards – the day Huerta had Victor killed.

"This road circles around and ends up near the upper ruins, about two miles," Garret shouted over the roar of the engine. "It'll give us enough time to do our business with Huerta and get you two the hell out of here, before Kopek realizes he's been played."

"I'm worried about Esperanza," Itzla said, firmly gripping the panic bar as the Jeep bounced in and out of potholes and over softball-sized rocks. "Is she being protected?"

Garret wrestled the Jeep around a few more holes, scaring a rabbit into the bushes on the side of the road then said, "Esperanza was born on this ranch. She knows every inch of it. They'll never get her. In fact, she'll probably take out one or two of them herself."

CHAPTER
TWENTY THREE

With the sun coming up over the mountains, lighting up the higher sections of ground, I saw that the road was leading us around the marijuana fields Garret had shown me the day before. The Ford tractor sat idling in the middle of the field while a few workers hacked at plants, seemingly unaware of the danger surrounding them. But knowing Mexico, I would bet the five hundred dollars I still had in the torn pocket of my shirt that they knew more than I did. The sun and the rising heat did little to take the unknown from my bones, and it didn't help that Manolo had shifted his bulk from his side of the Jeep and was now kneeling between the front seats, his massive shoulders nudging mine as I worked my way to the tailgate, out of his reach. Even though I trusted him, he was too quiet, and that was something I figured was dangerous. *It's always the quiet ones.*

Garret downshifted to avoid a pothole in the road then slowed to a stop. We were on the downside of a knoll looking back toward the marijuana fields. I slid myself next to Manolo, finding a space under the roll bar against the back of Itzla's seat, and put my hand on her shoulder. Without taking her eyes from the road, she reached up and placed her hand over mine. Her earlier tension seemed to have slackened. *Where did she find the strength?* Even Garret was unusually quiet, his normal bravado subdued. He had to be scared shitless behind that façade of cool, focused composure. And Manolo? What tangle of thoughts was going on in his head?

"We walk from here," Garret said, jamming the transmission into first gear and killing the engine. "Kopek can see and practically smell dust clouds miles away. He can't know we've left the compound. Not until we've finished with Huerta. We've got a half-mile walk down to the ruins once we're over this hill." He slapped the steering wheel and hopped out onto the road next to Manolo.

Manolo was one step ahead of Garret and had already unzipped the duffel, setting out the guns on the jump seat. Garret pulled the bag of diamonds from the duffel and stuffed them into the courier pouch, then threw the carrying strap over his head and onto his shoulder. "Winner takes all," he said, patting the pouch resting on his side. He took a .45 from Manolo, pulled the slide, chambered a round, and said, "God, I hate this shit."

Manolo picked up the Mossberg and hesitantly offered it to Itzla who decisively snatched it from his hands.

"Pick one, Skipper," Garret said. "No time for speculation or moralizing. They all kill."

I tensed for a moment, looked at Itzla confidently holding the Mossberg, then said, "Give me the damn Uzi!"

* * *

The rooftops of Teuchitlán were barely visible through a small window of trees and dense overgrowth at the top of the rise. Itzla sighed heavily after parting several branches with the muzzle of the shotgun. She stood for a moment, looking intently past the ruins of Guachimonton, to her Teuchitlán.

She suddenly jerked the muzzle away. The branch sprang back, closing the window. "It will never be the same," she said quietly to me.

"Nothing is ever the same," I said not knowing the full meaning of what I had just said. "What I mean is, change is what keeps us alive. And right now this and this," I said, indicating the Uzi at my side and the Mossberg she was holding, "could create major changes. Hopefully we won't have to use them."

"*Así es la vida*," she whispered. "It will be what it is."

Manolo had shouldered the duffel as Garret led us over the rise and into a wild growth of jungle plants. Neither Garret, nor Manolo, had said a word since we left the Jeep. Even the radios were quiet now.

We were picking our way through the branches when I heard the clicking of rifle bolts in the bushes ahead of us. I grabbed Itzla and pulled her behind me as the four guards he had sent down earlier pushed through the thicket checking their weapons.

"I told you once you'd never know they were there," Garret said, shaking his head.

Itzla looked quickly toward me, her eyes narrowing. She tightened her lips and cocked her head. I was getting used to that look. She gave me a small smile.

"You didn't have time to think when Kopek sabotaged my drug run, Skipper," Garret went on. "If you think about the situation you're in now, you may end up dead in the bushes. I need you to be sharp and focused."

"When was I ever not with you?" I said, checking the safety on the Uzi. "But let's get one thing clear, when this is over, I'm going to kick your ass."

He gave me a twisted smile and nodded toward Itzla. "I'm sorry you have to be involved, Itzla," he said. "You don't deserve this. I'll keep you out of it as much as possible."

"I may not deserve it," she said angrily, "but just try and keep me away from Huerta. Huerta is going to get what *he* deserves."

"Keep your anger checked," Garret warned. "Huerta isn't the only one we have to deal with. Kopek will be raging down the hill after us when he discovers we're not in the compound."

"What do you want us to do?' Itzla asked.

"You two stay with me," Garret said reaching into the duffel and removing a pair of binoculars. He began scanning the area. "Manolo knows what to do." As Manolo started off with the guards, Garret barked, "No radios. You know Kopek and Huerta are working the same frequencies."

In the silence that followed, Manolo strategically placed the guards behind bushes in a stand of trees growing on the uphill side of the open area of the ruins. One of the men disappeared behind the boulder that Kopek had used as cover the day before when he had Itzla and me pinned down by gunfire in the shaft tomb. When I saw the tomb opening itself and the splintered wooden ladder arms scattered like chopsticks around the lip of the entrance only fifty yards away, my stomach tightened.

Itzla had taken the binoculars from Garret and was panning the area when she spotted the plain, gray government car turning off Highway 15, making a speedy climb up the hill to Teuchitlan. "He's coming," she said coldly. "He's driving. There are others with him."

"As stupid as he is, he's not stupid enough to come alone. He's brought some muscle with him," Garret said.

"And by the looks of the dust he's kicking up, he doesn't have stealth in mind," I said. "Can you see your uncle?"

Itzla leaned forward, focusing the binoculars. "No. You don't suppose—"

"He's with him," I said in an attempt to ease Itzla's nervousness. "Huerta isn't doing this for fun."

"He doesn't have a sense of humor," Garret said with a grim chuckle, taking the binoculars from Itzla. "Lino's in that car. Huerta's stupidity has always exceeded his arrogance. He thinks he'll be protected under the cover of a government car." He exhaled deeply and mumbled, "Nice try, Huerta."

When the car reached the lower junction where the road split off into the secondary road that skirted behind the town, the car slowed. It appeared Huerta was thinking about the better of his options. He chose the town road.

"That arrogant son of a bitch," Garret said with a smirk. "He's going to parade Lino right through the damn town."

"Has he always had a death wish, or is he just plain crazy?" I asked. "Why would he broadcast his involvement?"

"As long as he has my uncle, no one in town will do anything," Itzla said. "Damn him!"

"Two killers in the car with him would tend to slow me down a bit, too," Garret said. He was scanning the area, looking up the hills into the trees behind us. "He knows we're watching him. It's a show. He wouldn't be doing this unless he felt he had some sort of advantage."

"Meaning?" I asked.

Garret seemed to wrestle over the question. After a moment he said almost apologetically, "I think he's putting all his money on Kopek."

If there was anything to laugh about, it would be Kopek's allegiance to anyone but himself. And if his and Huerta's IOUs were paid up, neither of them could resist disposing of the other. Given a different circumstance, it might have been amusing, but after Kopek's declaration of death to anyone even remotely involved with his mission, hilarity seemed as ludicrous as a hornless bull in the Plaza de Toros.

"Let's see where he's going with all this," Garret said.

We watched as Huerta slammed on the brakes and slid the car sideways in front of Lino's store. What greeted him was a brown veil of heavy dust, kicked up by his brazen display of primordial driving skills.

Even from 500 yards and with enough light now, I could see Huerta lay siege to the driver's door and having it snap back to catch his left leg in the door frame. "Ouch. That must have pissed him off," I said.

Huerta finally ejected himself, took a few swats with his cowboy hat trying to clear the thick dust swirling around his face, then jammed the hat on his head. He quickly brushed off the silver toes of his snakeskin boots with the back of his pants, then favoring his left leg, marched haughtily toward the door of the store. No one else got out.

"Something tells me he's not stopping for postcards," I said as Huerta tramped toward Vincencio who appeared to be repairing something near the entrance. Pepino, my little one-night stand burro friend, stood lazily next to Vincencio saddled with a basket of what looked like tools. When Vincencio pulled a machete out of the basket, Huerta stopped dead in his tracks.

Nailea seemed to have caught him off guard when she suddenly and angrily appeared at the door. She tried to weave around Huerta and run to the car, but Huerta was too quick for her. He grabbed her by the arms and threw her to the ground, sending her sprawling in the dirt. Vincencio raised his machete and started toward Huerta just as one of the guards flung his door open and jumped out next to Huerta waving a handgun. After a few heated words and seeing a crowd growing quickly, Vincencio lowered the machete to his side.

"Typically Huerta," Garret said. "Bullying the defenseless."

It was then I saw Benito with his conical Revolution hat and long-barreled rifle station himself against the wall outside the swinging doors of his cantina, one heel on the wall, stoically observing the happenings across the street.

C H A P T E R
TWENTY FOUR

Itzla was fuming as she slung the Mossberg over her shoulder and started sprinting down the hill. "Huerta can't get away with this!" she screamed. "I've got to help my family!"

She had covered about fifty feet when I caught up to her, grabbed her around the waist, and took her down to the ground. We rolled twice, stopped face down at the gaping mouth of the shaft tomb, our heads frozen over the lip. For an instant, I stared down into the dark shaft, remembering the bullets flying over our heads and then quickly rolled Itzla several feet away. "That isn't going to be our tomb," I said. But Itzla didn't seem to hear, her attention still focused on Huerta down the hill.

"He's hurt us enough already," she said attempting to get the Mossberg into firing position. "We have to stop him."

"That's what they want you to do, Itzla. They want to keep us off balance. We can't let that happen. They have to come to us."

The Mossberg was suddenly ripped out of Itzla's hands. I didn't have to look up to know that it was Manolo, the wide-cast shadow of his bulk giving him away. With the barrel of the Mossberg, he motioned us to move back up the hill.

"Maybe they're stronger than you think, Itzla," Garret said. He nodded to Manolo who tentatively handed the Mossberg back to her.

"Who?" Itzla asked, perplexed. She was again aiming the shotgun at Huerta.

"Those people in the town." Garret gently pushed the barrel of the Mossberg toward the ground. "Forget it. The shot would die fifty yards down the hill. Don't worry, you'll get your chance."

"I thought I just wanted him in jail," she said with a resentful stare. "Now I want him dead!"

* * *

The arguing in front of the store continued to heat up with Nailea back on her feet swinging her arms madly, trying to get to Lino who had briefly poked his head out the rear window of the car, but was quickly pulled back inside by the guard sitting next to him. It was, as Garret had mentioned earlier, Huerta's show. Vincencio and the others seemed helpless under Huerta's spell of power, not to mention Huerta's burly bodyguard standing next to his boss, undoubtedly displaying some type of weapon.

Discretion, I thought for the townspeople. *Be smarter than your tormentor.*

Discretion may be the better part of valor; but when Huerta finally shrugged, holding his palms out in front of him in a what-else-can-I-possibly-do gesture, my ire flared. I pictured a sardonic grin spreading across Huerta's wide, acne-scarred face and felt the gap closing between discretion and wanting to rip his head off. Manolo, unmoving, resolute, the cords of his neck standing out like cables, stood next to Garret who was panning the area with his field glasses. It was frightening to see the gelid calm in the Mexican's eyes. How narrow was the gap for Manolo? For Itzla? Her family? For Garret?

Huerta followed up by spinning on his right heel and limping back to the car, his left leg apparently still stinging from his mishap with the door. He scooted into the driver seat, slammed the door, and stabbed the accelerator, the car's tires spitting gravel and throwing dirt into the faces of Nailea and Vincencio who slowly disappeared behind the swirling vortex of dust.

What was Huerta's reason for wanting to anger Itzla's family even more than he had already? Was there something I wasn't getting? It didn't make sense. All Huerta had to do was skirt the town, do what he had to do to exchange Lino for the diamonds, and be on his way.

Forget it, Skip. Get a grip on that imagination. It's like Garret had said, "*It's just a show.*"

"It seems he has successfully reinforced his threat to kill everyone." It was Garret cutting into my thoughts as though I had asked him the questions. "There isn't any road out here," he went on. "It stops about a hundred yards from the ruins. He'll have to walk the rest of the way." He returned to scanning the hills behind us, a bone chilling reminder that Kopek and his nightmarish thrill killers were somewhere in those hills.

I knew the road. Itzla and I had walked the narrow horse path to get to the shaft tomb after her heated discussion with Vincencio and Nailea. I had parked her Toyota on flat ground at the junction of the pathway and the road that led to Garret's compound. Only now, within a few minutes, instead of Benito coming to our rescue, Huerta would be walking up the path with greed in his mind and a gun in his waistband, holding Itzla's uncle as his *triunfo*.

I wasn't wrong. Huerta was hurrying the car up the hill a few feet ahead of an angry dust cloud, bouncing it over ruts and potholes until he slid it to a stop in the middle of the small plateau at the junction. When the dust finally settled, I could see Huerta through the windshield cautiously appraising the area, his forearms spread over the top of the steering wheel, his head bobbing and rotating. He sat like that, tapping his fingers on the dashboard for a few tense moments. His guards were the first out, one manhandling Lino to the front of the car, the other standing rigidly next to Huerta's door.

Huerta slowly opened his door and began the walk toward the shaft tomb sandwiched between the two guards—one out front holding Lino and the other guard a few steps behind.

"Think they'll make it through the day after the exchange?" I asked Garret. It was an offhanded question, but the curious part of me wanted to know.

"Probably not," Garret responded glibly, motioning to Manolo to move Itzla and me farther back into the tree line under the cover of the dense bushes and large banana leaves. Itzla was settling in next to me when Garret adjusted the courier pouch over his shoulder, chambered a round into the .45, and walked out into the open. He covered thirty yards quickly, stopping just short of his side of the shaft tomb.

"Carlos, *mi amigo*," I heard him say as Huerta walked up to the other side of the tomb, his two truck-sized guards now flanking him, one nudging Lino along with his open hand, the other resolute in scanning the area for security. Their guns were still holstered. Huerta had his .45 tucked into the waistband on his right side, under his thin shirt, the grip a dead giveaway with its bulk. "Why is it we always seem to meet with guns in our hands?" Garret asked brashly.

Huerta showed more than just that sardonic grin of his beneath the brim of his black cowboy hat. "Guns have always made for a better understanding of purpose, Garret." There was an ugliness, a meanness in his face. Even at this time of the morning small circles of sweat were eroding the armpits of his light blue, short-sleeved guayabera shirt. Looking at the courier pouch hanging at Garret's side, Huerta said, "You brought the merchandise?"

"That was the deal."

Huerta pulled the pistol from his waistband and waved it at the ground in front of him. "Toss it, and you get the bitch's uncle."

Itzla's body tensed next to me, pulsing with angry, nervous energy. I felt the muscles of her arm flex as she clenched the stock of the Mossberg. "Bitch's uncle!" she whispered, her voice sharp and breathy. She was ready to pounce.

I gently grabbed her arm and said softly, "Trust Garret." *Even then,* I thought, *there are no guarantees.*

She took a deep breath and exhaled slowly. "It is hard to trust someone who kills."

"In this game," I answered, "it's hard to trust someone who doesn't."

Manolo, crouching next to us, put a finger to his lips. "*Silencio,*" he said under his breath as we watched Garret calmly slide the bag from his shoulder and pitch it across the gaping entrance of the shaft tomb. It landed on the toe of Huerta's reptilian boot with a thud worthy of a B movie.

Huerta nodded to the guard on his left, the one holding Lino. The guard tightened his grip on Lino's arm. The other guard tentatively squatted and picked up the pouch. After a few seconds of looking, the guard turned the pouch upside down, and with a quizzical look, shook the contents onto the ground. The shards of the Teuchitlán Warrior poured out and settled in a heap at Huerta's feet.

"What kind of shit game are you playing, Garret?" Huerta said furiously. He raised the .45 and shoved it into Lino's cheek. "I could shoot him right now. Where are the *fucking* diamonds?"

Itzla was instantly on her feet, nervously rocking back and forth, swinging the Mossberg from side to side in front of her. I popped up next to her, my adrenalin firing like pistons on a muscle car. Through the thick foliage, I thought I saw Huerta look toward the bushes where we were hidden.

"Don't worry about the diamonds," I heard Garret saying. "They're safe. And until Lino is safely out of your hands, that's where they stay."

"And what is this pile of shit at my feet?" Huerta kicked at the shards with the side of his boot, sending pieces of the broken Warrior over the lip of the shaft tomb. He pushed Lino onto his knees, aimed the barrel of his gun to the back of Lino's head.

"A reminder that we're holding the diamonds. They're safe," Garret repeated.

"Safe is what you're not, Garret."

"You know what those diamonds are worth, Huerta. Don't blow it. You really didn't think I was stupid enough to just turn them over to you."

"We have been in business for many years, my friend. If we can't trust each other, what is the purpose for continuing?"

"I understand your concern for our trust, Carlos. But that trust disappeared when you shot and killed Manolo's brother. When you had Kopek kidnap Lino. What was your deal with Kopek? Have him get rid of me so you wouldn't have to get your hands dirty?"

"You think I would kill you?" Huerta said, seemingly amused by Garret's statement. "My cash cow? You are seriously misunderstanding my intentions, Garret."

"Cut the crap, Huerta. You don't like leaving trails, and I'm not about to be at the end of it in a heap like that Warrior at your feet."

Huerta suddenly jerked Lino to his feet and slid his .45 back into his waistband. My throat turned as dry as the air around us when Huerta made a conciliatory gesture, shrugging and showing the palms of his hands. The same body language he had used with Nailea and Vincencio outside the store. *The patronizing son of a bitch. What had he told them?*

"The diamonds are mine," I heard Huerta say. His supercilious grin faded quickly. His face turned hard. "No one has to die."

"You are so noble-minded," Garret scoffed. "The trust between us is overrated. Is it because my men are out there? Or is it just your natural purity of heart?"

With a quick movement of his hand, Huerta pulled the gun from his waistband and slammed it into the side of Lino's face. Lino tumbled to the ground. A line of blood rolled down onto his neck. "Don't test me, Garret. My patience is wearing thin. The diamonds. Hand them over, and let's settle this thing."

I could feel Itzla seething next to me, hear her breath coming in hard, quick pants. She was holding the Mossberg with both hands across her chest. Her eyes were closed. She was standing steady as if reciting a small prayer.

CHAPTER
TWENTY FIVE

Manolo must have known what was going to happen next but either didn't care or had some plan of his own. You could never tell with Manolo. Either way, my anxiety was crushing at my chest as I watched him move farther away from us into the trees and disappear. It seemed we were on our own, both of us in a mind that could get us killed. I braced myself, took a few deep breaths. Nodding to Itzla, we both recklessly crashed through the ten feet of trees, branches and shrubs that were hiding us. We bolted toward Garret—Itzla carrying the Mossberg like she knew how to use it, I keeping the Uzi close to my side, finger on the trigger.

Huerta, seeing the charge, swiftly raised his gun in our direction. His guards whipped their pistols from their holsters, dropped to their knees, and took dead aim at the two of us.

Lino, lying at the knee of his guard, suddenly rolled over and shot a fist into the guard's groin. The guard groaned once and collapsed, the gun spinning out of his hand. The other guard seemingly confused as to what to do, turned toward Huerta for direction just as Lino clambered over the fallen guard to get to the gun. Huerta kicked the gun out of Lino's reach skidding it across the dirt and into the shaft tomb. He then stomped on Lino's fingers with the heel of his boot, hauled him up, and, holding him tightly as a shield, pressed the barrel of his gun into the side of Lino's forehead.

"That was a stupid thing to do," Garret said to us as we came up next to him. "Lower your weapons, you'll get us all killed."

I had the Uzi aimed at the guard who had picked himself up and was now standing useless, helpless, and pissed off, his potency having been trimmed by Huerta's boot that had sent the guard's gun into the tomb.

Itzla held a steady bead at Huerta with the Mossberg. She had to have seen the thin line of blood running down from under Lino's hairline onto his ear made by the blow Huerta had given him. "Are you alright, *Tio*?" she asked in Spanish. "The truth."

"Better than that *baboso* over there." He flicked his hand toward the unarmed guard he had taken down, and who had now positioned himself in as proud a posture as he could shake himself into. "I'm okay, *mi amada*," Lino declared.

Huerta suddenly burst out laughing. "Is this the best army you could muster, Garret? A museum director and… Mr. Reid, isn't it? I thought you were just passing through to Panama, but it seems you have encountered something of interest." He said this as he glared at Itzla. "I didn't think we'd meet again so soon, though."

I forced a grin to relieve some of the tension I was feeling. "I was hoping we'd never meet again," I said.

"And where is that ape man of yours, Garret?" Huerta said. He's not going to be a problem, is he?"

Garret raised his hand to signal his four guards out of hiding. They quickly surrounded Huerta and his men. Manolo was no where in sight. "You'll never see Manolo, Huerta, but he'll always know where you are."

Fear rose in Huerta's face as he evaluated his situation. He frantically turned toward the disarmed guard who seemed to be planted like a boulder next to him, all the while pressing the barrel of his .45 deeper into the skin of Lino's face. "You're useless!" he barked at the guard. "Get your damn gun out of that fucking hole!"

"Getting a little nervous, Huerta?" Garret asked, keeping an eye on the guard starting his climb down into the shaft on the fragile remains of the wooden ladder.

With his left arm clinched around Lino's neck, Huerta tried a grin that quickly collapsed under his own growing agitation. His eyes flickered back and forth to Garret's guards who were now twenty feet away, surrounding Huerta and his hired thug. When Huerta looked past the guards and into the trees, I knew he was looking for Manolo, still hidden somewhere inside the tree line.

"Nothing to be nervous about, my friend," Huerta said, the words not measuring up to his normal arrogance. "Like you, I, too, have friends."

The guard was well into the shaft when I heard his howl and remembered the missing sixth rung. I was close enough to see that he had fallen hard to the bottom, and with his weight had crumbled the remaining steps. The ladder had disintegrated and fallen to the bottom with him. He was on his back, impaled through the chest on a four-foot length of splintered side rail.

"I should have shot him," Huerta said as cold as the snakes he had in all likelihood shot to make his custom boots. "At least I wouldn't have to listen to his whining."

The word *snake* and Carlos Huerta had suddenly become indistinguishable from each other.

"If you're counting on Kopek to bail you out, that ain't gonna happen," Garret said. He scooted a good distance away from Itzla and me, covering the ground as lightly as a spider on water. He kept his gun at his side. Separation was good, I thought. At least Huerta wouldn't get all of us before he and his guard went down. "Tell him why, Skipper. Tell him what you heard."

My experience with negotiation up to this point had been little more than slapping around a few out-of-line hockey players and calming angry surfers who had been cut out of a wave by impatient weekenders. What was I supposed to say to a killer with a cocked gun rammed into the face of an innocent bus driver? "You already know he wants everything for himself," I started, rasping the words, not sure of where this was all going. I had lowered the Uzi, not wanting to stress Huerta anymore than he already was. Itzla, reluctantly, had dropped the barrel of the Mossberg toward the ground, both of us with the obvious thought that Garret's guards would take care of any misunderstandings.

When I found my voice, I said, "I was close enough to them to smell their sweat. Kopek could care less about any of us, and that definitely includes you, Huerta. He wants the files and the diamonds. He wants you and all of us out of the way, permanently."

There was a barely discernible slack in Huerta's jaw. He swiftly recovered and said with uncertainty, "He's here?"

"He's heading up to the compound right now," Garret stated. "When he discovers we've bugged out, he'll be down here faster than an M60 tracer round. Hand Lino over, and I'll get the damn stones to you. We don't have much time."

"Fuck you, Garret! Give me one good reason for me to believe that shit?"

"I'll give you a few right now," Garret said reaching into his front pocket and pulling out several pea-sized diamonds. He tossed them across the mouth of the shaft tomb at Huerta, who reflexively eased his grip on Lino while trying to snatch the tiny stones out of the air. "Don't get any crazy ideas that my pockets are full of diamonds, Carlos," Garret said. "Those are just a few to keep you interested. The most obvious reason is still to come. Kopek is here, and he's breathing down your neck."

Itzla raised the shotgun; but again, Huerta was too quick. He went taut, recoiling behind Lino, tightening his grip. Itzla held the Mossberg steady for a moment, then, perhaps thinking better of it, relaxed, slowly lowering the gun.

Huerta's shirt was now a patchwork of nervous sweat. He nodded to his guard, and again, sandwiched between him and Lino started backing down the path toward the car. "It sounds like we have to have another meeting, my friend," he fumed. "Perhaps after a few body parts show up at Nailea's front door?" He paused, waiting for that to sink in. Then, "Get the diamonds and we'll talk. Get them, or he becomes a jig-saw puzzle."

Garret still held the gun at his side. Itzla seethed next to me. Feeling a little uneasy, I raised the barrel of the Uzi toward Huerta. "If Kopek gets to me first, Huerta," Garret said, "this whole charade is mute. You could kill Lino, and for what? Some twenty-five year old bullshit betrayal? If I disappear, you'll never find the diamonds. What's my life worth to you?"

Huerta seemed to be melting in his own sweat. He had

stopped ten feet down the path; but before he could answer, the nerve-wracking, crackling sound of small arms'
fire began resonating in the hills near Garret's compound.
I caught a glimpse of Itzla's eyes. They looked the same
way I felt, pissed off and ready for battle. With any luck it
was Esperanza and Garret's guards taking out Kopek, Nuñez, and Casey. Whatever prescription for survival Garret
had set up for Esperanza and the guards, however, I still
couldn't help but think about Kopek's demonic laugh when
he told Casey and Nuñez that Garret's men would scatter
like quail after the first gun shot. But miracles sometimes
do happen. My money was still on Esperanza. It had to be.

"There's your obvious reason, Carlos," Garret stated.
"If Kopek makes it out of there, we'll have about ten minutes. It's your call."

We waited as Huerta grimaced and shifted his weight
against Lino. He looked toward the firefight up the hill
and, clearly unstrung, said, "Kopek owes me, Garret."

Garret, unwavering, retorted, "You're a fool, Carlos.
He wanted you taken out in Laos. He considered you a liability. You think he's going to race down here to save your
fat, brown ass?"

The gunfire was slowing with only the sounds of a
few random shots coming from the compound. Huerta
began moving unsteadily behind Lino, his body slowly
slacking into defeat. "Kopek and I have a deal," he said
unconvincingly.

"You don't have anything he wants," Garret said.
"You'll be the first one down."

The gunfire had stopped completely, leaving an eerie
quietness floating over the ruins and hills. I knew from
what Garret had told us coming down the hill that Esperanza and the guards would blow up the munitions bunker

if they were losing the battle, hopefully taking Kopek and his cohorts with it. He had instructed his guards to wire the bunker with Semtex and to set it off only as a last ditch effort to keep Kopek from adding to his munitions cache. An explosion could mean one of two things: that Kopek and his men had been killed in the blast, or that Esperanza and the guards were about to be routed. It was the quiet of the unknown that was unnerving.

Then it happened. The dreaded *whomp* of detonated Semtex. The explosion shattered the silence, the sound roaring down through the valley above our heads and across the ruins.

As the crack and snap of exploding ordnance filled the air, Itzla suddenly shouted, "*Tío! Pino! Pino!*"

A moment of slow motion followed Itzla's outburst. I looked to Itzla, hoping she wasn't thinking what I thought she was thinking. She was smiling. And as Lino returned her smile, she all the while, was raising the Mossberg toward Huerta. Sensing what was going to happen next, I slid the safety off the Uzi hanging at my side, and, fingering the trigger lightly, brought the gun up to my chest. Huerta's guard, seeing our slight movements jerked his .45 up in a two-handed grip aimed at us.

Huerta stood paralyzed at Itzla's unprompted clamor, and as he tried to compose himself, I noticed his grip loosen on Lino.

"*Pino!*" Itzla repeated more emphatically.

Lino, as though choreographed, dropped to his knees out of Huerta's grasp and rolled several yards away. Huerta reacted by diving behind Lino just as the shot from the Mossberg snapped across the surface of the ruins. The guard, apparently thinking Huerta had been hit by the blast, managed to trigger two rounds that hissed just above our heads. I swung the Uzi, stood on the trigger and sent a burst of rounds in the guard's direction. It was me and Itzla, or him; and the longer I stayed on the trigger, the better chance I had of taking him out. One of the bullets caught him in the left thigh and must have split open an artery. The growing smear on his light cotton pants told me he was giving up blood in a hurry. Struggling to stay upright, he was ready to fire again when another shot rang out, this time from inside the tree line, dropping the guard hard like a puppet with severed strings. He lay sprawled in a pool of his own blood, face down in the dirt, the back of his head blown away.

Garret was lowering his gun, looking past Huerta, toward the tree line. "Looks like Manolo beat me to it," he said.

"Call him off!" Huerta ordered after catching sight of Garret's lieutenant emerging from the trees, his rifle trained on Huerta.

"He has his orders, Carlos," Garret said calmly, "but sometimes his emotions get in the way of them. Release Lino, or I release Manolo. None of us want a senseless slaughter."

With both his bodyguards out of the game, Huerta worked Lino to his knees, keeping him between himself and Itzla, maneuvering for position. He pulled Lino to his feet, and with difficulty wrapped his left arm around Lino's throat, steadily nudging the gun just under Lino's ear. It appeared Itzla hadn't missed. I could see the upper sleeve of Huerta's shirt turning crimson, the blood from his bicep seeping through what was left of the fabric that had been ripped open from the shotgun blast. With Manolo now thirty feet away, Huerta, his wounded arm obviously failing him, was trying desperately to maintain his grip on Lino.

"And you'd better hurry," Garret went on after slowing Manolo and the four guards with a hand signal. Manolo then began a deliberate pacing behind Huerta who jerked Lino around to keep the big Mexican in sight. "You know damn well Kopek heard those shots," Garret added.

"What guarantee do I have that you won't kill me after I give you Lino?" Huerta asked, shuffling around in his dusty boots, his eyes flicking about at the four guards surrounding him. "And that you'll even hand over the diamonds if I do give him up?"

"I can only guarantee that *I* won't kill you," Garret said, "but there are at least three others out here that probably wouldn't even flinch about putting a hollow point in your head. Give him up, you get the diamonds. That's the only guarantee I can give you."

Again, Huerta started backing down the path toward the car, but the weight of the gun against Lino's neck seemed to be taxing his wounded arm; and it began to sag to Lino's chest. Manolo, apparently sensing Huerta's move to escape, turned and fired two shots, exploding two tires of the government car.

Huerta moved to Lino's side in an attempt to shield himself from Manolo. Itzla took advantage. She lowered the Mossberg's barrel, settling her aim just below Huerta's oversized silver belt buckle.

"Itzla, *cariño*," Huerta pleaded, not knowing which way to turn. "What lies have they been giving you?"

"*¿Mentiras*, Carlos?" she asked a bit too calmly. "You took my parents from me. You murdered them. And now you're threatening to kill my uncle." Her words suddenly turned acidic. "Don't tell me about lies, *car-i-ño*."

Don't do it, Itzla. Her readiness to take Huerta out was

admirable, but the Mossberg's shot pattern would probably rip Lino apart, too. I hoped she knew that.

"You want to know about lies?" Huerta was frantically wheeling Lino around trying to find safety from Itzla's shotgun and from Manolo who had been working his way up behind him. "There are more lies than you can handle. Kill me and the answers get buried with me. Put the gun down before you ruin your life, too."

Itzla scoffed. "Don't count on my sympathy, Carlos."

Huerta struggled to tighten his hold on Lino, saying, "With that high-priced education you have, the one I paid for, you still don't understand anything, do you?"

Itzla looked almost amused. "You have a better card than that, Carlos. I don't owe you a thing except to make sure that you're buried deep somewhere. Had I known who you really were, I would have burned all your fucking guilt money."

Her fuse is lit, Carlos. Don't piss her off.

Through a nervous smile, Huerta said, "All that supposed 'guilt money' paid your way out of this dirt hole, *cariño*. By now you'd probably be spending your days raising six kids and pounding laundry on river rocks. You should be thanking me."

That pissed me off. "You self-serving son-of-a-bitch," I said, angrily taking a few steps toward Huerta, my finger tensed against the trigger of the Uzi. Huerta smiled, somehow finding the strength to lift Lino's chin with the barrel of his .45. I backed off.

"You can't change the past," Huerta said, his arrogance fading. "It wasn't supposed to happen that way."

The shock wave of Huerta's statement whipped through the air like a snapped power line, jarring Itzla's focus for a moment. "What wasn't?" Itzla pushed the question. "You're telling me there was a plan?"

Huerta rocked back and forth. Eyeing the guards and scuffling behind Lino for cover, he pressed the .45 into Lino's neck just below the ear.

I could almost taste the bitterness in Itzla's voice as she said, "Before I shoot you again, I want to know why."

Huerta hesitated, glaring at Itzla, then said in a tone drier than the dirt at his feet, "Maybe you should ask your uncle that question? Feel like talking, Lino?"

There was no time for an answer. Lino had brought his fist down hard onto Huerta's weakened arm, the force of the blow knocking the gun out of Huerta's hand. Huerta, with his good arm, tried to restrain Lino, but his hold loosened as Lino continued pounding on his bloody arm. Lino finally broke his hold and squirmed away. Spinning to the side, he picked up the gun, and for a brief moment held it steadily at Huerta's chest. He looked at Itzla standing ready with the shotgun and said, "*No vale la pena*," and threw the gun into the shaft tomb.

Lino was probably right, I thought, it wasn't worth it. Itzla, however, seemed to have other ideas about how to handle the situation. When Lino was safely at her side, she raised the Mossberg. I looked at Garret, thinking he might intervene, but all I got was a hard grin. Manolo had moved to the side, out of the way. They were enjoying this.

CHAPTER
TWENTY SIX

When Itzla pulled the trigger, shards of limestone blasted off the rock lip of the shaft tomb between her and Huerta. By the time I could get my hand on the barrel of the Mossberg to stop her, she had fired again, this time in the dirt near Huerta's feet. Huerta, after dancing to his right in anticipation of a third shot, seemed to give up. He straightened his body, and said with lapsed bravado, "It seems I am going to die here, *cariño*. I never thought it would be by your hands." Then throwing his shoulders back, exclaimed, "Shoot me! Shoot me if you have the *cojónes*!"

I had my hand wrapped around the barrel of the Mossberg and was struggling with her to keep it aimed away from anything that could die. "Think about it, Itzla," I said, wrestling the barrel of the gun toward the ground. "You're not a killer, and I'm not going to let you become one."

"I'll become whatever I choose." She glared at me, her dark, angry brown eyes as hot and deadly as the shotgun she was raising toward Huerta, reminding me of the afternoon in the shaft tomb when Kopek had us pinned down, when she let her anger fly. She had needed time to settle herself then. But now, time wasn't an available luxury.

The more we struggled, the more I could feel her angst giving way, the tension in her body slackening. I saw the hard lines in her face softening. When I felt her fingers loosen around the trigger guard and saw her calmly, yet hatefully, glaring at Huerta, I eased my grip.

She nosed the shotgun toward the ground then wrapped her arm around Lino's shoulder in that same tender way she had walked him back to his house the night she rescued him from Benito's cantina.

"*No vale la pena*," she said, repeating her uncle's words. Unlike Huerta, she had given in to her small voice of conscience.

"I'm sorry, *hijita*," I heard Lino say. "This is not your problem."

"It has become my problem," Itzla said. "We'll talk about this later."

I could only imagine what her conversation with Lino would drag up after all this was over, but right now all of us had a bigger problem. Even with two dead here at the ruins and Huerta under control, what had happened up the hill at the compound was anybody's guess.

"Shit!" Garret grumbled, moving quickly around the rim of the tomb toward Manolo who had started a slow walk toward Huerta, the rifle cradled in his arm.

Itzla took hold of my arm, flexing her fingers nervously as Garret jumped between Manolo and Huerta to stop his lieutenant from getting to Huerta. It only took a second for Garret to see what I saw in Manolo's eyes; and when he saw it, he stood down, and backed away. It would take a bullet to Manolo's heart to stop him, and I was certain Garret was not going to shoot his friend.

Huerta scuffled backwards trying to keep out of Manolo's range. "Garret! For Christ's sake!" he yelled. "You got what you wanted. You can keep the fucking stones. Just keep him off me."

"You're a little late, Carlos," Garret said. "You should have thought about it before you had his brother steal the Warrior." Manolo was closing in, now fifteen feet from Huerta. "I've covered your ass long enough," Garret said. "I'm done."

"You're going to let him kill me?"

"You were begging to die a minute ago."

Huerta gave Itzla a quick, pitiful look. "I knew she wouldn't have the guts to do it." Then just as quickly turned back to keep his eye on Manolo who had closed the distance to ten feet. "What do you want from me, Garret?"

"There's nothing you can give me any more, Carlos. Like I said, I'm done."

Manolo faked a lunge at Huerta. Huerta jumped back, catching his heel on the leg of his downed guard, sending Huerta into a spin that landed him face up on the guard's back. Manolo uncradled his rifle and walked the remaining few steps to where Huerta lay. He stuck the barrel up under the brim of Huerta's cowboy hat and flicked the *cobarde's* hat onto the ground next to him. After a brief look into his eyes, Manolo then purposefully waved the barrel at Huerta's right knee. "*Para mi hermano,*" he said, "*para Jorge.*" And without blinking, pulled the trigger.

The retort of the rifle sent a burn up my spine. Itzla gasped and turned away, burying her face in my shoulder. Huerta's scream was unnatural, haunting, a high-pitched howl of pain and fear. Writhing in the dirt at Manolo's feet, and holding what was left of his shattered knee with his good arm, he pleaded, "Don't do this, Garret! Tell me what you want!"

"It's no good, Carlos," Garret said, his attention momentarily diverted to the hills behind us. "It's not what I want that matters."

In his panic, Huerta rolled off the guard's sprawled body and began dragging himself across the gritty, limestone dust near the shaft tomb. Within seconds his wounded arm gave out. He inched his way pathetically across the dirt with his right elbow and left knee, the blood from his mangled knee seeping through his linen slacks, leaving an iron-red trail in the sand.

Manolo followed Huerta with a slow, measured stride. He rammed the barrel into Huerta's side twice then kicked him over onto his back. Sand had mixed with the blood leaching from his wounds and the sweat on his body giving the appearance of a beached, decaying sand shark. The only similarity being that they both knew how to wallow.

"Look at me!" Manolo demanded, taking hold of Huerta's shirt and jerking him into a sitting position. He looked hard at Huerta. Huerta flinched and raised his right hand to shade his eyes. Manolo then said with cool calculation, "I want you to see your killer."

I could only imagine what was going on in Huerta's mind as he looked into the eyes of his assassin. For a few seconds they stared at each other, until Huerta made a futile attempt to scoot away. Manolo slowly moved the rifle barrel down to Huerta's groin. He stabbed at Huerta's genitals twice then moved the barrel inches away and fired once into the sand between Huerta's legs. Manolo then set the barrel on Huerta's other knee cap and smiled. Huerta howled in agony as his knee was blown apart. Manolo brought the butt of his rifle down hard into Huerta's face. I heard the bones crunch and saw more blood pour from Huerta's nose and cheek. Shouldering his rifle, Manolo then grabbed the whimpering Huerta by the waistband and hauled his limp body up out of the dirt. Even with Huerta's significant weight, Manolo made him seem feather light as he raised the man up over his head. Walking the short distance to the rim of the shaft tomb, Manolo unmercifully pitched Huerta into the shaft.

I heard a thump and a groan and then Huerta saying in a painful whisper, *"Por favor."*

Manolo leaned over the edge. *"Si está vivos mañana, voy a matarte."*

If you are alive tomorrow, I will kill you.

"Enough! *Bastante!"* Garret demanded. Manolo, still breathing heavily, was slowly coming out of his murderous stupor. He turned away from the shaft tomb and marched over to Garret where they both studied the body of Huerta's guard that still lay face down near the lip of the shaft tomb. Garret poked the body with the end of his shoe. He pried the guard's gun from his hand and tossed it to Manolo. "Leave it here," he said to Manolo, nodding toward the body. "It's good to have a corpse lying around. For effect. And send the guards back up the hill to help Esperanza. We've got it covered here." He then sent Manolo to retrieve the duffel bag he had left just outside the clearing.

I didn't feel like becoming a shooting gallery target, nor did I want to become a part of the "effect" Garret was trying to create. With the guards gone, standing in the open was a sure invitation for Kopek to take a few unobstructed shots at us if he was lucky enough to survive the firestorm up at the compound. I wanted to believe that he was dead and that this nightmare would be over. I wanted to believe that Esperanza and Garret's guards had prevailed. But those assumptions could get us all killed. Until I knew for certain that Kopek had been taken out, I could only assume that he and Nuñez and Casey were heading down the hill at that moment to kill us.

Garret rushed around the shaft tomb to us, intently searching the trees and bushes for any signs of movement. "Get behind those rocks and stay there," he ordered, herding us behind a rock outcropping away from the trees. "Manolo's bringing enough firepower to wipeout a platoon."

As we took up positions behind the boulders, I said to Itzla, "If you know any Aztec gods of good fortune, I only hope you're in good standing with them. We're going to need all the luck any of them can give us."

She put her hand on my cheek and kissed me quickly, her smile fading into a mist of concern. "We will make our own luck, *cariño*," she said. "The day of the Dead is for celebrating, not for dying. But if you need something more to believe in, pray to *Macuilxochitl*."

"Easy for you to say," I said. "I'll trust in *us*."

When Manolo returned he tossed the duffel at our feet. He seemed to be back to his usual stoic self. He unzipped the bag and dumped a handful of automatic weapons and full clips onto the ground. A letter-sized courier folder fell out onto the pile of guns along with a few diamonds that had spilled out of a small cloth bag. Manolo quickly grabbed them and threw them back into the duffel. Garret noticed my interest and said, "Files and photos. Incriminating evidence. If I don't make it out of here, do what you want with them. Same with the diamonds." He nodded toward the bag. "I don't think Huerta wants them anymore. Kopek is going to try like hell to get them and the files. And I don't really give a damn about any of this shit." He picked up one of the automatics, shoved a clip into it, and pressed it and a second clip into Lino's hands. "*¿Sabe usted como utilizarlo?*"

"He grew up with guns," Itzla said. "He knows how they work, and he's not afraid to use them."

Lino pulled the slide back and chambered a round. Garret caught the action and smiled. "No one is going to hurt my Itzla," Lino said with such resolve that I felt myself rocking on my heels away from Itzla. Finding a safe spot between an avenging uncle holding an automatic weapon and a determined niece with a shotgun wasn't my idea of a romantic interlude, but I wasn't going to let anyone harm her either. When Lino smiled at me and flicked his head toward Itzla, I realized he knew that. I was at least on safe ground with him. After flashing an endearing look at his niece, he spun around and dropped flat across a boulder, watching.

"Put this in your pocket," Garret said, handing me an extra banana clip for the Uzi. "And hit something when you pull the trigger. Then hit it again. These guys won't go down easy. Itzla, keep the shotgun. You seem to know what to do with it."

After several minutes of gunfire coming from the compound up the hill, it suddenly went quiet. I could only hope that Esperanza and the guards had taken care of Kopek, Nuñez, and Casey. "Maybe they're dead," I said before a short burst of gunfire erupted up the hill.

"Still think so?" Garret said, moving slowly away from the protection of the rocks, heading toward the tree line, Manolo following a few yards behind. Garret had seen my concern. "This is the best place to be," he said over his shoulder. "Just don't go anywhere. Manolo and I are going in. See if we can head them off. If they come out, I'd better hear some shots."

As they disappeared into the trees, Itzla moved closer to me, her breath coming in short bursts. She pressed her back to the wall of rock next to Lino. "I would have killed him," she said.

"Huerta's as good as dead, Itzla," I said. "He's lying in

his own tomb. You don't need nightmares for the rest of your life."

"I'm living one, *cariño,*" she declared, clutching the shotgun to her breast.

I couldn't deny her that. Up to this point we had been trudging along in the fires of hell, and now the devil was about to appear. Kopek was somewhere near, he and his band of killers, and I hoped that Garret and Manolo would find them before we had to face them. What chance would we have against trained killers?

I looked at the duffel that Manolo had thrown down at our feet, saw the stray diamonds glistening in shards of the sun, and saw the file folder that these men were willing to kill for.

"Jesus!" I spit the words out. "Talk about a nightmare! We're standing on what they want! I'm not going to be anywhere near the main attraction if they come down the hill. Sit still. I'll be back in a minute. This stuff has got to be buried."

It was a short distance away in another cluster of rocks that I found an opening between two boulders that was perfect for hiding the duffel. I started to jam it into the crevice when several photographs slipped out of the file— a shirtless Kopek next to Garret, standing like warlords on a four-foot pile of heroin bricks surrounded by high-ranking Laotian, Thai, and Vietnamese officers. Nuñez and Casey standing to the side holding up chains of ears and other body parts. On the back was written, "Vientiane." Obviously a heroin distribution center. Another photo of Huerta, smiling, holding a gun to a young girl's head. Still another with the words "Interrogation at 3000 ft." boldly written across its face showing Kopek swinging a black clad body by the ankles outside the door of a helicopter.

This man needs to die, I thought.

I rifled through some of the letters and memos signed by ranking U.S. military personnel and U.S. senators requisitioning the use of military aircraft to fly into and out of a place called Long Tieng, the headquarters for CIA operations in northern Laos. A General Vang Pao was commander of the CIA's Secret Army in Long Tieng and was apparently in charge of a CIA sponsored heroin factory there. Garret's and Kopek's names were constantly turning up, as was Carlos Huerta's.

No wonder they are such a CIA priority, I thought as I shoved the bag into the crevice. Who knows what else was happening over there? There were hundreds of photos and papers, any one of them would be incriminating evidence that showed the depth of CIA operations in Southeast Asia. Bringing the files back to Langley would be a definite coup for Kopek, and he could live quite comfortably with millions of dollars worth of diamonds. All he had to do was find the duffel and…. What would he do with us if he did?

My thoughts spun back to Itzla and Lino hiding in the rocks across the small open space from where I was stashing the duffel. I made short work of concealing the bag by filling the crevice with stone rubble and sage then made a low crouching dash back to where I had left the two of them.

I wasn't fast enough. Both Itzla and Lino had disappeared. Thinking they may have taken off into the trees for a more secure place, I started out from behind the rocks only to find Lino on his side, sprawled in the sand. He wasn't moving. His gun was gone. Itzla was nowhere to be seen. The Mossberg lay next to Lino, its clip removed.

CHAPTER
TWENTY SEVEN

I pulled Lino behind the protection of the boulder. He groaned and rolled onto his back. Except for a growing lump and a trickle of blood matting his hair, I saw no other traces of blood. He had been hit hard and knocked out for as long as it took Itzla to disappear. By all accounts, he'd been lucky.

I propped him up against the rock and kneeled on one knee next to him. "*¿Qué paso?* What happened? Are you alright?" I asked in my most urgent Spanish. "Where is Itzla?"

"Something hit me from behind," he said, shaking his head slowly, straining to focus. "I only know I am awake now." He touched the knot on his head, rolling the blood around on his fingertips. Then he noticed the shotgun lying nearby. "Itzla!" he snarled as he struggled to get to his feet. "They have Itzla!"

"Not for long," I said, fingering the safety off the Uzi. I raised my hand to Lino and whispered, "*Silencio.*"

The silence that followed was unbearable. It was the quiet of deep water where the only available sense is visual, and even that was limited by the stillness of the trees and leaves rimming the ruins. I hugged the rock, slowly worming my way up until I could see the tree line fifty feet to my left. To my right was nothing but a few smaller rocks and high sage. The open area was the size of a football field with a few leveled remnants of ancient foundations, and Huerta's car sitting at the far end.

Where had they taken her? And so quickly. And where were Garret and Manolo? My stomach twisted into a tight ball, and I was heated with anger and panic for leaving Itzla and Lino alone.

Focus, Skipper. No time for regrets or hesitation. Shake it off.

As I slid down next to Lino, protected on three sides by high rocks, it suddenly occurred to me that Kopek might not know I was here with them. It was speculation, I realized, but other than his seeing me with Itzla at the ruins, and being run off by Benito, the chances were pretty good that I was invisible up here. And that I could use to my advantage.

Think, Skipper.

"Lino," I whispered, peeking through a crack between boulders where I could see the open area clearly. "Listen to me. We're going to get her back. They won't hurt her. They'll use her like Huerta used you."

Lino shot me a sideways glance. "And when they get what they want?"

"They won't," I declared.

No sooner had I said this when a repulsive, demonic laugh came from somewhere inside the undergrowth. Nuñez burst forth into the open, gripping Itzla tightly around the waist and holding his combat knife to her throat. He dragged her around the lifeless body of Huerta's guard and through the small patches of sage to the rim of the shaft tomb directly in front of me. In the early morning light, I could see a scar that ran from his left ear to just under his left eye. It fit him. I saw the blood stains on the back of his head where I had hit him with the tree branch. Kopek was no where in sight, nor was Casey.

"Garret!" Nuñez hollered into the trees after looking down at the bloodied, half decapitated guard. "*I* would have used a knife. It is much more efficient."

"Those bastards!" Lino said under his breath. "I want the honor of killing them."

"You may get your chance," I said. "But right now, stay calm, and stay put. I'm pretty sure they don't know I'm here."

Lino tapped the Uzi in my hand. "Use it," he said.

"Nothing would give me more pleasure," I said, "but I don't trust this thing for accuracy. I'm not going to risk hitting Itzla. And I don't think Garret or Manolo will risk it either. Besides, Kopek and Casey may still be out there."

"You will know when to use it," he said. "I am sorry I am of no use to you."

"You're safe," I said. "Let's keep it that way."

Then, Nuñez, with lethal finesse, trailed his knife down across Itzla's breasts, running it up and down to her groin. Itzla squirmed and kicked at his legs. That's when I saw the knife rip across her upper thigh, putting a neat slice in her slacks, drawing blood. Nuñez yanked at her hair, pulling her head back, exposing the carotid arteries, and raised the knife to her throat. "Cunt," he said tight-lipped. "You want to play nasty with me?" He spun her around hard toward the shaft tomb. "You want to go in there in pieces, bitch?" Then as though reminded of something more important, he backed off. Still holding the knife to her throat, he yelled again into the trees. "Garret! Drop your weapons and get your fucking ass out here where I can see you. I want your goon right next to you with his hands in the air."

After a tense moment of silence, Garret's voice boomed from down the tree line. "Stand down, Sergeant. That's an order."

"This ain't 'Nam, Garret," Nuñez retorted, turning Itzla toward the sound of Garret's voice. "Your orders don't mean shit here, *Capitan*. And don't count on your guards. They've been taken care of. You think the two of you and that punk Mexican bus driver can take us out?"

Two? They don't know I'm here.

Lino tensed his body next to me. "*Cabrones*," he muttered.

"You're not worth the dialog, Nuñez," I heard Garret declare. "My business is with Kopek. When he comes out, we come out. And you're smart enough to know that if anything happens to the girl, you're dead where you stand."

"She's just another bitch, Garret." Nuñez waved the knife in front of Itzla's face, his sadistic laugh ripping through the air, not a hint of expression on his gristly face. "A very pretty bitch," he said, yanking her hair back and licking her cheek.

I wanted to rip Nuñez's throat out, but I'd have little chance of getting to him before he could do his damage to Itzla. He seemed stoned and crazy enough to jeopardize the diamonds and the files in order to fulfill some sadistic rite of passage. Feeling helpless, I hunkered down and waited, my finger on the trigger of the Uzi. At that moment a banana leaf would have been more powerful in my hand.

"In the open, Garret," Kopek hollered from somewhere inside the tree line. "Let's do this."

Kopek was alone, dressed in jungle fatigues, carrying only a handgun when he came out of the jungle thirty yards to my left. Garret and Manolo pushed through the undergrowth forty yards from Kopek. I had to assume Casey was embedded somewhere inside the tree line covering his boss. Garret and Manolo were side by side several yards apart. Garret had a two-handed grip on his .45 aimed at Kopek. Manolo had a bead on Nuñez with his rifle.

Kopek surveyed the area, assessing the situation. "Do I look worried, Garret?" he said contemptuously as he walked to within ten feet of Nuñez, his gun hanging from his hand at his side. "You know how Nuñez operates. I'd hate to see him take this pretty lady apart."

"Let her go," Garret said. "This isn't her fight."

My finger pulsed on the trigger guard as Kopek looked at Itzla obscenely. She was frozen under Nuñez's blade at her throat. "It became her fight when Nuñez found her with the shotgun," Kopek said. "Feisty bitch. She'd be a lot of fun. But there's no way she's leaving here."

One shot at that insane asshole Nuñez, I thought. *Just one shot.*

"We'll get to her later," Kopek continued, looking at Huerta's guard lying in the dirt. "I see you've made my work easier. The arrogant fuck even came in his official vehicle. What did you do with him?"

"He's no longer a problem," Garret said. "Let's get this done."

"Give us the shit," Kopek snapped. "We'll torch the files right here. Be done with it. You give us the stones, and we're out of your life."

"And disobey your prime directive?" Garret asked.

Kopek forced a laugh. "Of course, you would know that. I forget you still have friends."

"In some strange places," Garret said and lowered his gun slightly. "You're a liability anyway you look at it. They aren't going to let you live knowing what you know. And if you turn the files over to your handlers, they'd have no reason to keep you around."

"Immunity, Garret," Kopek said haughtily. "Remember your first lesson in 'Nam? CYA. Cover your ass."

"You think the Agency gives a damn about your ass?" Garret said. "Illicit drug dealing and war crimes aren't their idea of front page at the *Washington Post*." He looked to Nuñez then back to Kopek. "Where the hell is Casey? Get Casey out here!" he demanded. "I know he's aching to put a bullet in my back."

Kopek flicked his hand in indifference. "He ate it up the hill."

"You expect me to believe that?" Garret said. "CYA. Somebody always has *your* back."

"Believe what you want, Garret," Kopek said. "I'm through fucking around with you. Get the stuff, or she starts coming apart." He abruptly raised his pistol toward Itzla. She jerked to her left just as Kopek fired. The bullet nicked her right arm as it hissed by her and ricocheted off the rocks behind her and Nuñez.

My stomach turned and my mouth went dry as my hand tightened around the barrel of the Uzi. I could smell the adrenaline in my sweat.

Nuñez, momentarily caught off balance, had ducked to his left, loosening his grip on Itzla, his upper body leaning out over the shaft tomb. "Fuck you doing man?" he shouted, trying to gain control of Itzla. "Damn near smoked *me*!"

"Next time it'll find bitch meat," Kopek said icily. "Take off a little at a time." His eyes snapped back to Garret. "It's your call, Garret. The shit for the bitch."

In the confusion Itzla broke Nuñez's hold. She slid down until she was squatting in front of him then shot her right elbow backwards, missing his groin by inches. Nuñez grabbed her hair and pulled her to her feet; but he was off balance and Itzla swung again, this time landing her forearm squarely into Nuñez's balls. He fell away from her just as the hollow pop of a bullet reverberated from down inside the tomb. The bullet ripped through Nuñez's chin, exiting out the back of his head. Nuñez dropped to his knees. His head lolled, and he rolled face forward onto the blade of his knife. Carlos Huerta had taken his last shot.

Kopek, seeing Nuñez go down, must have thought that Garret or Manolo had taken the shot. He spun and fired at Garret. Manolo, always one step ahead, jumped in front of Garret and took the bullet in his right shoulder. But crashing into Garret, he knocked the .45 out of Garret's hand.

I had a clear shot at Kopek now; but knowing Casey was probably waiting in the undergrowth salivating for a fire fight, and with Manolo down, I couldn't risk it. One shot from me and we all could die.

"Casey!" Kopek yelled.

Casey was already on the run, hustling through the bushes and out into the open when a bullet came out of nowhere and tore into his stomach. A second later another bullet ripped his left shoulder apart.

Who in the hell was out there?

Kopek was desperately looking around for the shooter when Garret scrambled away from Manolo, diving for his .45 laying a few yards away. Kopek spun toward Garret. Before he could pull the trigger to fire again, I jumped from behind the boulder and pulled the trigger on the Uzi. One of the bullets ripped through Kopek's left leg as he wheeled around and dropped to one knee, bringing the pistol up with both hands, locking the sight on my chest. A look of shock and surprise twisted over his face.

He laughed. "You," he said disdainfully.

I dropped behind the rock just before he fired. The snap of the bullet hissed over my head then another ricocheted off the top of the rock, the sting of rock fragments burning into the side of my face as the bullet splintered the limestone above me. I cleared my eyes with the back of my hand and felt the slickness of blood on my cheek.

I was pinned down, and I knew he would be going after Garret again. I couldn't let that happen. I jumped out from behind the rock and fired a quick burst, hitting Kopek in the side, but it was too late. Kopek had taken his shot. I saw the bullet hit Garret, saw him go down, saw the blood on his chest.

Kopek looked toward Itzla who was stumbling away from the tomb. He started toward her, seemingly unaffected by the bullet in his leg and side. She was his last hope for staying alive and I wasn't about to let him get to her.

"Touch her, you're dead!" I shouted.

"You," he said again, turning and firing another round that whistled by my ear.

"Me," I said and squeezed the trigger of the automatic. He danced like a psychotic puppet, his limbs flailing as the flurry of .9 millimeter bullets hammered into his body. He fell face up next to Nuñez without firing another shot. He was still breathing when I kicked the gun out of his hand. We stared at each other for a moment. He blinked, shook his head, and said in a raspy whisper, "A fucking surfer."

Itzla had run to me and was holding me around the waist, pressing hard into my back, looking down at the growing pools of blood around Kopek's body. When I saw his body go slack, I threw the heated Uzi onto the ground and turned to hold her. Over her shoulder, I saw Manolo, thirty feet away, sitting in the dirt, holding Garret propped against his chest.

I backed away from Itzla when Lino came out of hiding. *"Atende de ella,"* I said to him and hurried over to where Garret and Manolo lay, both bleeding freely from their wounds.

Manolo had ripped open his shirt. He had been hit in the upper chest. He was bleeding onto Garret's right shoulder. Manolo's hands were covered with blood as he pressed hard trying to stop the flow of blood pouring from Garret's chest wound. It looked like the bullet had entered Garret close to his heart. He was still alive. I dropped onto my knees next to him, listening to his labored breathing.

"Are you okay?" he wheezed. The words rattled out of his chest.

I nodded and said, "Itzla and Lino are safe. Everyone else is dead."

"Kopek?"

"Dead."

He coughed. A trickle of pink, foamy blood rolled out of his mouth. "You've got balls, Skipper. You didn't run out."

"Nothing to do with balls. It was stupidity and morbid curiosity, plus the fact you made it clear in the boat at Chapala that a bullet would be chasing me around Mexico if I bailed on you."

"You are gullible and can write. I needed you. You were never in any danger from me."

I gave him a half-hearted smile. "Now you tell me. Don't talk. We have to get you taken care of."

"Forget it, Skipper. I'm done." He coughed deeply, blood and tissue rattling a dirge in his chest. "We still have a deal?" he asked, the words nearly inaudible now.

"The deal is still on, my friend," I said, fingering my

shirt pocket, amazed that the five one-hundred-dollar bills were still there. I pulled them out and fanned them in front of his eyes.

He smiled painfully. The metallic odor of his blood, mixed with the musty dust and sweet sweat smoldered in my nose. "Burn the files, Skipper. Throw them in the damn hole with the rest of the garbage." His voice was weakening. I leaned in closer, putting my ear to his lips. "They don't mean shit anymore. Do that for me, and I can leave here with a clean conscience."

"Yes, sir," I said, pulling away for a moment and giving him a two-fingered salute.

He moved his hand toward his face, but it fell useless onto his chest. I leaned again toward his mouth. "The diamonds," he said on a breath of air, "they died with the dead. They're untraceable." He looked past me to where Itzla and Lino were standing. "Looks like you could have a damn good future, Skipper."

I was about to tell him that it would be even better if he were in it when I heard a sudden rustling in the foliage next to us. I spun around, weaponless, only to see Esperanza frantically clawing her way through the thick, low-hanging branches of a pine tree, beating limbs out of her way with the barrel of her rifle, her medicine pouch slung by a strap over her shoulder.

"I did what I could for the men in the compound," she said as she rushed to us, "but I'm afraid I was of little help." She made a quick sign of the cross and dropped down on her knees next to her son. She began prodding his wound.

Manolo waved her off. "*Atende a Garret,*" he said. "*Estoy bien.*"

I pictured the men in Garret's compound putting up a

good fight; but like the bulls in the *corrido de toros*, the odds were against them.

As Esperanza feverishly worked on Garret's wound, Benito came up over the rise behind Huerta's car, his horse following closely behind. He was wearing his dirty, conical hat and leather vest. The bandolier of rifle shells was stretched tightly across his chest.

"I am not too late?" he asked as he walked proudly over the sandstone toward us holding his rifle high in the air, his posture like that of a nineteen-year-old standing next to Pancho Villa on the caboose of a stolen train some sixty years before. He looked around at the carnage spread over the dirt and shook his head. "I have not seen such bloodshed since Durango during the Revolution." He waved his rifle at Esperanza in recognition. Esperanza gave him a quick nod and then shook her head over Garret's body. "I am getting too old for seeing men bleed," he said. He pointed his rifle at Garret. "Take this one away. Leave the rest to rot." Then sighing said, "Perhaps I will open a surfing *tienda* in Puerto Vallarta. It is a good business, no?"

I followed Benito's gaze to Casey sprawled on his side, lifeless, the hand of his only good arm draped over his bleeding gut. "That was you?"

He caressed the long barrel of his ancient rifle and said with a mixture of pride and sadness, "My eyes, they are still good. This time I did not miss."

"We're running up a tab with you, Benito," I said. "That's twice you've saved us."

"You owe me nothing. These *babosos* they think they know the land and the people."

"That was their mistake," I said.

EPILOGUE

Our room at the Camino Real Hotel in Puerto Vallarta overlooked the pool and the Pacific. We were wrapped in humidity, sitting quietly at a metal-grated table on the open balcony listening to thunder thudding in the distance, watching lightning light up the midnight sky. I had just finished a bottle of Dos XX and was admiring Itzla in her form-fitting shorts and soft cotton top as she sedately sipped on a long-stemmed glass of merlot.

I tapped her glass in salute after snapping the cap off another beer. "I praise the museum board for giving you these two weeks."

She smiled, took my hand, and stared out across the sand to the surf roughing up the beach. "You're awfully smug tonight, *cariño*."

"Escaping death tends to lift my spirits," I said, following her gaze out over the water. Even with the files burned and the bulk of the diamonds safely tucked away in a safe deposit box in Guadalajara and with Garret being formally buried near the fountain in the compound for more than a week, I was still looking over my shoulder for the shadows of trained killers. "Don't let my glibness fool you. It's a façade for every mistake I've ever made."

She stood and walked to the railing. Even in the heat, her fingers were cool as she slid her hand across my bare shoulders. She was facing me, leaning against the railing. The two-inch cut on her thigh glowed red around the incrustation. Seven stitches.

She saw me looking. "I know you have been concerned. It is better than yesterday, no?"

"It will be a reminder," I said.

"That will go away, too," she said, gently running her index finger over the wound.

"Now who's being smug?" I mused.

She pushed herself off the railing and kissed me softly. "That's for helping my family."

My grin was purposely wry. I said, "What do I get for any lost relatives, friends, or even pets?"

"Is your imagination failing you already, Mr. Reid?"

I squirmed in my chair, a slight twitch moving things around in my swim trunks. "I haven't had to imagine much since we got here," I admitted.

She had returned to the railing and was watching the lightning flashes rip through the clouds when the first drops of warm rain began smacking the metal table like errant marbles. "It's cleansing," she said, lifting her face and arms to meet the rain.

I uncoiled from my chair and wrapped my arms around her waist. "It's a relief knowing Lino had nothing to do with the theft or any conspiracy," I said, thinking back to Lino's apologetic confession the morning after Carlos died in the shaft tomb. We were sitting in Nailea's kitchen in the back of the store. Nailea brought food. No one ate. Lino explained how horrifying it was for him to have caught Carlos lighting the torch that had killed her parents; how

Carlos kept wrestling him away from the flames outside the burning house; how Carlos had told him he would kill all of them if Lino exposed him.

For the moment, I kept a lid on those hellish thoughts. Itzla didn't need reminders.

"What could I do?" Lino had said. "It has been sitting like a rough stone in my stomach for twenty-five years, but now it is finished. The fear is now gone with the man." He had looked at Itzla sitting across from him, the sadness in his eyes apparent, and then he stared at his hands lying open-palmed on the table. "The dirt on these is all that is left."

Itzla had reached across the table and stroked his calloused hands. "But you told some of the others," she said. "That took courage."

"I couldn't bear the secret alone," he had said, "and who was going to talk? We did not want you hurt."

I slowly backed Itzla under the cover of the balcony above us, out of the downpour. She spun around to face me. "What really makes me angry is the cover up. No one will ever know the truth about Carlos Huerta. Even the newspapers have caved in, honoring him as a champion of the people."

"Politics," I ventured, practically spitting the words out. "As we've learned, no government will suffer bad press."

Carlos Huerta was definitely not a hero in our eyes, but the news media was reporting otherwise. The same day Lino had told us his story, front page features were declaring Carlos a hero, a man committed to negotiating with Leftists who had been holed up in the ruins near Teuchitlán, where he and his two bodyguards had been shot and killed by members of that group. It was publicized as part of the "Dirty War" where more than fifteen hundred Leftists were either killed or had disappeared.

We had learned through one of Itzla's friends at Interpol that the entire incident had been conveniently forgotten by the CIA after it was discovered that the files had been destroyed and that no one was being held accountable for the deaths of the eight men found at the ruins. The CIA in conjunction with Mexico's Federal Security Directorate made sure there was no leak.

"*Así es la vida.*" Such is life. Itzla shrugged and walked to the table. I poured her another glass of wine. The rain had soaked through her thin top, pressing the cotton against her olive skin. "Stranger things have happened, Mr. Reid. Mexico is a constant surprise."

I had to admit that the country had a few bolts that needed tightening. "Strange things don't have much oomph for me right now," I said. "I'm preferring the familiar more and more."

"Maybe you should take Manolo and Esperanza up on their offer of a room at the ranch," she said. "You could write Garret's *corrido* in familiar territory."

"When it's cleaned up and the guns are gone, I just might. I hate guns."

"They have more than enough money to do it now, thanks to you." She looked at me curiously then said softly, "While you were in between surfing and writing this afternoon, I received a phone call from the museum directors in Guadalajara. They have offered me the opportunity to explore an archeological site at a newly-found ruin west of Tikal called El Peru-Waka in Guatemala."

I squinted at her, took another sip of beer. "Are you going to take it?"

"I would be working in conjunction with the Guatemala Historical Society. It's a one month dig in the middle of the jungle."

"Are you going?" I repeated, eyeing her cautiously.

"We'd be camping near a town called Paso del Caballos near Lake Peten Itza in the high country. You could write there, too."

"I like the 'we' part," I said with a playful grin. "And isn't Tikal on the way to Panama?"

Garr Kuhl is a novelist, play-wright, and award winning short story writer. He lives on Whidbey Island in the Pacific Northwest with his wife, Tia, and their dog Tanner.

Garr Kuhl is available for select readings and lectures. To inquire about a possible appearance please contact garrkuhl@whidbey.net

photo by Michael Stadler